I0547960

A Stirring in
The Blood

CHRIS NIBLOCK

Copyright © Chris Niblock 2017

The right of Christopher Niblock to be
Identified as the Author of the Work has been
Asserted by him in accordance with the Copyright,
Designs And Patents Act 1988.

All rights reserved.
Apart from any use permitted under UK
Copyright law no part of this publication may be
Reproduced, stored in a retrieval system, or
Transmitted, in any form or by any means without
The prior written permission of the publisher.

All characters in this publication are fictitious
And any resemblance to real persons, living or
Dead, is purely coincidental.

ISBN 978-0-9572442-9-0

Published by Focalpoint
5 Vernon House, Watling Street South
Church Stretton SY6 7BG

DEDICATION

For William and Biddy

BY THE SAME AUTHOR

Back Dated

Soul Trader

THANKS TO

Lesley Douglas and Kristen Stone for their invaluable assistance in proofreading the text; any errors and omissions that remain are mine and mine alone. Thanks also to, Maggie Booth and Colum Ryan, for their advice and encouragement.

One may smile, and smile, and be a villain.

Hamlet Act 1, scene 5

CHAPTER ONE

INSOMNIACS do sleep, they just don't get much of it, and Harry Paget was no exception. So, when he found himself awake in the middle of the night, he didn't immediately look for a reason for his sudden wakefulness. It was just how it was and had been for the past 730 sleepless nights. Nor did he open his eyes straight away, preferring to keep them shut in the vain hope that he might, just might, against all the odds, drift off again.

When a floorboard creaked, he wasn't alarmed. Harry had grown used to lying in bed just listening to the sounds his old house made in the depths of the night; the ticking of a cooling radiator or the creak of the woodwork as it contracted. Some nights he imagined himself alone at the wheel of a sailing ship in the middle of a dark ocean, with only the groan of the ship's timbers and the crack of the wind in the sails for company.

As the seconds ticked by, he became conscious of the wider world beyond his bedroom; the sighing of the wind in the trees that lined the avenue, and the distant barking of a dog. A car pulled up to the junction and waited for the lights to change. Its idling engine and the muted sounds of the car's radio carried up to him on the still night air – 'You've got a friend,' sang James Taylor – one of Annie's favourites. The music took Harry's mind shooting straight back to the 70's when he and Annie were courting. That song had been their song, but he was abruptly dragged back to the present by the familiar sound of a dressing table drawer being slowly withdrawn.

Harry froze. That drawer couldn't have moved by itself…

His mind racing almost as fast as his heart, he cautiously opened one eye to find a dark figure peering at him, the face a ghastly red, caught in the glow from the bedside clock radio's digital display. In his gloved hands he held Annie's jewellery box. Before Harry could say or do anything, the intruder brought the box smashing down on his face and made for the door. But he had to run round the bed to get to it and, with an agility that surprised both men, Harry rolled out on the opposite side of the bed and hurled himself at the fleeing burglar. The impetus of Harry's dive sent the man crashing against the wall, dislodging one of Annie's framed watercolours. All three tumbled to the floor. As the man attempted to get to his feet, Harry jumped on his back, wrapped both arms around his neck, and clung on like a limpet as the man sought to shrug him off.

'Get off me, you dirty old bastard!' growled the man, and Harry caught the whiff of stale cigarette smoke on his breath.

Harry hadn't worn pyjamas for years and his pale limbs showed up ghostly white in the darkness. In any other circumstances, he would have found the situation amusing. His intruder was clearly more alarmed at the prospect of being buggered by a naked, middle-aged man, than he was of being arrested. The impression Harry had was of a young man and a strong one, and he wondered how much longer he could hold onto him.

'I just want my wife's jewellery box,' he said, through gritted teeth.

'I dropped it when you jumped me, didn't I.'

Harry cast around. His eyes had grown more accustomed to the darkness, but his night-time vision wasn't good.

'I can't see it.'

'Fuck sake! I'm lying on it,' snarled the intruder. 'If you want it, you'll have to get off me.'

Harry was quite prepared to let the thief go if that meant he got Annie's jewellery back. But, and it was a big but, could he rely on this vicious criminal to keep his word?

'Hurry up, this thing's digging in me.' whined his assailant.

It was risky but he would have to go with it. 'All right, but you keep one knee on the floor. You hand me the jewellery box, and then you leave. OK?' His captive grunted. 'OK?' Harry repeated, this time louder.

'Yeah, yeah. Just get off me.'

Harry slowly withdrew his arms from around the man's neck. He was half expecting a trick of some kind, but was still caught off balance, when the young burglar brought his head whipping back into Harry's face, smashing his nose. He felt the warm gush of blood and his hands shot up to stem it. At that same moment an elbow was driven with great force into his abdomen. Harry rolled off onto his side where he lay doubled up, and gasping for air.

Bleeding and winded, Harry was defenceless as his assailant jumped to his feet and, accompanied by a stream of expletives, delivered a series of kicks to his body. The last thing Harry saw was a large boot coming towards his head, and then blissful unconsciousness; sleep of a kind, a rare event since losing his beloved Annie.

CHAPTER TWO

DETECTIVE SERGEANT Glyn Tudor rubbed his unshaven jowls and stared across Harry Paget's narrow kitchen table at the man's battered features. He didn't see this kind of thing very often in a low crime area like Stretton Spa; the population was largely made up of the elderly and early retirees from the south east of England. The latter had cashed in their million pound, three bedroom semis and were enjoying the good life in South Shropshire. Following his divorce, Tudor had been unable to afford anything larger than a small, two bedroom-flat in his home county, and this was a source of some resentment.

He had no idea which category to place Paget in. Despite a trip to A & E, his face was such a mess, it was hard to determine his age. Still, Tudor couldn't help but feel sorry for him. Butterfly sutures traversed his left eyebrow, the bridge of his nose and the left cheekbone. Whilst the pale blue eyes, one barely open, that stared out from under his thinning grey hair were tiny islands set in a purple sea.

PC Maggie Mellor stirred a heaped teaspoon of sugar into a mug of tea and brought it over to the table. She set it down in front of Harry and

Tudor looked up sharply.

'Where's mine, Mellor?' he asked.

'Sorry Sarge, that was the last of the milk,' she said with a mischievous smile. Young and pretty with soft, brown eyes, she was used to dealing with misogynists like Tudor, having grown up with three older brothers.

Tudor, who, along with his shave had skipped breakfast that morning and at this rate would miss lunch too, eyed the mug of tea enviously. That and a bacon butty would have gone down a treat.

'The garage over the road sells milk,' said Harry nasally.

He'd said very little so far and Tudor's head went swivelling back to him; a widower, he'd said. Another poor sod unable to look after himself. He'd seen that often enough round here. Men who had found themselves back on their own after decades of marriage and couldn't hack it.

'It's all right, Mr Paget. I'll have one later. Now, I know you've already spoken to PC Mellor here and her colleague but, if you wouldn't mind, I'd like you to go over it again with me. Got your note book handy, Mellor?'

The PC dipped a slim hand into the top pocket of her uniform jacket and fished out a small, black notebook and pencil.

'Ready when you are, Mr Paget,' she said.

Harry wasn't listening. His mind was elsewhere as he tried to gather his thoughts. When he'd regained consciousness earlier that morning, daylight was already seeping in under the heavy bedroom curtains. He didn't know how long he'd been out for, but it must have been some time. Almost immediately he began to shiver as his dormant body sought to restore normal functionality. With this restoration had come pain, and

Harry was made aware of his various injuries; a sharp stab in his right side every time he breathed in, the throbbing pain in his face, and the mother of all headaches. But his greatest hurt came from the loss of the jewellery box and the precious artefacts contained in it. It was a wound that would not heal until the box was returned to him.

'Mr Paget…'

Harry realised he'd been staring abstractedly out of the window and turned his attention back to the room. The two police officers were eyeing him expectantly.

'Sorry, what…?'

'I said, would it help at all if we went upstairs? You could walk me through what happened.' Tudor pronounced each word very slowly as if speaking to someone with hearing difficulties.

'We can do this another day, Mr Paget, if you don't feel up to it,' Mellor suggested kindly.

'No, no, I want to do it now,' said Harry with some vehemence. 'You will catch him, won't you?'

Tudor and Mellor exchanged meaningful looks.

'We'll do our best, Mr Paget. Was the jewellery insured?' asked Tudor.

'What? Yes, but I don't care about the money. I just want Annie's jewellery back.'

Tudor was used to the man of the house going 'Bruce Willis' on him; describing in lurid detail what they would do to the violator of their home, should they ever get their hands on them. So he was puzzled by Paget's lack of anger or desire for revenge, considering the amount of violence that had been visited upon him. It was sad, but chances were he'd never see that jewellery again…

'I understand that sir. Was that all… I mean, has anything else been taken?'

'Just some cash I left on the side there,' Harry indicated the work surface behind them. ''bout thirty pounds and some change.'

Mellor noted that down. 'The guy was in the lounge too, Sarge, been poking about in a bureau.'

'Do you keep anything of value in the bureau, Mr Paget?'

'No, it's where I keep the household bills, insurance documents – that kind of thing.'

'Ok. Odds are he was looking for cash. And where do we think he got in, Mellor?'

'These houses are quite old Sarge. They have a pantry...'

She took a few steps across Paget's cramped kitchen to a narrow door and opened it. Tudor followed and peered in over her shoulder. The pantry had become an extension of the under stair's cupboard. Its shelves were stacked, not with cans of food, but with cans of paint. There was also a selection of light bulbs, cleaning materials, boxes of screws and a collection of hand tools. An ironing board stood against one wall and beside it a vacuum cleaner.

'All the other windows are uPVC. This one's wood and rotten in places. Prised it open with a screwdriver, by the look of it.'

'Be a bit of a squeeze, wouldn't it?' observed Tudor.

'You wouldn't get through it, Sarge, but a slim, fit, young man could slip through easily enough,' said Mellor archly.

'Mind you don't cut yourself on that tongue of yours, Mellor,' Tudor murmured into her ear. He returned to stand beside the chair he'd recently vacated. 'OK, Mr Paget. Shall we go upstairs?'

The bedroom was in darkness, the heavy curtains still closed. Harry hovered on the threshold for a moment before switching on the light and walking in. Despite the familiar furniture and the Laura Ashley wallpaper that Annie had loved so much, the room seemed alien; one that belonged to someone else. The two police officers pulled on surgical gloves and disposable overshoes before following him in.

DS Tudor positioned himself at the foot of the bed; a stocky figure with coalminer's shoulders and a shock of dark hair, greying at the sides. His blue-grey eyes darted this way and that as he surveyed the crime scene.

'Which side of the bed were you sleeping on, Mr Paget?'

'The side nearest the window.' It had been Annie's side.

Tudor's gaze travelled from the bed to the window and the dressing table that stood in its bay. His eye was caught by a framed photograph of a smiling woman and a young gap-toothed child that stood on top of it; Paget's late wife and their daughter, he assumed.

The top drawer on the left-hand side of the dressing table hung out like a dangling tongue.

'I realise this must be difficult for you sir, but could you just take us through what happened?'

Difficult just didn't cover it as far as Harry was concerned, but once he got started, he couldn't stop talking and his story just poured out of him. Annie's death, his insomnia, the realisation that somebody was in the room, the ghastly face looming over him…

'You saw the man's face?' Tudor shot a glance at Mellor. 'Young or old?'

'He was young, early twenties perhaps...'

'OK… can you describe him?'

Harry tried to visualize his assailant but struggled to bring him into

14

sharp focus.

'About my height, I think…' he said, then fell silent again as the shadowy image he was trying to hold in his head faded.

'Hair colour?' Tudor prompted.

'Brown… or it could have been black. Sorry, I'm being so vague, but it's hard to tell the difference in the dark.'

'It's all right, Mr Paget, you're doing really well,' said PC Mellor encouragingly.

Tudor gave a discreet cough. 'If we could just concentrate on his face for the moment, Mr Paget, did our young friend have any distinguishing features – scars, piercings, that sort of thing?'

Harry thought hard. 'Not that I remember. To be honest, I only glimpsed his face for a second before he hit me, and the only light in the room was coming from that clock radio.' He pointed to the digital display.

Tudor went over to the bedside table and, cupping a hand over the clock's display, examined his other hand in its glow.

'Umm,' he said. The detective stretched himself out on the bed, hands by his side like a corpse. 'Shut the door and turn the light off will you, Mellor.'

Mellor could guess what was coming next; the sergeant had something of a reputation amongst the PCs for pulling this kind of stunt, but did as she was told. When the light went off, the room was plunged into darkness except for the eerie, red glow from the clock face.

'Now, come over here.'

Mellor felt her way round the bed and stood over the horizontal Tudor.

'Lean over me,' he said.

Tudor was enjoying this, she thought. He'd tried it on with her several times in the past few months. On each occasion she'd knocked him back, but the stupid man kept coming back for more.

'No, he's right. You're unrecognisable in this light, Mellor.'

There was a tap on the door and a uniformed officer stepped just inside the room. Tudor leapt up off of the bed and Maggie was forced to hop backwards in order to avoid a clash of heads.

'Sorry to disturb you, Sarge,' the officer said with a smirk, 'SOCO's here. Can I send them up?'

'We just need a few more minutes,' Tudor told him, then realising how that might be misconstrued, switched to the offensive. 'How's the house-to-house going, Crawford – got anything to report?'

'Nothing so far, Sarge. None of the immediate neighbours saw or heard anything.' Then, deadpan, 'The lady two doors down asked me to find her missing cat – should I...?'

'All right, that's enough of that. Back to work, Crawford, and put the light on as you go, there's a good lad.' As the light came on, Tudor turned to Mellor. 'Comical your oppo, isn't he?'

'He thinks so,' she said drily.

Tudor turned to Harry. 'Sorry, Mr Paget, but I'm afraid we'll have to leave it there for the moment and let the forensic boys and girls do their work. If you could let us have a list of the missing items and any photos you have of them, we'll get that circulated. I'll phone you later with a crime number for your insurance company.' Taking a business card from a leather card case, he handed it to Harry. 'If you think of anything else that might help us, give me a ring. Right then, it's back to house-to-house for you, Mellor and the station for me. I'll give some of our regulars a pull, see if they know anything about Mr Paget's missing jewellery.'

The SOCO team were waiting at the bottom of the stairs, their silver metal equipment cases at their feet. Tudor stopped to give them a quick briefing, leaving Mellor to escort Harry back to the kitchen. Paget eased himself down into his chair, took a sip of tea and grimaced.

'Gone cold, has it?' said, Mellor with a sympathetic smile. 'Never mind, I'll pop over to that garage and get you some milk. Make you a fresh one. Nothing like a nice, hot cuppa, is there?'

Tudor was just leaving as Mellor stepped into the sunlit hallway and she followed him out into the street. The hills above the town were vivid green against the clear blue sky, and a glider appeared to hang motionless, like a huge bird of prey, in the air above the Long Mynd.

'You shouldn't have got on that bed Sarge,' Mellor told him, as she closed the wrought iron front gate behind her. 'You're not Sherlock Holmes.'

'That guy, Paget, seems to think I am. What?' She was giving him a reproving look. 'Oh, come on, Mellor, you know as well as I do there's not much chance of him getting that jewellery back.'

With the two police officers gone, Harry's kitchen seemed very empty. Suddenly he felt lonelier than ever. When Annie had become terminally ill, he'd taken early retirement to look after her, and he found himself wondering, as he had done every morning for the past two years, what the hell he was going to do with the rest of his life? The despair he had been fighting to hold back gripped him, his shoulders heaved and, with a howl more animal than human, he burst into tears. Harry did not often give in to self-pity like this; he considered it unmanly – big boys didn't cry. Staring into a black hole that threatened to swallow him if he let it, Harry blamed himself and, even more so, the young burglar, for this unwelcome revisiting of old sorrows.

He was still quietly sobbing into his hands when he heard footsteps in the hall and realised Mellor had returned with the milk. Harry did not want the girl to see him like this, and hurriedly dabbed the tears from his eyes with his shirt sleeve. In his haste he forgot about his injured nose and let out a startled yelp.

'Mr Paget… are you all right?'

'Fine,' he said, avoiding her gaze.

'You don't sound fine.'

Mellor came around the table and examined Harry's stricken face.

'Oh,' she said. 'Do you want to talk about it?'

'It's nothing. Things just got the better of me, that's all.'

'Hardly surprising after what you've been through.'

Mellor set the bottle of milk down on the table and slipped into the empty chair.

'You're in shock, Mr Paget. It's a perfectly normal reaction to this kind of trauma. I've seen it dozens of times.'

'I was so strong, you know; when my wife died, I mean. I had to be, my daughter was in bits. When people told me I should sort out my wife's things, I did. It was hard, but I did it. That jewellery and a handful of her watercolours was all I hung on to. He could have taken anything else, and I wouldn't have given a damn. But he had to take her things and he might just as well have ripped out my heart.'

Unable to come up with any suitable words of consolation, Mellor fell back on the great British standby in times of crisis, 'I'll just make that tea,' she said quietly. Taking two clean mugs out of the cupboard, she popped a tea bag into each of them and set the kettle to boil.

'I'm not going to get that jewellery back, am I?' said Harry when Mellor returned to the table with the tea.

Maggie Mellor sighed. 'I won't lie to you, Mr Paget. We'll do our best but the statistics aren't good. You want your wife's jewellery back? My advice is to take your story to the media. Get it in the papers or on TV. You never know, our light-fingered friend may have a conscience. It's been known. And if he hasn't, then maybe one of the women in his life, his mother or his girlfriend will have one.'

CHAPTER THREE

DS TUDOR pulled up on the car park of the Jasper Arms and surveyed the half dozen vehicles parked there. One in particular caught his eye; an orange Fiesta with 'go faster' stripes along the side. He glanced at his watch. It was 11.15 am. The pub didn't open until eleven but then, the owners of these vehicles had probably been waiting outside the door when the landlord opened up.

In its Victorian heyday, The Jasper had been a rather grand hotel with terraced lawns and tennis courts. Those days were long gone and most of the land had been sold off over the years for redevelopment. The car park was all that remained of the once extensive grounds. The ornate Victorian exterior at least still hinted at the building's rather more glamorous past.

The detective locked his car and went in through the rear entrance. A small vestibule with a door on either side gave access to the lounge bar and a pool room. Tudor pushed against the door for the latter.

Inside, sunlight, streaming through the blinds of the large window which fronted the street, banded the scrubbed wooden floor and faded, dark red wallpaper. Two youths were playing pool. A dark haired young man in T shirt and jeans was crouched over the table, whilst his sandy-haired opponent stood to one side, his cue resting in the crook of his arm like a rifle. As Tudor came through the door, 'sandy hair' looked up and nudged his friend just as he was about to take his shot. The cue skidded over the cue ball and the dark-haired youth went sprawling over the table. He leapt back up and rounded on his friend.

'Jimmie! Whadya doing? You stupid fuck…'

Jimmie was still staring at Tudor and the dark-haired youth followed his gaze.

'Ooops,' said Tudor with a grin.

'Oh, it's you,' said the dark-haired youth and looked sullen. He had a narrow face, thin lips and prominent eyebrows which almost met in the middle.

Tudor strode over to the pool table and stood directly in front of Shaun, fixed him with a hard-eyed stare. Shaun stared back with blood shot eyes. It all came down to who would blink first.

'You don't seem pleased to see me, Shaun. Why is that, I wonder?'

'I just missed my shot, thanks to you.'

'Foul play, wasn't it? I thought that was your speciality, Shaun?'

Shaun held his gaze for a moment longer but then turned away. Retrieving his pint from the bar, he took a swig. Wiping the back of his hand across his mouth he said, 'Did you want something, Mr Tudor? Only, as you can see, I'm in the middle of a game of pool with my mate, Jimmie, here.'

'I'll come straight to the point then. Where were you last night?'

Shaun leaned back against the bar and furrowed his brows as if deep in thought. 'Ooh now, let me think. Where were we last night, Jimmie?' Jimmie grinned. 'Oh yeah, we were here!' he said, as if it came as a sudden revelation.

'What, all night?'

'Pretty much, yeah. It was a lock-in. I got so pissed, Jimmie here had to take me home. That's right, isn't it, Jimbo?'

'That's right, rat-arsed, he was,' Jimmie confirmed.

It was like talking to Laurel and Hardy. Except that Jimmie, though gormless, was the chubby one. He couldn't have got through Paget's pantry window, but Shaun was slim enough.

'Anybody else there who could confirm your story?' he asked.

'Are you saying I'm making this up, Mr Tudor?'

Tudor narrowed his eyes, 'Don't push your luck, sonny. I'm a vindictive bastard and I've got a long memory.'

Chastened, Shaun proceeded to recite a list of names and Tudor jotted them down. Tudor was familiar with all of them. Most had previous. He added Shaun and his chubby pal to the list.

'All the usual suspects, eh, Shaun? Let's see... Darren Parfitt; convictions for assault and petty theft...Tommy Russell; receiving stolen goods...Oh, and Pete Goodhall; two counts of burglary...' Tudor paused, tried to gauge Shaun's reaction but could discern none. 'Dave Maddox, he continued; 'taking cars without the owners' permission, and last but not least, Alun Edwards; possession of a Class A drug. Nice company you keep. And no doubt these paragons of virtue will vouch for the fact that you never left their sight. So, just to get it straight, you were drinking in here until the early hours of the morning – how many pints do you reckon you consumed in that time?'

Shaun silently mouthed the numbers as he attempted to add them up, a task which ultimately proved beyond him.

'I dunno, 'bout twelve,' he said.

'Well, it's a nice round number at any rate. Twelve pints of... lager, was it?' Shaun pointed to the name emblazoned on his pint glass. 'All right, if you want to be pedantic, twelve pints of Heineken at what...three quid a pint? That's thirty six of Her Majesty's pounds. You drink in here most days, don't you.' He stated it as a fact rather than a question. 'Over the course of a week that must cost a bit. You're not working so, where did you get the money to pay for all that booze, never mind run that pimped up fiesta outside?'

Shaun took another long sip at his pint.

'That's what job-seekers is for, init, Jimmie?' Jimmie grinned and raised his glass.

'A lot of people would disagree with you,' said Tudor. Me for one, he thought. He didn't go to work and pay his taxes to provide beer money for tow-rags like Shaun Tomlins. 'So, you're *actively* seeking work, are you, Shaun?' Tudor was unable to keep the disbelief out of his voice.

'Oh yeah, deffo, Mr Tudor. Trouble is, I'm a watchamacallit... a square peg in a round hole. I'm difficult to place.'

Not for me, laddie, Tudor was tempted to say, *I've got a cosy prison cell that would be a perfect fit for a square peg like you.* Frustratingly, it would take a lot more than mere suspicion to put Shaun in there for any length of time. Tudor cast a jaundiced eye over the pool room with its shabby furniture and the yellowed prints of dogs playing billiards that hung on its walls.

'Well, you deffo won't find a job in here lads,' he told them. 'I'll be back,' he added by way of a parting shot.

Back in his car, Tudor opened a window and lit a cigarette. Inhaling deeply, he let the smoke escape slowly from the corner of his mouth, then opened his notebook and went down the list again, tracing the names with his finger. Two of them, Pete Goodhall and Shaun Tomlins, were of particular interest as both had previous convictions for burglary and he decided to concentrate on them for the time being.

His mobile rang. Tudor snatched it up from the seat beside him and checked the caller ID; Maggie Mellor. *Perhaps she'd changed her mind about going for that drink...*

'Missing me already, are you?' he said playfully.

'Me and the entire squad, Sarge; saw Crawford crying earlier.'

He could hear the laughter in her voice and felt crushed.

'OK, OK. So, what's up?'

'Just been talking to one of the neighbours, says she saw a young guy hanging around outside Paget's house that afternoon.'

'She give you a description?'

'Yes, but it's pretty vague; medium height, dark hair... doesn't narrow it down much.'

'Oh, I wouldn't say that. I'm looking at someone right now who matches that description perfectly...'

Shaun had just come out of the pub and head down, was hurrying over to his car. Tudor dived down behind the dashboard as his suspect cast a furtive glance in his direction. 'Now, where's he off to in such a hurry?' he muttered to himself.

'Sarge? Sarge...are you still there?'

'Sorry, Mellor, gotta go. Suspect's on the move.'

He ended the call and stuffed the phone in his jacket pocket. Moments later, he heard the throaty rumble of the souped-up fiesta being started.

Risking a quick peep, Tudor was in time to see the boy racer sweep past him as he headed up towards the car park's exit, where he signalled a right-hand turn. Tudor waited until the fiesta had cleared the car park then, tossing the stub-end of the cigarette out of the window, followed him out onto the Shrewsbury road. He joined the traffic four cars behind Shaun's but the Fiesta's distinctive colour scheme made it easy to follow from a distance. Besides, Shaun was boxed in behind a Land Rover with a trailer, and a white transit van. So, for the moment at least, he wasn't going anywhere fast.

The little convoy snaked its way at a leisurely pace along the Shrewsbury Road and past the school playing fields. Across the fields, Caradoc's hill fort stood sentinel over the approach to the town; a brooding presence even with a clear blue sky behind it. When the convoy entered All Stretton, the car immediately in front of Tudor turned off, reducing the gap between him and his suspect. The rest, including Shaun Tomlins, proceeded to drive straight through the village, and it became apparent to Tudor that Shaun was heading for the A49. Once on the trunk road, it would be much easier for a 'boy racer' like Shaun to overtake the vehicles that boxed him in and take off.

As Tudor had foreseen, the moment they joined the A49, Shaun began swinging out into the oncoming traffic, chancing his luck in a bid to overtake the vehicles that blocked his way. Each time he was forced to swing back in again. These manoeuvres of Shaun's grew increasingly reckless, to the point where Tudor began to fear he would lose his chief suspect to a fatal road accident.

They were approaching a straight stretch and the detective knew that, when Shaun made his move, he would have to go with him. High speed pursuit had not featured much in Tudor's career so far, and he began to feel nervous at the prospect of risking his neck on what could turn out to be a wild goose chase. He was still considering this when, with a squirt of black smoke from the exhaust, the Fiesta shot out from behind the transit van. Instinctively, Tudor slammed the gear stick into third and stamped his foot down hard on the accelerator. The Mondeo seemed to hesitate for a moment then lunged forward and he narrowly missed clipping the car in front, as he swung out into the opposite carriageway. Tudor still had three vehicles to get past as Shaun whipped in front of the Land Rover. The Mondeo was barrelling along, its engine growling like a cave full of angry bears. In the distance, a lorry was approaching. Straining forward in his seat, Tudor held the wheel in a dead man's grip and, with the pedal flat to the floor, willed the Mondeo to go faster.

The lorry loomed larger in his windscreen by the second. The driver flashed his lights. Gritting his teeth, Tudor ignored him. Only the Land Rover to get past and it was down to seconds. It was reckless to go on but the fiesta was pulling away from him. With the rev counter red-lining, the lorry was almost on top of him.

'Jesus! Come on, come on,' screamed Tudor.

The squeal of brakes echoed his scream, the lorry juddered and its tyres smoked. The pungent smell of burning rubber filled the Mondeo's cabin as Tudor shot through the narrowest of gaps, pursued by the sound of honking motorists. In his rear view mirror he could see the Land Rover driver mouthing obscenities and shaking his fist at him. He didn't blame him, it had been an appalling piece of driving on his part, verging on the suicidal, almost. Did he hold his life so cheap, that he was prepared to throw it away in pursuit of a worthless scrote like Tomlins?

In his head, he could hear Maggie Mellor scolding him, "*You're not a stunt driver, Sarge. You could have caused a major accident.*"

The thought was a sobering one and Tudor eased his foot off the accelerator and shifted into fifth. Shaun's fiesta, though some distance away, was still clearly visible, thanks to its bright paintwork and the owner's bad taste. Tudor gradually closed the gap and, by the time they reached the outskirts of Shrewsbury, he was only three cars behind him once more.

They entered the town via Frankwell and crossed The Severn at the Welsh Bridge. The traffic was busier here and progress was slow. As they waited for the lights ahead to change, Tudor found himself thinking about Mellor again. He'd worked with her on and off for about eighteen months now and still knew very little about her life outside the force. She was secretive, that one, and gave very little away, but that only made her all the more alluring. Tudor was well aware of how pathetic his pursuit of her must seem. Maggie had made it quite clear on a number of occasions now that she wasn't interested. She was too young for him, in any case.

This damned job, he thought, it made it so difficult to maintain a relationship. Sally, his ex, had never accepted that. A couple, with two children of a similar age to his own, passed by and he experienced a sudden overpowering sense of loss. He missed his kids, Gareth and Cerys, so much. Close to tears, he stared out at the brown river which curved away to his left to form a loop around the town. In that moment, it seemed to Tudor that life itself was flowing away from him and he was swimming against the tide.

The lights changed and Shaun was on the move again. Banishing these unhappy thoughts to the back of his mind, Tudor followed him under the railway bridge into Castle Foregate. They were heading away from town now, and he was starting to wonder how much longer it would

27

be before they reached their destination when, without signalling, Shaun shot off to the right. Oncoming traffic prevented Tudor from doing the same and, powerless to do anything about it, he could only watch as the fiesta raced down the road and disappeared from sight.

For the second time that day, Tudor showed a total lack of consideration for other motorists. Impatiently revving the engine, he forced his way across the path of the oncoming vehicles and went roaring after Shaun. Rounding a bend, he spotted the fiesta parked outside a house on the right. He was going too fast to pull up and park without attracting attention, so he decided to drive on past and park further up the street. Shaun was already out of his car and walking up the driveway of the modest semi. In his rear view mirror, Tudor watched him open a side door and go inside.

The detective gave it a further couple of minutes then got out of his car and walked back down the street. The house Shaun had entered was one of a row of older, red brick houses with grey slate roofs. This one had a smart new block-paved driveway. Tudor glanced up and down the street. Two doors down a young postman in grey shorts and a Royal Mail sweatshirt was coming down the path. Tudor met him at the gate and flashed his warrant card.

'Got anything for number seventy-nine?' he asked.

The young postman, it seemed, was a bit of a jobsworth. 'I didn't get a proper look,' he complained. 'Could I see it again, please?'

Watching for any signs of movement in the upper windows of number 79, Tudor brandished his warrant card in front of the young man's face. The postman scrutinised it carefully and, apparently satisfied, pulled two envelopes from the bundle he was clutching and handed them to the detective. Pocketing his warrant card, Tudor made a note of the name and the full address.

'Thanks, he said, offering him the envelopes. 'You can pop them through the letterbox now.'

'What's he done?' asked the postman, ignoring them.

'Nothing, as far as I know, routine enquiry, that's all.' Tudor thrust the letters into the postie's hands. 'On your bike then,' he said firmly.

'It's a van, not a bike,' he heard the young man mutter as he returned to his daily routine.

Tudor got back in his car and requested a criminal records check on a Mr G. Edkins, the occupant of number 79. He could hear the rattle of fingers on the keyboard as the details were typed into the computer. While he waited, he kept a watchful eye on the house through his rear view mirror.

'Right, got him,' said a voice in his ear. Gary Edkins, aged 38, two convictions for assault and one for receiving. Last arrest was two years ago.'

'Thank you. You just made my day. Oh, hold on, this could be him now. If it is, he couldn't have timed it better.'

A black 4 x 4 had pulled onto the block-paved driveway. As Tudor watched, a tall well-built individual with a shaved head and tattooed forearms got out of the vehicle and let himself in through the front door of number 79.

'Looks like Mr Edkins is in da house,' said Tudor triumphantly. 'Laters,' he added, sticking with the street argot and ended the call. He was considering his next move which, without a warrant, was problematical, when he heard a woman scream. He couldn't be certain but it seemed to come from the Edkins' residence. Tudor was out of the car and walking back to the house, when a naked woman came stumbling out of number 79. The hysterical woman was struggling to pull a flimsy negligee around her as she ran barefoot up her neighbour's driveway and hammered on the front door with her fists.

'Help me. For God's sake, help me. He's going to kill 'im!' she screamed.

Tudor called for back-up and an ambulance. This was a gift from the gods. He could now legally enter and search number 79 – he was about to save a man's life.

The woman was still furiously banging on the door; her nakedness still clearly visible beneath the flimsy, black negligee.

'Need some help, luv?' Tudor called from the foot of the driveway.

The woman ceased her pounding. She turned and Tudor was treated to the full frontal view, which was even more interesting than the rear had been. The woman was about thirty-five; a petite blonde, though it was evident to Tudor this was not her natural hair colour. In contrast to her rounded figure, she had a slightly pinched, but none-the-less, attractive face which betrayed no sign of embarrassment before Tudor's brazen stare. It wasn't the first time in his career that he'd come across a naked woman – the important difference being that, unlike the others, this one was very much alive.

'Oh, thank God for that,' she cried. 'Quick, it's my husband, he's going to kill the lad if you don't stop him.'

'Show me,' said Tudor, then realised the irony of making such a statement to a woman who had just shown him everything.

With a glance back over her shoulder to make sure Tudor was following her, the woman ran back round to number 79, the filmy negligee floating up behind her. The lads would be buying him pints for months on the strength of this story.

At the doorway, the woman stood aside to allow Tudor to enter first. 'Upstairs, back bedroom,' she said.

That much Tudor had gathered; the ceiling reverberated with the stamp of heavy feet. An angry voice spat out a string of expletives in a deep basso; each one punctuated by the sickening thud of a fist colliding with solid flesh, and answered in a terrified falsetto. Tudor had a fair idea which of those two voices belonged to the young Shaun Tomlins.

'What's your name, luv?' asked Tudor.

'Karen,' the woman replied, shaking.

'OK, Karen. You stay here. Reinforcements and an ambulance are on the way.'

A thump much louder than the others and the splintering of furniture had Tudor bounding up the stairs. The door immediately facing the top of the stairs was open. Through it he could see the burly form of Gary Edkins crouched down at the side of a double bed whose bedding was in disarray. It bore all the hallmarks of a spare bedroom; plainly furnished and with very little in the way of decoration. Karen had at least had the decency not to sully the bed she shared with Edkins. Stepping inside, it became apparent to Tudor that the outraged husband had just extracted the luckless Tomlins from the wreckage of a cheap built-in wardrobe. Becoming aware of the detective's presence, Edkins turned a baleful face in his direction and slowly came to his feet.

'Who the fuck, are you?' he growled.

'Police,' Tudor calmly informed him, and showed the man his warrant card. 'You're under arrest. You do not have to say... anything, but... it may harm your defence if you do not mention, when questioned, something which you later rely on in court. Anything you do say may be given in evidence.'

'What's the charge?'

Tudor stared at the man in disbelief, then at the battered figure lying at his feet, and back again. In the silence, the familiar wail of a police patrol car siren could be heard; for the moment distant but growing louder by the second. Shaun, naked and spattered with blood, managed to raise himself up onto one elbow.

'Oh, fuck, it's you,' he groaned and fell back again.

'Causing grievous bodily harm to Mr Tomlins will do for now,' intoned Tudor. 'But, we could be looking at attempted murder.'

'I caught 'im shaggin' my missus, what would you expect me to do?'

Tudor had some sympathy with this argument. What would he have done, he wondered, had he caught his ex, Sally, *in flagrante delicto* with her lover, now her second husband, that smarmy bastard, James Sadler?

These reflections were interrupted by the sound of heavy boots on the stairs and two male police officers appeared in the doorway.

'Hands together behind your back now please, Gary,' Tudor ordered.

Edkins glanced towards the two officers. His face wore the look of a trapped animal; the lips drawn back revealed yellowed teeth, whilst the hands held at his sides remained bunched into fists.

'Don't even think about it,' Tudor warned.

Edkins continued to defy him for a moment longer, then turning away from them, held his hands out behind his back.

'Cuff him and take him down to the car,' Tudor told the waiting constables. He pointed to the prone figure at the side of the bed. 'This one's for the ambulance.'

With Edkins gone, Tudor knelt down beside the injured Shaun. So, his mad dash into town had simply been a hormone rush at the thought of getting his end away. 'You really like to live dangerously, don't you, son,' he said. 'Still, I imagine she was worth it.'

Tudor pictured Karen on her neighbour's doorstep, her naked back towards him, but when he called to her and she turned around, it was Maggie Mellor he was staring at. He shook the disturbing thought away. The only naked body here was Shaun's.

Beaten but unbowed, Tomlins summoned all his remaining strength to push himself up into a sitting position. 'Fuck you,' he spat through bloodied lips.

'That's the spirit,' said Tudor, patting him on the shoulder.

There was a tap on the door and an overweight, bespectacled paramedic in his yellow, high vis jacket stepped into the room.

'OK mate, he's all yours,' Tudor told him.

He was about to get up and out of the paramedic's way, when he spotted some boxes lying in the bottom of the shattered wardrobe. Tudor reached in and, pushing some shards of wood aside, took one out; it was a brand new, unopened iPhone. There were dozens of them. He stood up and opened another of the built-in wardrobe's doors and found an even bigger stash of consumer goodies.

The detective took out his phone and rang the station; he was going to need some more help…

CHAPTER FOUR

LYING ON his back, his eyes closed, as he drifted in that half-world between sleep and wakefulness, Harry felt a warm breath against his ear.

'Harry...Har-ree, are you awake?' That familiar voice; soft but insistent, whispered in his ear.

'Hmmm,' he murmured, and turning on his side, rolled into Annie's arms. She held him to her and he breathed in the scent of her warm skin.

'Wake up, darling,' she said, her voice husky with desire, and carefully placed a kiss on each eyelid. 'And, about time too,' she chided, as his eyes blinked open and he took in her smiling face. 'For a man who says he can't sleep, you take a lot of waking up.'

'Why, what's the matter?' he asked, trying to shake off the last vestiges of slumber.

'Oh, Harry. You are slow on the uptake this morning.'

She cradled his face in her hands and pressed her lips hard against his. Something cold and metallic dangled against his cheek.

'You slept in your earrings? You've never done that before,' he said.

'You've never bought me diamonds before. I love them so much, I'm never going to take them out,' she replied and kissed him again. 'And…I know it was my special birthday but I think you deserve a present too.'

'Oh, you don't have to...'

'Shhhhh,' she said, and pressed a finger to his lips. 'You don't know what it is yet.'

She took the finger away and, slipping her hand beneath the duvet, reached between his legs. Harry closed his eyes and, with a low groan that came from deep within him, surrendered to her touch…

When he opened his eyes again, he was wide awake and alone in his darkened bedroom. Annie, such a physical presence a moment ago, seemingly so real that he could feel her touch, smell her perfume, had returned to whatever recess of his mind she still lived in.

Annie had come to him many times before in this way. Each time it was a different version of the girl he'd first met when he was just twelve and she was eleven; sometimes the younger, sometimes the older Annie. But just as on every previous occasion, he felt that same keen sense of loss and a reluctance to let her go. He supposed he was in denial, that awful piece of psychobabble that, along with closure, people trotted out at times like this. But Harry didn't want closure. He had no wish to get over Annie and move on, to consign to the past the woman he'd loved for the best part of fifty years.

Harry glanced over at the bedside clock; the large, red numbers showed it was 3:30 am. It would be several hours before daylight brought some relief from the darkness of the night, but the gloom he harboured within him would remain.

CHAPTER FIVE

THE DRUMMER raised his sticks above his head and brought them together four times to count *RockFace* in and lead guitarist, Paul Hudson, launched into 'Brown Sugar'. Crouched over his stratocaster, he blasted out the intro as if it was a machine gun he held in his hand. The response from the small crowd was immediate; the women jumped to their feet, began dancing and singing along with the band. And by the first chorus, their husbands and boyfriends had abandoned their pints and joined them. It worked every time.

On electric bass, Glyn Tudor was enjoying a rare moment of happiness. He lived for nights like this; an appreciative audience and a feeling that he could do no wrong; that he was master of his instrument. For him the gig was a fitting celebration, one that marked the end of what had been a very satisfying day; Gary Edkins was locked up for the night and would be charged in the morning. And he was hopeful that the cuckolded Edkins would provide him with the evidence he needed to bang Shaun Tomlins up with him.

Glyn glanced across at Paul Hudson. As usual, all the best looking women in the room had gathered in front of him. Head back, eyes closed, he was shamelessly playing up to his audience giving them his impression of a rock-god. Blond-haired and blue-eyed, he was good looking in a rugged sort of way. He looked like a bad boy and the women loved him for it. Lead guitarists the world over, professional or amateur, invariably got the pick of the women. Nobody took much notice of the bass guitarist; they just weren't sexy. But for tonight at least, Glyn didn't care; he was on a promise of sorts. A half promise anyway. More a non-committal maybe, now he thought about it. The tantalising Maggie Mellor had said she might pop down to the Crown and Anchor to see the band play. He scanned the audience but couldn't see her anywhere.

Now that they'd got them dancing, Paul didn't want them to stop and with a nod to the drummer, Steve Sallis, and keyboards player, Ray Tanner, went straight into that other crowd pleaser, 'All right now'. They'd just started the second verse when Glyn saw her walk in. She was wearing a dark blue jacket over a white T-shirt and a pair of blue denim jeans. Disappointingly, she hadn't come alone but at least her friend was female; a tall, red-head, and not a boyfriend. They stood at the back, near the bar. Maggie caught his eye and gave him a self-conscious wave.

In return, Glyn gave her a nervous smile. Desperate to impress the girl, he turned up the volume on his bass guitar and began improvising around the song's usual bassline. Paul's head came swivelling round. He glared at his bass man but Tudor was too wrapped up in his playing to notice. Annoyed at this intrusion into what he considered to be his province, Hudson increased the volume of his own instrument. When this failed to bring his band-mate to heel, he grudgingly ceased playing and with just the drums for accompaniment, let Tudor have his few minutes of glory.

Glyn was on a roll. He was playing riffs he didn't even know he could play and getting away with it. He even threw in some 'slap' bass and the crowd went wild. So much so, that when Paul came in again, Glyn got a round of applause – he couldn't remember the last time that had happened.

When they came to the end of the number, Paul announced they were taking a break and would be back in twenty minutes. *He must really have his arse in his hand*, Glyn realised – they weren't officially due to take a break for at least another quarter of an hour.

The second the *stratocaster* was safely perched on its stand, Paul stormed over to confront Glyn.

'What the fuck was that?' he fumed.

'Just freshening it up a bit, Paul…you know, updating it a little…'

'We're a fucking covers band, Glyn – our audience expect us to sound exactly like the original.'

Our audience. Who the hell did he think he was? The Pompous twat. Glyn stole a quick glance towards the bar. A tall guy in a leather jacket appeared to be chatting up Maggie's red-headed friend. This was no time to argue the toss, he decided; Leather Jacket might have a mate…

'Stick to the original. Got it,' he said and handing Paul his bass, rushed off to buy Maggie Mellor a drink before some other guy beat him to it.

A mystified Paul turned to the drummer and asked, 'What am I, his roadie?'

The area around the bar was crowded. Punters, most of them men, were jostling for drinks; they obviously found dancing a thirsty business. Tudor searched for Mellor but could see only her tall friend, now in animated conversation with Mr Leather Jacket. His spirits sank. The girl had probably taken one look at the place and walked back out again. The

Crown and Anchor wasn't exactly the most salubrious of watering holes. The Landlord and his wife were a couple of aging rockers; he still wore his hair down to his shoulders, even though it had all but disappeared from the top of his head and turned grey. She wore leather skirts that were far too short for her and black fishnet stockings. The pub itself was a prime example of a mid-twentieth century pub, complete with tobacco-stained ceilings.

And a covers band playing mainly sixties rock was hardly likely to float her boat either. It just proved how little he knew her, he supposed. No doubt her friend had only stayed on because she'd pulled. He was about to get himself a drink when there was a tap on his shoulder. He spun round and there she was.

'Evenin', Sarge,' she said. Was she mocking him? He couldn't be sure.

Her sudden appearance took him by surprise in more ways than one. He'd been too busy grandstanding earlier to fully appreciate how much more attractive she was out of uniform and, with her dark, shoulder length hair down rather than pinned up under her cap, she looked gorgeous.

'There you are, I thought you'd…'

'What?' she said.

'It doesn't matter. Can I get you a drink?'

'Got one in, Sarge.' She held up a wine glass that was three quarters full. There was an imprint of her lower lip in red lipstick on the rim, he noticed.

'I think we can dispense with the Sarge as we're off duty, don't you?' Tudor nodded towards her girlfriend. 'She didn't waste much time.'

Maggie took a sip of her wine and, when she lowered her glass, her lips glistened invitingly. 'That's Elli for you. She attracts men like moths to a candle flame.'

'She sounds dangerous...' said Tudor.

'When you play with fire...' said Maggie, with a glance at her friend. 'I just hope she remembers to give me a ride home.'

As they watched, Leather Jacket slipped his arm around the red-head's waist and tried to pull her into a clinch. Deftly sidestepping his mouth, Elli, her face pressed up against the man's cheek, glanced back over his shoulder and gave Maggie the thumbs up.

'Oh, my god, what is she like,' said Maggie, staring down into her glass and pretending not to know her.

'You know, I can give you a lift home, if you need one...' Tudor offered, careful not to sound too eager. Having got her to himself at last, he didn't want to frighten the girl off.

'Thanks, but she's just toying with him. Elli's the cat and he's the dead mouse – he just doesn't know it yet.' Her brown eyes engaged with his. 'Anyway, why are we talking about Elli when your day sounds so much more exciting?'

Tudor found himself blushing. 'Exciting is putting it a bit strong...'

'What?' she exclaimed. 'You're the talk of the station.' And she proceeded to count off the main highlights on her fingers. 'A naked blonde, her blood splattered lover, her cuckolded husband and a stack of stolen booty? Looks like you've solved the case, Sherlock.'

'I wish you wouldn't keep calling me that,' pleaded Tudor. 'I may have solved *a* case... I'm just not sure if it's *the* case. They're still searching the Edkins' house but so far there's no sign of Paget's jewellery.'

'But, you're convinced this Shaun Tomlins is the thief?'

'I'd bet a week's wages on it. It's got that little scrote's fingerprints all over it.'

'Sounds like you two have got some history.'

'Our paths have crossed a few times...' Tudor admitted, his blue-grey eyes turning visibly colder at the remembrance.

'And you don't like him?'

'He preys on the elderly and infirm – what's to like?' said Tudor, as if the fact of the young burglar's existence on the same planet was an offence to him.

'I'd hate to get on the wrong side of you,' observed Maggie.

'You're all right, you're one of us,' Tudor assured her.

'I'm hoping to be...'

It took him a moment to decode what she'd said.

'Oh, I see. After my job, are you, Mellor?' He'd often wondered if that sharp humour of hers was a cloak for ambition, and here was the proof.

'I was intending to aim a bit higher than that, Sarge,' she said, in that teasing manner of hers that left him wondering if she was joking or not. 'And I seem to remember you saying it was first names only tonight.'

'You're right, I did.'

Tudor stole an envious glance towards the bar, looking for an escape. Maggie was staring at him expectantly – waiting for him to comment; offer some encouragement for her aspiration, perhaps? The pressure for him to say something, anything, soon became unbearable.

'No, you go for it,' he found himself saying. 'We need more women in the CID.'

They both knew he didn't mean a word of it. Maggie was about to say so when she saw the band's lank-haired drummer looking pale-faced and anxious, hurrying towards them.

'Hello, what's up with your mate,' she said.

Tudor turned and, when he saw Steve Sallis's face, he groaned. 'I've got a pretty good idea,' he said.

'Sorry luv, I need to borrow Glyn for a minute,' Steve said, pulling Tudor to one side.

'Don't tell me,' said Tudor. 'Some bloke's caught Paul snoggin' his wife.'

'Girlfriend,' Steve gasped, a little out of breath. 'Yours is fit, by the way.'

'Where is he?' said Tudor, secretly flattered that Steve had automatically assumed that the gorgeous Maggie was his girlfriend.

'Round the back, on the car park,' said Steve.

'OK, I'll just let Maggie know where I'm going.'

'Well, make it quick, will you. Wonderboy's in big trouble this time.'

Tudor went back to Maggie and quickly explained the situation.

'Don't go away. I'll be back as soon as I can,' he said, whilst vowing to himself that next time this happened he was going leave Paul to take his punishment like the hapless Tomlins had.

'You're joking,' she said. 'I'm coming with you.'

Maggie hadn't met the band's lothario yet and he preferred to keep it that way. On the other hand if he left her behind, he risked losing her to another pick-up merchant like Leather Jacket.

'OK, but take it from me, Paul's an arse.'

*

The drummer led them out into a stone-flagged passageway, past the gents' toilets and down a short flight of steps to the pub's rear entrance. The pub backed on to open fields. It was a dark, starless night and the car

42

park was poorly lit. Staring out into the darkness, Glyn could see very little beyond the yellow crescent cast by the porch light but he could hear the sound of raised voices somewhere off to the left.

'Where is he? I can't see him,' he said, his breath opaque on the cold air.

'Over there in the corner,' said Steve, pointing.

Tudor moved beyond the arc of light over ground that was uneven and dotted with potholes. He cursed as his foot went down into one of these cavities and he felt the shock of cold water closing over his shoe. In the far left corner of the car park he could see an oak tree. Beneath it stood a rather large gentleman in a rugby shirt. Seemingly impervious to the cold, he was shaking a huge fist at a pale figure perched in the lower branches and, in a voice laden with Welsh cadences, called on him to, 'Come down yere and face me like a man.'

Tudor knew there was no way Paul was going to do that. Hudson was a ladies man; his forte was foreplay not fisticuffs. And even if he had been handy with his fists, a man of Paul's slender build stood no chance against this man mountain from Wales. And, after a moment's consideration, Tudor decided that he didn't either.

The detective dropped behind his companions and, delving into his trouser pocket, pulled out a crumpled packet of cigarettes and a zippo lighter. Lighting up he took in a deep lungful and, closing his eyes, released a great plume of blue smoke. He knew he should give it up but at moments like these, smoking was deeply satisfying.

Realising that Tudor was no longer with them, Steve and Maggie turned back.

'What are you doing?' asked Maggie.

'I'm assessing the situation,' Tudor replied, offering Steve a cigarette.

The drummer took one and Tudor lit it for him.

'Hello?' said Maggie. 'The guy over there has chased your bandmate up a tree and he's going to be there all night unless we do something about it.'

'Yes, he is, isn't he?' observed Tudor with some satisfaction.

'You're enjoying this, aren't you,' she said.

'Yes, I am.' He caught Maggie's sideways look. 'And you needn't look at me like that. I wouldn't hesitate if it was in the line of duty, but I've lost count of the number of times I've had to step in to save that idiot's neck. He just can't keep it in his trousers, that's his trouble. Beats me what these women see in him.'

'You mean, apart from the blond hair, the blue eyes and the rugged good looks?' said Maggie.

'Oh, don't tell me you fancy him too, Mellor…' Tudor groaned.

'Not me, Sarge, I much prefer the knight in shining armour type who slays the dragon and saves the girl…'

'What girl?'

Tudor hadn't noticed her till now; a diminutive brunette with a surprisingly large bust for one so small. She was standing several metres away from her boyfriend and was shivering, or perhaps she was crying, he couldn't tell which. 'Where did she spring from?' asked Tudor.

'She was hiding behind the tree,' Steve supplied.

'What about her?' said Tudor, his resolve beginning to slip.

'She looks upset,' said Maggie

'Oh, she'll get over *him* soon enough, I expect' said Tudor. 'I'm sure half of 'em only snog Paul in order to get their boyfriend's attention.'

'And what sort of attention do you think Taffy over there is likely to give her if Paul continues to taunt him from the safety of that tree?'

asked Maggie.

Tudor took another look at the girl and decided she was crying, after all. Damn her and damn Paul, he thought, but it made no difference; to hold back any longer would scupper any chance he might have of a relationship with Mellor. Besides, they couldn't complete the gig without Paul. Tudor took one last drag on his cigarette and, throwing it down, stubbed it out. 'Come on then,' he said.

Several of the pub's patrons had followed them outside to have a smoke and now watched the trio with interest as they picked their way across the pot-holed car park.

'Oh great. Now we have an audience. That's all we need,' complained Tudor. 'Right, Mellor, you see to the girl,' he instructed. 'And Steve, I want you to hang back a bit. We don't want to crowd him. But be ready to give Paul a hand, if he needs one. In my limited experience, it's a lot easier to climb a tree than it is to get back down again.'

Tudor sauntered up to the Welshman. Up close, the man was enormous. Square jawed and powerfully built, it would take an entire forward pack to subdue him. This is how the Christians must have felt when they went into the arena and came face to face with a muscle-bound gladiator, he thought. For his part the Welshman barely spared the detective a glance, but steadfastly maintained his watch on the figure in the tree.

'What's going on?' asked Tudor, keeping his tone neutral.

'Thank God,' he heard Paul murmur.

The Welshman looked him up and down. 'Nothing that need concern you,' he said.

'Let me guess, then,' said Tudor with a glance at his band mate. 'Our guitar hero up there was messing with your girl and now you want to beat seven shades out of him. That about right, Paul?'

'Glyn, that's not helpful,' came a tremulous voice from the oak.

The Welshman rushed at the tree and placed two huge hands on either side of its trunk as if he intended to shake Paul out of its branches. 'Paul, is it? He was snogging 'er face off,' he growled then, turning to Tudor, 'You know this joker, do you?'

'I'm in the band...' he said and wondered what more it would take, other than performing in a clown costume, before audiences remembered him.

The big man appeared doubtful. 'Are you?' he said. 'Which one are you then?'

Tudor sighed. 'Mr. Invisible, the bass player.'

'You're kidding. That's not you're real name, is it?'

'No, it's my stage name. Look, the thing is... sorry, what's your name?'

'O-wen,' the Welshman supplied.

'Thing is Owen...' Tudor consulted his watch. 'We should have been on stage five minutes ago and if we don't get back in there and finish our set, we won't get paid. Now, I consider myself a pretty good judge of character and you strike me as being a fair-minded sort of bloke so, I'm sure you wouldn't want to spoil everybody's evening by forcing us to cancel the gig...' Out of the corner of his eye he saw Maggie place a consoling arm around Owen's sobbing girlfriend and wondered how deep the big man's feelings went for the girl. 'So, I'm proposing that you postpone retribution until we've finished playing...'

There was a strangled cry of protest from Paul.

'Although, if that was my girl over there,' he nodded towards the tiny girl who now had her head nestled against Maggie's neck, 'and I really cared about her, I'd take her home and forget about loverboy up there, he really isn't worth the time or trouble. Anyway, it's up to you. Meanwhile, do we have a deal?'

Tudor extended a hand and, after some hesitation, Owen grasped it in a finger numbing grip.

'Good man,' said Tudor. 'Now let's get inside, it's bloody freezing out here.' And, leaving Steve to help the reprieved lothario down from his arboreal sanctuary, he hustled Owen, his penitent girlfriend and Maggie back inside.

CHAPTER SIX

From the Shropshire Post

WIDOWER BRUTALLY
BEATEN BY INTRUDER

By Holly Ryder

Widower, Harry Paget (61) woke in the early hours of Tuesday morning to find an intruder looming over his bed. When Mr Paget bravely tackled the man, he was cruelly beaten to the ground and left unconscious. The plucky widower was taken to A & E where he was found to have a broken nose, a hairline fracture of the left cheekbone, a fractured rib and numerous cuts and bruises. The thief, believed to be in his twenties and of medium height with dark brown or black hair, fled with jewellery belonging to Harry's late wife, Annie. She and Harry were childhood sweethearts and had been married for 36 years. At his home today, Mr Paget pleaded with the thief to return the jewellery, which is of great sentimental value, and offered a reward for its return.

And, in a new development, police today arrested one man and are waiting to interview another who was taken to hospital with serious injuries. However, the police spokesperson refused to confirm if the arrest was connected to the burglary.

Sandwiched between the reporter's byline and the article was a large colour photograph of Harry's bruised and swollen face, which rendered his injuries in such clarity it made Harry wince. It was the same story every time he caught sight of himself in a mirror; as if he'd dived into a wormhole, his mind took him racing back in time to the moment he'd opened his eyes and seen that ghastly, red face peering down at him.

Harry shook the image away and re-read the article's final paragraph. The news that a man had been arrested came as a complete surprise as he hadn't heard from DS Tudor or that nice young policewoman since they'd interviewed him. It wasn't good enough, he decided, especially when they had assured him that he would be informed of any new developments. Harry felt badly let down. He'd read often enough of victims and their relatives complaining that the criminals got more consideration than they did. Well, he wasn't going to let that happen to him.

Heaving himself out of his armchair and ignoring the stab of pain from his bruised ribs, he hobbled over to the bureau and, opening one of the drawers, took out DS Tudor's business card. Snatching up the phone from its base on top of the bureau, Harry dialled the number on the card and asked for Detective Sergeant Tudor. After listening to several

49

minutes of Musak, designed no doubt to reduce irate callers to something approaching a vegetative state, the desk sergeant came back on the line to inform Harry that DS Tudor was unavailable at present. Could he take a message?

The Musak had done nothing to improve his mood but there was little Harry could do, other than request that DS Tudor phone him back when he was free.

Harry replaced the phone and, going to the patio door, stared out at his garden; his mood mirrored in the bleakness of the world he saw outside. The early morning sun, with its promise of a bright new day, had been extinguished by a blanket of iron-grey cloud. As Harry gazed at it he felt the weight of that heavy sky settle around his shoulders.

The feeling was a familiar one; an old friend in a perverse way but still, an unwelcome visitor. Harry's life had not been touched by depression until Annie died. He managed to keep the 'black dog' at bay most of the time yet, like the demon hound, it stalked him.

Restless, his thoughts returned to the article in *The Shropshire Post*. Was it wise, he wondered in retrospect, to draw further attention to himself when, for three days now, he hadn't dared leave the house; unable to face the curious stares and the inevitable questions his changed appearance would draw from the neighbours, acquaintances and shopkeepers of the town.

So far he'd allowed only Colin Turner and his wife Sue, two of his oldest friends, to see him in his present state. The couple ran a small bed and breakfast establishment and, after fetching him home from A & E, had wanted Harry to stay with them for a few weeks. It was a kind offer but Harry had lived on his own long enough now to know that, staying with them for any length of time, would only make it harder for him to go back to his solitary existence. *When you fell off a horse it was best to get straight back on it; to do anything else risked losing one's nerve.*

For the past three days Harry had been worrying over what, if anything, he should tell his daughter Julia. She was studying for her final exams and Harry didn't want to worry the girl at what he knew would be a stressful time for her. She was a bright kid but academic success didn't come easily to her, and she'd always had to work hard for it. He knew that if he told Julia, she would drop everything and rush back home to look after him. She had done the same when her mother became ill, taken a gap year and stayed at home to help him nurse her. On the other hand, he didn't want her hearing the story from anyone else and publication of the article guaranteed that sooner or later she would. It was unlikely she would pick up a copy of The Shropshire Post in Leeds but some of her friends still lived in Shropshire and were in contact with her. With a sigh, Harry picked up the phone and dialled his daughter's mobile...

CHAPTER SEVEN

FRIDAY MORNING and he'd got a whole weekend off; an empty prospect for Tudor ordinarily, unless it was his turn to have the kids. But this weekend promised to be anything but ordinary; last night's gig had ended with a kiss on the cheek from the lovely Maggie Mellor and a date – lunch on Saturday at a riverside pub. A minor conquest by Paul Hudson's standards, but look where his blitzkrieg approach had got him; chased up a tree by an angry Welsh giant and then, too afraid to come down, he'd had to be rescued by the band's Mr Invisible. Tudor smiled at the recollection; Paul had been crapping his pants up in that tree. Not that he felt much sympathy for him. Wonderboy had been pushing his luck for years. You couldn't plough another man's furrow as often as he did, without one of them planting one on you, sooner or later. It was a close run thing but, in the end, the Welshman had decided to heed Tudor's advice and take his repentant girlfriend home. He didn't deserve it, but the randy guitarist had the luck of the devil.

Still, all things considered, it was the best possible result and Tudor had come out on top. His was the greater prize – a date with Maggie Mellor, a proper one this time. Feeling pretty lucky himself, Tudor ran a razor over his stubbled chin, and imagined he and Maggie hand-in-hand, as they took a *postprandial* stroll across Abraham Darby's famous Iron Bridge. He was getting ahead of himself, he knew, but for the first time in years everything seemed to be going his way and he was feeling optimistic. Tudor had almost forgotten how that felt and was determined to embrace the moment. Half an hour later, he set off for the station in Monkmoor with a light heart and a spring in his step.

*

The atmosphere in interview room 2 was veritably monastic in its silence; Gary Edkins had not uttered a word so far whilst his solicitor, a tall, hawk-faced man, had spoken only to introduce himself. Tudor unwrapped two fresh tapes and loaded them into the machine, checked they were correctly aligned and, pressing record, sat down opposite his suspect. Edkins' face remained impassive while they waited for the alarm to stop ringing, indicating that the tape leader had run through. As he was obliged to do, Tudor explained at every stage what he was doing and why, though he knew from the man's record he was well versed in the procedure.

'This interview is being recorded,' pronounced Tudor in a sonorous voice. 'This is an interview with... state you full name please,' he prompted Edkins.

Gary gave his name in a gruff monotone and continued in the same manner as he was asked to state his address and date of birth.

'I'm Detective Sergeant Tudor,' Glyn continued. 'Also present are; Detective Chief Inspector Tom Dudley, and Mr Edkins' solicitor, Mr Brian Awbridge. There are no other persons present.' Stating the date, time and their location he then addressed his suspect directly, 'At the conclusion of the interview, I will give you a form which will explain the

53

procedure for dealing with this recording and how you can have access to it. You do not have to say anything but it may harm your defence if you do not mention when questioned something, which you later rely on in court. Anything you do say may be given in evidence.' He paused before continuing, 'Do you understand?'

Gary nodded his head.

'Mr Edkins is nodding his head,' Tudor explained for the tape. 'Could you say it aloud please, Mr Edkins.'

'Yes,' said Edkins mechanically.

Tudor opened the file on the desk in front of him and consulted his notes.

'We're here today, Mr Edkins, to talk to you about events that occurred at your home on the 19th of this month. In particular, the assault on, Mr Shaun Tomlins and the large number of iPhone and other devices found in the bedroom, in which the assault took place.' Tudor produced one of the phones, still in its evidence bag, from a briefcase at the side of his chair. 'I'm showing Mr Edkins an iPhone, one of fifty such devices that were found at his home.'

The hawk-faced solicitor cleared his throat. 'With your permission, DS Tudor, at this point, my client would like me to make a statement on his behalf.'

Awbridge flipped up the catches on his expensive leather briefcase, which had probably cost him more than the suit Dudley was wearing, thought Tudor, and took out a typed sheet of A4.

The two detectives exchanged glances and Dudley nodded his assent.

'You may proceed, Mr Awbridge,' said Tudor, intrigued.

'My client is prepared to admit to assaulting Shaun Tomlins, having been provoked beyond endurance after finding him *in flagrante delicto*

54

with his wife. It was therefore a crime of passion. Gary and his wife, Karen, have been experiencing marital difficulties for some months and, during that time, he has been absent from the marital home for long periods. He only returned on the day in question to collect some more of his belongings. As for the iPhones and other devices, he was unaware of their presence in the house and can only assume that his wife and her lover, Mr Tomlins, are responsible for them being there.'

They had agreed to suspend the interview at that point. The two detectives were lounging against the rear wall of the station, an area overlooking a small, sparse lawn that had unofficially become a retreat for smokers.

'We're going to have to let him go,' said Dudley and his craggy cheeks hollowed out as he took a long suck on his E-cigarette; a pipe-like device which gave Tudor's solemn-faced boss the jaunty look of a penny whistle player.

'Yeah, I know,' said Tudor, lighting up the real thing. 'Which is it today?' he asked, as Dudley exhaled a cloud of vapour, 'The fruity one or the herbal?'

'Butterscotch.'

'Lovely,' said Tudor and grimaced.

'It's not that bad. You should try it.'

'Thanks, but I'll take your word for it,' said Tudor.

Dudley's face took on the stricken expression of a mourner at a funeral. This was his latest attempt to stop smoking. He'd already tried nicotine gum, patches, and, on one disastrous occasion, had gone cold turkey. Tudor wondered why he bothered – he had no real desire to give up smoking – it was his wife who wanted him to stop. Until Dudley himself determined to give up the dreaded weed, the enterprise was doomed to failure. Meanwhile, it succeeded only in making him irritable and unhappy.

Ten years older than his sergeant, Dudley's straight, black hair was brushed with grey at the temples, while his brown, puppy-dog eyes concealed a sharp intelligence and a steely determination. Slightly built but taller than Tudor, he lacked the pitman's shoulders, but Dudley had come up through the ranks and was harder than he looked. His apparent gentleness made him the perfect foil to Tudor's bad cop when it came to interrogations.

Dudley pushed away from the wall and slipped the vaping device into his pocket.

'OK,' he said. 'We bail Edkins on the assault charge, pending further investigations. Is this Tomlins guy still in hospital?' Tudor nodded his agreement. 'Right, take him some grapes and get his side of the story. I'll get a couple of the uniforms to interview the neighbours, see if they confirm Edkins and his wife have been living apart. Oh, and you'd better have a word with her while you're at it.' He paused for effect. 'Just make sure she has some clothes on this time…'

'You heard about that?'

'Boys will be boys, you know what the lads are like. Liberated young woman by all accounts.'

'None of us will be wearing clothes when they're all as liberated as that one,' observed Tudor, drily.

*

A freckle-faced nurse pulled pastel blue curtains around Shaun Tomlins's bed and Tudor sat down.

'Fifteen minutes, Sergeant,' she said. 'And no more, Mr Tomlins needs to rest.' Swivelling on her heel, she was gone; her rubber-soled shoes squeaking on the smooth vinyl flooring.

The detective barely recognised the young burglar; his narrow face was now as round as a football and the thin lips were a celebrity's Botox nightmare. Shaun's blackened eyes described a lazy arc which brought them in line with Tudor's own.

'Wot, no grapes, Mr Tudor?' he croaked, and despite his injuries, managed to put a smirk on his face.

'Soz. Maybe next time, eh,' said Tudor without conviction. His searching gaze took in the single get-well card and the bunch of grapes on top of Shaun's bedside cabinet, and wondered if Karen Edkins had brought them in. 'Are they looking after you in here?' he inquired.

'Like you care.'

'OK,' Tudor was happy to concede, 'That's got the social niceties out of the way.' He leaned in closer to the recumbent form and lowered his voice, aware that beyond the thin curtains, other ears were listening. 'Well, this is weird, isn't it? *Me* interviewing Shaun Tomlins; a victim of a crime, rather than the perpetrator? Phew. Finding it hard to get my head around it. But there it is, your erstwhile friend, Gary, has just been charged with causing you grievous bodily harm.' Tudor had decided that, for the time being, he would withhold the news that Edkins had been bailed, pending further enquiries. 'He says he was driven to it when he came home and found you screwing the arse off his wife. That would do it for me. Claims he knows nothing about the stolen iPhones we found in the wardrobe he shoved your head through. Reckons you and the lovely Karen must have put them there.' Tudor let this last sentence sink in before adding, 'Care to comment?'

'He would say that, wouldn't he,' said Shaun, with all the distain a man can muster, when his lips are swollen to three times their normal size.

'Who are you, Mandy Rice Davies?' said Tudor. He had the lips for it. With that mouth he could out-pout Marilyn Monroe.

Shaun simply looked blank.

'Wu?' he said, through puckered lips and winced.

He wouldn't be kissing anyone for a while, Tudor concluded, but felt scant sympathy for him. He remained convinced that it was Shaun who had battered Harry Paget, and in his book, had deserved the beating he'd received at the hands of the cuckolded Edkins.

'Forget it,' said Tudor with a sigh. 'So, that's all you've got to say for yourself, is it? You surprise me; I never had you down as the forgiving sort.'

'Whot do ya mean?'

'It's obvious, isn't it? Gary knows he's going down and wants to take you with him. He won't want you and Karen playing happy families, while he's banged up 22hrs a day. Not while he's sharing a cell with some heavily tattooed psycho, who wants him to be his valentine. But, if you're happy to let Gary put you in the frame for receiving those stolen iPhones…'

Shaun's eyes were slits beneath his swollen lids. 'Naah, I'm not buying it. You're trying to play me.' His voice took on a loftier tone, 'As you have previously admitted, Mr Tudor,' (he pronounced it Chew-door) 'I am the innocent party in this matter.'

Hardly innocent…

'As for the aforementioned iPhones, I only became aware of their existence after Mr Edkins had put my head through that wardrobe door. I am therefore unable to help you with your enquiries, as I have no knowledge of how they came to be there or where they came from.'

If nothing else, young Shaun's frequent brushes with the law had taught him a second language,' thought Tudor. The little scrote was almost fluent in legalese.

CHAPTER EIGHT

SATURDAY MORNING dawned bright and Tudor woke before his alarm went off. Rolling onto his side, he checked the bedside clock: 7.30 – he'd hoped for a longer lie in; less time then to wait before lunchtime came around. He was feeling nervous. It had been a long time, he realised, since he'd experienced anything like this sense of anticipation about a date and he began to have serious doubts that it could possibly live up to his expectations.

Calm down, he told himself, *you've waited this long, you can manage a few more hours.*

As he turned onto his back and shutting his eyes, tried to get back to sleep, his landline began to ring. Before he could answer it, the line went dead and his mobile took over. It could only mean one thing; someone was about to piss all over his parade.

He snatched up the mobile. It was Dudley.

'Boss,' he said, with a sense of impending gloom.

'Morning, Glyn. Sorry to get you out of bed this early but there's been an incident over at Morecroft Hall. The owner's dead; some rock singer…'

'Rik Haymer,' Tudor supplied.

'You know him…?'

'Know of him, yes. The guy's a rock legend. 'The Axeman Cometh?''

'Yeah? Well, he's goneth now,' Dudley quipped. As gallows humour went, it was unusually witty for Dudley. 'Anyway, it's more your territory than mine. I'm on my way right now. Meet me there as soon as you can, will you? This guy was high profile and the press are going to be all over it.'

'Hold on, Boss,' Tudor protested but Dudley had also 'goneth' and was no longer listening. 'I'd got plans…' he added with a sigh.

*

Tudor was still stewing over his broken date when he presented his warrant card to the uniformed man at the main entrance and was waved through. Morecroft Hall, with its gothic spires and turrets, rose up like a fairy-tale castle at the head of a long, gravelled drive. Its mellow stonework, set against the darker backdrop of a wooded hill, glowed like honey in the early morning sunlight. It was a strange mixture of styles which, to Tudor's eyes, looked like the architect had somehow got the plans for a castle and a cathedral jumbled up and this was the result. Though he could see why Haymer would have been attracted to the place; the guitarist had been a leading light in the Goth scene of the early 80's.

He pulled up beside Dudley's BMW and switched off the engine. A further half dozen police vehicles, including the forensic team's van, were scattered across a large parking area in front of the house. It was 8.45; he considered phoning Maggie but instead, sent a brief text message. He was hopeful that Mellor would understand; she'd been in the force long enough to know that sometimes you had no choice but to answer the call, whether you were on duty or not.

A short flight of stone steps led up to an arched doorway. Stepping inside, he was greeted by another uniformed officer, a familiar face this time; Bill Wharton, one of the lads from Shrewsbury nick. While Tudor sorted through a box of coveralls for a pair that would fit him, Wharton got on his radio.

'DS Tudor has arrived, sir,' he reported.

The response was faint and crackly, as though Dudley was standing in a cave, but Tudor caught the gist of it; his boss was sending someone to collect him.

'You'll need a guide, it's like a bloody labyrinth in there,' said Wharton.

The exterior of Morecroft Hall might have looked like a fairy-tale castle but, as he moved further inside, Tudor felt he had wandered onto the set of a Hammer horror film. This impression deepened as he followed a member of the forensics team, wraith-like in her white coveralls and hood, along dimly lit galleries, whose pillared arches and elaborate ironwork had more than a whiff of a Victorian Mausoleum about them. At the end of this maze of corridors his guide led him down a narrow stone staircase which spiralled into a basement area. Passing through another arched doorway, the place was full of them, Tudor found himself in a cavernous underground Roman baths. Light bouncing off the surface of a full-sized swimming pool marbled a painted ceiling where naked revellers cavorted in an orgy of lustful coupling. This bacchanalian fantasy was supported by a series of Doric columns that formed a curtain between the pool and the changing rooms and saunas which surrounded it. Stone plinths positioned at intervals along each wall displayed life-sized busts of gods from the Roman pantheon. As blind as Samson in the temple, they stared down with godlike indifference at the tragedy that had unfolded before their stony gaze.

Dudley was at the far end of the pool where the water was deepest. From the poolside he directed two police divers in wetsuits, who bobbed up and down in the water like playful seals. They were not alone in the pool. Beneath them, distorted by refraction and distance, something dark and shadowy swayed in the slight eddy generated by the divers' movements. Dudley glanced up and seeing Tudor, urged him to join him with an impatient wave of his hand. As Tudor padded across the tiled floor, he marvelled at Haymer's rock star lifestyle; couldn't help wondering if the orgy depicted on the painted ceiling had ever inspired the real thing. Or perhaps it had been the other way round. Either way, the place would, he imagined, be a wet dream for his priapic bandmate, Paul Hudson. Fortunately for the guardians of the nation's morals, Paul, talented guitarist though he was, could only dream of enjoying this level of excess.

One of the divers submerged. Moments later, the cold, white light from an electronic flash lit up the bizarre figure of a man performing a handstand on the blue-tiled floor of the pool.

Tudor joined his boss in gazing down at the drowned rock star. From here he could see the man was anchored to the bottom by an electric guitar that was slung around his neck. Fully clothed, he was dressed as if for a gig, in a black hussar jacket richly decorated with gold frogging, black jeans and boots. His shoulder length black hair – he'd probably been dyeing it for years now – billowed out behind him, creating the illusion of movement; as if he was falling rather than floating.

The diver with the camera surfaced. He swam to the side and handed it up to one of the SOCO team.

'Got everything you need now?' Dudley asked him.

'Yes, sir.'

'Right. Let's have him out then.'

The two divers went back down. One of them held the guitar, while the other unhooked the leather strap. When they brought it to the surface, it was Tudor who took the instrument from them and gently laid it down on some plastic sheeting. The guitar had probably cost Haymer several thousand pounds but, now he was dead, it would fetch tens of thousands as a piece of rock memorabilia.

Though freed from his anchor, Haymer continued to hang motionless in the water like a submerged log or an insect trapped in a piece of amber. The divers caught hold of him and gently rolled him over, before bringing the body to the surface. In a scene reminiscent of a horror movie, Haymer's upraised hands slowly rose out of the water as if making one last desperate appeal for help. With one diver at his head and the other stationed at his feet they swam with him to the shallow end, where a stretcher was handed down to them. Passing it underneath him, they lifted Haymer's body clear of the water and, holding him at chest height, waded over to a flight of tiled steps. As they bore him up onto the poolside, excess water from the stretcher cascaded onto the tiles and poured back into the pool.

Tudor and Dudley had followed them down to the shallow end and now, along with members of the forensics team, they gathered around the water-logged corpse. Haymer's face showed signs of lividity; his features marked by the distinctive purple discolouration of pooled blood. Tudor knelt down beside him and examined him more closely. Haymer wore an open-mouthed look of surprise, though Tudor presumed this was due to rigor mortis, rather than astonishment, which he judged by the rigidity of the upraised arms and torso to be well advanced. He was surprised by how much smaller Haymer was in death than he remembered him being in life. They say you shouldn't meet your heroes because you will never feel the same about them afterwards. In his younger days, Tudor had been a big fan of the 'axeman', he'd even seen him perform live once at some festival or other but, had resisted the urge to go backstage and meet him. Was it more or less of a disappointment meeting him like this? Hadn't he known all along that Haymer was as mortal as everyone else?

Not quite true, he decided on reflection, Haymer's back catalogue would ensure he achieved an immortality of sorts.

'He's all yours,' said Tudor to the SOCO team as he got to his feet.

Leaving them to get on with their grisly task, the two detectives adjourned to the deep end.

'What do you think?' asked Dudley.

Tudor just wanted to get away to keep his lunch date with Maggie Mellor, but he knew that no matter what he thought, he wouldn't be going home for hours yet.

'It's looking like suicide to me,' he said, with a glance back over his shoulder at the grim tableau taking place at the shallow end.

'I know,' said Dudley. 'But it's a weird one, isn't it; him dressing up like that and jumping in with his guitar? Almost like it was staged.'

'Presumably that's the way he wanted to go – he was very flamboyant on stage, some would say over the top. His extended guitar solos were legendary.'

'I'll take your word for it. Prefer something a little more tuneful myself.'

Dudley and his wife, he knew, were Andrew Lloyd Webber fans. Well, somebody had to be, Tudor supposed. 'But you're right,' he agreed. 'Until we get the post-mortem results, we can't rule out foul play. Who found him?' he asked.

His superior was pacing up and down. Tudor recognised the signs; his boss was desperate for a smoke, even if it was just an E-Cigarette. 'Alex Rainesford,' said Dudley, after several more turns.

'Want me to talk to him?' Tudor offered.

Dudley stopped pacing, and his mood visibly lightened at the prospect of a nicotine fix. 'He's a she; short for Alexandra, been Haymer's PA for the past five years. Rather attractive in a stand-offish sort of way.'

'Just my type, then,' said Tudor, with a conviction born of bitter experience. 'And where will I find this ice maiden?'

'It's easier if I show you,' Dudley replied. 'I've got to fetch something from my car, anyway.' They both knew he was lying.

Arriving at the head of the staircase that wound up from the pool, Tudor remembered something. 'Haymer married a young Swedish actress. Must have been ten years ago now, if not more. Is she still around?'

'Yes, but she was in London last night at the premier of the new James Bond film. When I left her, Ms Rainesford was trying to contact her.'

'Ah, that's right. She was a Bond girl herself once...Ingrid something or other'

'Ingrid Sandstrom,' Dudley supplied.

They walked the rest of the way in silence; Tudor impressed, and not for the first time, by Dudley's uncanny ability to find his way around an unfamiliar space. He could have been living at Morecroft Hall for years, the unerring way he found his way back to the impressive entrance hall; a bright spot amidst the gloom where diffused sunlight filtered through a glass atrium. Here a pillared archway gave access to the main ground floor rooms, while twin staircases led off on either side to a galleried landing above. All the way up the stairs the walls were lined with gloomy 19th century landscapes, their colours muddied by age. A job lot perhaps, that Haymer, lacking grand portraits of his ancestors, had bought at auction to go with the house's gothic interior.

Pausing to remove their coveralls, surgical gloves and shoe covers, they crossed the marbled entrance hall and through an arch which brought them into a narrow hallway. Time had moved on here. The wall coverings were lighter and the gloomy Victorian landscapes had been replaced by framed photos of Haymer and his band, album covers, tour posters and other memorabilia. From a room at the end of the corridor came the strangled whispers of two people having an argument and trying hard not to be overheard. Tudor assumed that the female voice he could hear belonged to Alex Rainesford. He had no idea who the male with her might be, but in the light of the rock star's death, he was keen to know what they were arguing about. It seemed that Dudley was just as curious as himself, for he began to steal down the hallway like an alley cat on the prowl. Frustratingly, just as they neared the door, a filing cabinet drawer was slammed shut and the conversation abruptly ceased. Dudley stifled a groan, gave a sharp tap on the door and, without waiting to be invited, walked straight in.

A lean-looking individual lounged against the window, one arm draped along the sill. Red-faced, his brown eyes still burned with residual anger. Full lips were framed by a white Van Dyke beard and his long, white hair was scraped back from a wide forehead and tied in a ponytail. Tudor recognised him immediately – it was Mike Moretti, Haymer's long-time collaborator and the band's bass guitarist and occasional keyboards player. Between them, they were responsible for most of the band's material. It was no secret that the pair didn't get on; detailed accounts of their frequent busts-ups, punch ups and break-ups had been circulating for years. And YouTube hosted dozens of recordings of some of the most spectacular.

To the right of him, Alex Rainesford sat rigidly upright at her desk. 'Do come in, Inspector,' she said, in a welcome that came with a side order of sarcasm.

Dudley had been right about her, thought Tudor; Alex Rainesford *was* a 24 carat ball-breaker, but a diamond, though flawed, still has the power to dazzle. And he could imagine this woman dazzling a man with her dark auburn curls and pursed lips that seemed set in a permanent pout.

Moretti drew himself up – puffed himself up, as Tudor saw it, and assumed an exaggeratedly masculine stance; feet apart, chest pushed out, balled fists held ready at his side. Was this display of machismo down to the man's Italian ancestry, he wondered, or was he just an arrogant arse?

'Are you going to take a statement from me or what?' Moretti demanded.

About to address Ms Rainesford, Dudley turned and eyed him coldly. 'We have a job to do here, Mr Moretti, and it can't be rushed. I'll get to you in a moment,' he said with studied politeness.

But Moretti was not to be put off so easily.

'With all due respect, Inspector, that selfish bastard downstairs has just thrown a massive spanner in the works and I have to get back to London and salvage what I can from the wreckage. We all had a lot riding on this project.'

'Some more than others,' Ms Rainesford added sotto voce.

Moretti, his face crimson, rushed at her, but Dudley intercepted him and held him back. Straining to get past, he bellowed at her over the Inspector's shoulder, 'I warned you to keep your nose out of my damned business.'

'Calm down, Mr Moretti,' said Dudley firmly. 'And show a little respect. A man is dead. And however inconvenient that might be for you, no one is leaving here before we have their statement. Now, if you'll just give me a moment,' and here he turned to Haymer's PA, 'Ms Rainesford, did you manage to contact Mrs Haymer?'

Ms Rainesford appeared untroubled by Moretti's outburst and her icy composure remained intact. 'Ms Sandstrom, Inspector. Ingrid prefers to be known by her professional name. But, in answer to your question, yes I have spoken to her and she's returning immediately. I'm expecting her back here by mid-afternoon.'

'Thank you,' he said. Dudley waved Glyn forward. 'Detective Sergeant Tudor here will take your statement. I'd like to interview Mr. Moretti separately. Is there another room we can use?'

'Ms Sandstrom's office is next door. You can use that.'

'Excellent. Come along then Mr. Moretti...'

Like a boxer returning to his corner, Moretti had gone back to the window and was staring out of it.

'Mr Moretti?' Dudley repeated. Moretti turned. He was still red in the face but the fire in his eyes had died and he seemed much calmer. 'Shall we?' invited Dudley and indicated the door.

The man shot a final hate-filled glance at Alex Rainesford and, with studied insolence, strode through the door that Dudley had opened for him. They were met in the in the hallway by PC Wharton who had a fair-haired youth in tow.

'Not now, Wharton,' said Dudley who, faced with the prospect of a long delay before he could nip outside for a smoke, was growing increasingly irritable.

'But Sir, I thought you'd want to see him. He was driving Haymer's car.'

'Mr Haymer said I could borrow it,' asserted the youth.

Moretti gave a derisive snort. 'Kid's a liar. Look at him; he's got guilty written all over his face,' he said and laughed.

Tudor heard these exchanges through the open door. As he closed it, he caught a glimpse of the boy's face; Moretti was right – the lad did look guilty.

Tudor took up Moretti's place at the window and got out his notebook. At the same time he was aware that Alex Rainesford was giving him the once over. He looked up to find her staring at him. Judging by her expression, she was unimpressed by what she'd seen.

'When you're ready, Inspector,' she said.

Had she really not heard Dudley introduce him as a Detective Sergeant? He doubted it. Remembering people's names and titles was part of her job. And, from what he'd seen of her so far, Alex Rainesford was little Miss Efficiency personified. No, she was a lot more subtle about it than Moretti had been but there was no mistaking the icy disdain in her voice. Having promoted him to a higher rank, he would now be forced to correct her apparent misapprehension and thereby belittle himself.

'Thanks for the promotion, but it's Detective Sergeant,' he said. Not a flicker from her. 'So, it was you who found Mr Haymer. What time was that?'

'A little after 6.30,' she said.

'Bit early for a dip, isn't it?' queried Tudor.

'I take a swim every morning before breakfast. I find it invigorating.'

'And do you just splash about or are you one of those people who like to swim up and down without stopping until they're ready to get out?'

She gave him a withering look. 'I swim to keep fit,' she said. That much he could believe; there wasn't an ounce of spare flesh on her as far as he could tell. 'So no, I don't just splash about, that's strictly for kids.'

'You're a strong swimmer then...' he glanced at her perfectly coiffured hair. 'Did you dive in and try and pull him out?'

'No.'

'No? Why not?'

'There didn't seem much point. The open mouth, the vacant look in his eyes... it was pretty obvious he was way beyond saving.'

Tudor tried to picture the dead man, head down in the water. How much of his face had been visible? Was it possible for her to have looked into Haymer's eyes without getting into the pool? He made a note to check the photos the SOCO team had taken from the poolside. 'So, what did you do?'

'I... phoned the emergency services.'

It was the briefest of pauses but it was the first time he had seen her hesitate or appear unsure of herself. 'Did you phone them from the pool or did you go back upstairs?'

'No, I phoned them from the pool. Is this going to take much longer sergeant? Only I have work to do?'

'You're right of course; best to keep busy at times like this. I'm almost finished,' he said. 'Tell me, who else was in the house last night apart from Rik, yourself and Mr Moretti... I'm assuming he *was* staying here…'

'Yes, he's been here all week. He and Rik were planning a new project. So, with Ms Sandstrom and Rik's driver away in London, there was just Mrs Curtis and her husband here. Between them they look after the house and gardens.'

Tudor made a note of their names. 'Right, I'll have a word with them in a moment. Just one more thing…' Alex Rainesford let out an impatient sigh. 'What were you and Mr Moretti arguing about before the inspector and I arrived?'

'That? Oh, it was nothing really…'

'Mr Moretti seemed pretty worked up about it…'

A Mona Lisa smile. 'Mr Moretti is a very angry person. It doesn't take much to get him agitated. The result of living in someone else's shadow, I expect. You know what that's like, don't you, Sergeant?'

Did she really dislike him or was she trying to distract him and so avoid answering the question? The look Moretti had given her as he left was one of pure hatred; a bit extreme, even for a man of his fiery temperament, if it was nothing more than a minor disagreement.

'Nothing? Ms Rainesford. If looks could kill, I would have the unhappy task of investigating your death as well as that of your employer. So, exactly what was Mr Moretti referring to when he warned you to stay out of his business?'

She gave him a searching look and appeared to be weighing up her options. Tudor knew when to press a witness and when to hold off and give them some space. Finally, after taking a deep breath, she said, 'It's bound to come out now, anyway… I suspected Mike had taken a large amount of cash out of a joint account that he and Rik had set up to finance their new venture. Yesterday afternoon, I tackled him about it.

72

He denied it of course; claimed Rik must have had the money. But when I said I would check with Rik, he became very aggressive; grabbed me by the throat and threatened to kill me if I said anything.'

'Did he … So you hadn't told Rik, then?'

'No, I wanted to give Mike the chance to put the money back before Rik noticed it was missing. The success of the project depended on them working together. Neither of them could afford to have it fail.'

'This project – what was it – a new album?'

'I'm not at liberty to say. You'll have to ask Mike. I suppose it's his project now.'

'You're sworn to secrecy, are you?'

'That's show business, Sergeant. It's all about timing and managing expectations. Are we done?' she said, and the ice maiden was back. Getting up from her desk, she stepped over to a counter and poured herself a cup of coffee from a vacuum jug. The fragrant aroma filled Tudor's nostrils and he suddenly felt very thirsty. He would have welcomed a cup himself but the offer wasn't forthcoming.

'Not quite.' This drew another impatient sigh from Ms Rainesford. 'What did the three of you do yesterday evening?'

She came around the desk and perched herself on the edge of it, took a sip of her coffee, savoured it. She had nice legs, he noticed and very slender ankles.

'We all had dinner together here, then Rik and Mike closeted themselves in Rik's recording studio. That young lad was with them for a time but then he went out and didn't come back until just now. I went to my room and watched television until 10.30, then went to bed.'

'Young man? You mean the one who was in the hall? Who is he? What does he do around here?'

'Jack Barclay? Oh, he's one of Rik's strays.' she said, with a dismissive wave of a hand. 'He helped him set up the studio and he's been doing some work on Rik's archive, I believe.'

With practised ease, Alex Rainesford slipped off the desk without exposing any more leg and returning to the counter, refilled her cup. She took it to her desk and opening a laptop, switched it on.

'Right,' said a disgruntled Tudor. 'Well, I'll leave you to get on with your work and go and have a word with him. You'll let one of us know when Mrs… Ms Sandstrom returns?'

'Of course,' she said without looking up from her screen.

Tudor was glad to be out of there; the smell of that coffee was driving him mad. In the hallway, he wondered if this Mrs Harris could rustle up a hot drink for himself and the rest of the team. Of course, he'd have to find her first which, in the labyrinth that was Morecroft Hall, could take more time than he had to spare.

Taking out his mobile he checked for incoming text messages; nothing from Maggie Mellor, just a reminder from Paul Hudson that they had a band practice on Sunday afternoon. Did Maggie's failure to reply mean he'd blown it or was it simply a tacit acceptance on her part that he would be too busy to read anything she sent?

On the wall beside him, a youthful Rik Haymer smiled down from a framed photo of himself and the band. Standing behind him, a dark-haired Mike Moretti scowled back at the camera. But it was the guitar that Rik held in his hand that caught Tudor's eye – it was the black Fender Stratocaster that had anchored him to the bottom of the swimming pool.

CHAPTER NINE

IN THE WAKE of the burglary, the realisation that his home was no longer his castle, had burrowed deep into Harry's psyche. His home had always been a refuge from the rest of the world – the one place where he could be sure of feeling safe; if he was no longer secure within its protective walls, then where? Alone and growing more paranoid by the day, those natural creaks and groans which previously had seemed comforting, now filled him with anxiety. If a floorboard squeaked in an upstairs room or the wind rattled the back door, he almost jumped out of his skin. So, when he heard the front door being opened that Saturday afternoon, Harry was up out of his chair and reaching for one of the heavy brass candlesticks that stood on the mantelpiece.

There came a rattling sound and then his daughter's voice, 'Dad you've left the chain on.'

Harry had forgotten about the door chain; since the break-in he'd been leaving it on even in the daytime. His heart still racing, Harry shouted 'Coming,' and, moving as quickly as his protesting body would allow, made his way to the door. As he stepped into the hallway, he could see his daughter's worried face peering at him through the narrow gap between door and jamb. 'Hold on, I'll have to close it again before I can take the chain off,' he explained. The chain released, Harry threw the door open.

'OH, MY GOD! *D-a-d,* is that really you?' Julia's face, the image of her mother's at her age, expressed the same horror as Colin Turner's had done when he had fetched Harry home from A & E. Throwing her arms around his shoulders, Julia hugged her father so tightly, it made him wince.

'Thanks for coming luv,' he said. 'But really, there was no need for you to come rushing down here. I'm fine, honestly. It looks far worse than it is.'

Julia pulled back and held him at arm's length. 'Dad, you look like a gargoyle!'

'You should have seen what I did to the other guy,' said Harry in a lame attempt to lighten the mood.

'It's not funny Dad,' she chided.

'I know, I know... anyway, we don't want to discuss it out here. Come inside. I'll put the kettle on.'

Harry stepped aside to let his daughter pass. As he watched her walk down the hallway, it was as if the last 6 or 7 years hadn't happened; Julia looked like a teenager still with her blonde hair in a ponytail and a pink knapsack slung over her shoulder. For a moment, he could almost believe that, when they walked into the kitchen, her mother would be there with a mug of tea and a slice of carrot cake ready on the table.

With a heavy sigh, Harry followed his daughter into the kitchen and set about making them both a mug of tea.

While he did so, Julia went round opening each cupboard in turn, then checked the freezer. 'What have you been living on? There's hardly anything to eat in this place.'

'I haven't been outside the door since Colin brought me home, haven't wanted to.'

'Oh Dad.' Harry gave her a lop-sided smile. 'Right,' she said. 'I need paper and pen. I'm going to make a list. As soon as I've finished this cup of tea, I'm going to do a big shop and make sure there is enough food in this house to keep you going for a while. Did they say at the hospital how long it will be before your face is back to normal?'

'Should be looking pretty normal in a month or two, they reckon.'

'Your freezer isn't big enough to store enough for one month, never mind two. You need someone to look after you.'

'That's what Colin and Sue said. They offered to put me up at their place.'

'So, why didn't you take them up on it?'

Harry shrugged his shoulders. 'I prefer to have my own things around me. Besides, they've got a business to run. One look at this,' he indicated his swollen face, 'And their guests would be booking straight out again.

'I think you're exaggerating.'

'Oh, come on, you said yourself I look like a flippin' gargoyle.'

'Then maybe I exaggerated.'

'Stop fussing. I can look after myself,' he said, rather more vehemently than he intended to.

'Oh, really?' Julia indicated the empty cupboards. 'I know what you're like,' she chided. 'It was the same when mum was ill.'

'That was different.'

'In what way different? You refused to admit you needed help then and you're doing it again now. Why are you being so stubborn about accepting a little help from your friends when you need it?'

Harry shifted uncomfortably on his bar stool. 'I'm not being stubborn.' Julia rolled her eyes. 'All right, I am, but it's because I value my independence. I'm only sixty-one, for God's sake. I'm not a helpless geriatric.'

Julia reached across the table and took one of his freckled hands in hers. 'I'm not suggesting for one minute that you are, but you've taken quite a beating at the hands of this thug and I don't want you staying here alone while he's on the loose. What are the police doing about catching him?'

'According to The Post, the police have arrested somebody, but they refused to confirm if the arrest was connected with the burglary.'

'Useful. Have you phoned them?'

'Y-e-s, just before I phoned you, but Sergeant Tudor was unavailable. I left a message for him to phone me back but I've not heard from him yet.'

'Sergeant Tudor?'

'The detective in charge of the investigation. He seemed quite confident of recovering your Mum's jewellery, but when I had a quiet word with the pretty, young PC who was with him, (Harry omitted to mention that he was having a tearful moment at the time), she admitted that it was unlikely. It was her who advised me to tell my story to the papers in the hope that someone close to the thief might turn him in.'

'I see, doesn't exactly fill you with confidence, does it?'

'Don't worry, I'll phone Tudor again on Monday morning if I haven't heard from him by then. 'Now, how's the revision going?'

CHAPTER TEN

AFTER INTERVIEWING Rik Haymer's young 'stray', Tudor wandered outside to get some fresh air and found his boss sitting on the steps. Dudley had finally got his nicotine fix and was contentedly puffing on his 'penny whistle' e-cigarette. Tudor pulled out a pack of the real things and, ignoring the dire warnings of an early death printed front and back, lit one.

'Those things will kill you,' said Dudley as Tudor sat down beside him.

'Don't preach or I'll confiscate your penny whistle,' said Tudor good-naturedly. He took a long pull on his cigarette and the two men sat smoking and staring at the distant blue-green of the Clee Hills.

'OK, you first,' said Dudley, after several minutes of silent contemplation. 'What did you learn from the frosty Ms Rainesford?'

'That she doesn't like to share, for a start; helped herself to two cups of coffee while I was with her and didn't offer me any.'

'An only child, probably – so she's never had to,' said Dudley. 'Just as well I got Mrs Harris to rustle up a brew then. She's got an urn, apparently.'

'That doesn't surprise me,' said Tudor. 'Place is like a mausoleum. I think I'd top myself too, if I had to live there.' He jabbed a thumb at the Hall behind them.

'I think we can assume that the late, Mr Haymer chose to live here,' said Dudley. 'More to the point, did you learn anything of relevance to our enquiry?'

Tudor took a last pull on his cigarette and stubbed it out in the stone vase at his side, one of two that stood either side of the topmost step. 'She told me what she and Mike Moretti had been arguing about. According to her, 'Mr Angry' has been helping himself from a joint account he and Haymer had set up to fund a new project. When she confronted him about it, he threatened to kill her if she said anything. Grabbed her by the throat, she says...'

'She says… you don't believe her?'

'Well, you saw them. Did you get the impression she was at all scared of him? She didn't even flinch when Moretti lunged at her.'

'So, what are you saying?'

'I dunno, exactly. I just felt I was being played; that she was trying to set Moretti up.'

'I can see why she might want to do that,' said Dudley. 'There's no love lost between those two and I can vouch for the fact that Mr Moretti isn't an easy man to like.'

'Same goes for La Rainesford.'

'She really got under your skin, didn't she?' Dudley put his pipe down and turned to face Tudor. 'A word of advice, and I say this as a friend, you're a good copper, Glyn but you have a tendency to take things a little too personally sometimes. You can't afford to do that in this job, clouds your judgement.'

'I know, ignore me – I'm just in a bad mood.'

Dudley gave him a knowing smile. 'Ah yes, you had plans…'

This had Tudor wondering how much Dudley knew about his growing friendship with Maggie Mellor. But Dudley took up his pipe and it was back to the job in hand.

'Friend Moretti, you won't be surprised to hear, tells it differently. He called Ms Rainesford, "Rik's Rottweiler"; reckons she wears the trousers round here and has got some sort of hold over him and his wife. Says she was always coming between him and Rik and trying to stir up trouble for him. When I asked him where he was last night, he told me he'd spent the evening with Rik in the studio they've got here, drinking and working on a new album. Moretti went to bed around 1.00 am leaving Rik to finish the bottle.'

'So, it was a new album… Alex Rainesford refused to tell me when I asked her.'

'Tends to confirm what Moretti said about her. Bit of a control freak by the sounds of it.'

'Do we know precisely when he heard that Rik was dead?'

Dudley consulted his notebook. 'Says he was woken up around 6.45 when Ms Rainesford phoned him from the pool.'

'Now, that is interesting…' Tudor felt a quickening of his pulse. 'Alex Rainesford said she found Haymer at 6.30 – she has a swim at that time every morning – I asked her if she'd tried to pull him out and she said no. So, what was she doing between 6.30 and 6.45? We need to check what time her call to the emergency services came in. Be worth listening to the recording itself – get some idea what sort of state she was in.'

Dudley made a note. 'Anything else?' he asked.

'I've had a word with Jack Barclay.' Dudley looked puzzled. 'The young man who was driving Haymer's car,' Tudor explained. 'Barclay has worked here for the last couple of months on a free bed and board and a bit of pocket money basis. He was at the house for the early part of the evening, but then went into Ludlow. He got off with some girl he met in the pub and spent the night at her flat. The lad was a bit hazy about the address, but the girl had given him her phone number. I've just spoken to her and she confirms Barclay was with her all night. Alex Rainesford can also vouch for the fact that he went out and didn't come back until this morning.'

'Oh, to be young again, eh?' mused Dudley. 'At it all night long...'

'I wouldn't know,' said Tudor. 'Pandas have more sex than I do.'

Dudley chuckled. Edinburgh zoo's attempts to mate their two Chinese Pandas had been in the news a lot recently and their sex lives discussed in some detail. The female only comes into season on one day each year so the male Panda has to get in quick.

'We never watch nature programmes,' said Dudley. 'All that sex and violence, upsets the wife.'

Tudor was never quite sure if his boss was joking or not when he came out with stuff like that. But his off the cuff comment had painted a picture of contented domesticity that he couldn't help but envy. What was their secret, he wondered? How had the Dudleys managed to sustain their marriage despite the enormous strains that police work, by its very nature, placed on a relationship?

He was still pondering this anomaly when the crunch of tyres on gravel announced the arrival of a police patrol car. He watched it swing into the parking area and come to a halt. The passenger door opened and PC Mellor, who was cradling a large cardboard box in her arms, got out and walked towards them. Moments later, PC Crawford emerged from the driver's side and hurried after her.

'Hopefully this will improve your mood,' said Dudley, with a nod towards the girl.

So, it would appear that Dudley was aware of their budding relationship...

Just then Maggie glanced up at the house and stared directly at him. Tudor felt the blood rush to his cheeks; he hadn't been made to feel this self-conscious in years. It revived memories of the first time he'd invited a girl home for tea. He must have been about 11 years old at the time. His mother had worn this silly smirk on her face throughout the proceedings and afterwards had teased him unmercifully. He'd often wondered if that one incident was responsible for him becoming a shy, awkward teenager, but had eventually concluded that it was probably the fate of most adolescents, as he'd rarely met anyone who would want to revisit that time in their lives.

'What's that, Sir?' he said, affecting a deep interest in the fluting on the stone vase at his elbow.

'Sandwiches, man... what did you think I meant?'

Unable to come up with a satisfactory reply, Tudor simply shrugged his shoulders.

'Well, I don't know about you, but I'm starving,' said Dudley, rubbing his hands in gleeful anticipation. 'Didn't have time for breakfast this morning and there's a bacon butty in that box with my name on it.'

Maggie Mellor was at the foot of the steps, Crawford at her shoulder. Tudor cringed as he recalled the constable stepping into Paget's darkened bedroom; the smirk on his face when he saw him lying on the bed with Mellor leaning over him. Crawford, who fancied himself as something of a comedian, could this day get any more fucked up?

Mellor came on up the steps leaving Crawford down below. Tudor was surprised at how much younger she seemed compared to the last time he'd seen her and the old reservations about the difference in their ages assailed him. How old was she… twenty-six, twenty-seven? He was a good ten years older. What a fool he'd been to think he could ever have a relationship with a girl like her? It was doomed from the start just as their lunch date had been.

Mellor greeted his boss with a deference that Tudor hadn't witnessed before. Sarcasm was something she reserved solely for the lower ranks, apparently. It revealed a whole new side to her. She didn't even acknowledge him, he noted.

Maggie reached into the cardboard box, which had originally contained Walkers crisps. 'Here you are, Sir,' she said, and handed Dudley his sandwich.

'Still warm. Well done, Mellor. How much do I owe you?'

'Twenty-five pounds, Sir, all told.'

'Did you get a receipt?'

'Yes, Sir,' she said and held it out to him.

Producing his wallet, Dudley handed her the money and pocketing the proffered receipt, proceeded to devour his sandwich with gusto.

Aware that Crawford was eyeballing him from the foot of the steps, Tudor hadn't dared look at Maggie while this exchange was taking place, but now he was forced to as she turned to him and said, 'What about you Sergeant? There's cheese and cucumber, ham and tomato or chicken salad…'

'I'm not fussy,' replied Tudor, sounding sulky and, reaching into the box, chose one at random. His petulance backfired on him for, when he deciphered the spidery handwriting on the bag, he discovered he'd chosen cheese and cucumber. He didn't like cucumber, it gave him indigestion.

Dudley noisily swallowed his last mouthful of sandwich, 'That went down a treat,' he said, and, wiping his mouth on the back of his hand, carefully folded the empty paper bag into a small, neat square and slipped it into his jacket pocket. He got to his feet and seemed to notice Crawford for the first time. 'You will have had your lunch, I expect,' he said, in a manner that would brook no denial.

'Yes, Sir,' the constable replied in a monotone.

'Get yourself down to the main gate then and relieve the man on duty there; send him up here for a sarnie and a cuppa.'

'Yes, Sir,' said Crawford, his voice betraying a distinct lack of enthusiasm for the task assigned to him.

Tudor was filled with guilty pleasure as Crawford began his long trudge to the Hall's front gates. His retreating back, with its sagging shoulders, was a picture of dejection.

'Right, I'll go and chase up that tea,' announced Dudley and went off to find the elusive Mrs Harris and her tea urn.

'Didn't expect to see you here,' said Tudor, as Maggie took up Dudley's place on the step beside him.

'Yeah well, this guy I was supposed to be having lunch with stood me up, didn't he? So I thought, what the hell, I might as well go in to work.'

'Sorry about that, but duty called.'

'Yes, he called me too; wants me here when the grieving widow gets home.' She batted those big brown eyes at him, 'A beautiful Swedish actress and former Bond Girl, so the inspector was saying... My name's

Tudor, Glyn Tudor,' she intoned in a surprisingly deep voice. 'A fan, are you, by any chance?'

Tudor laughed. 'Of the late, great Rik Haymer, yes. The man was the god of rock. He'll be sadly missed.'

'Before my time, Sarge, I'm afraid.'

'Mine too,' said Tudor, a little too defensively. 'He was in his forties by the time I got into his stuff. Rik Haymer's the reason I bought my first guitar. Unfortunately, I hadn't got his talent for playing lead so I switched to playing bass instead.'

Tudor's mind flashed back to the moment he saw the rock star's arms slowly rise out of the water as if in supplication. Had the one-time bad boy of British rock music been seeking forgiveness for his sins or had he simply grown tired of his dissolute life? If fame had been hard to cope with, how much harder had it been for him to adjust to growing old and seeing younger musicians shooting up past him on their way to the top? Rock stars like Rik Haymer were meant to die before they grew old. Still, the question remained; had he jumped into the pool of his own volition or had he been pushed?

Mellor broke into these deliberations. 'So, what happened in there then?'

Tudor stopped staring into the distance. 'Ah well, it seems my hero put on his stage clothes, picked up his guitar and, jumping into his private pool, tried to perform a farewell concert underwater.'

'But, why would he do that?'

'I dunno… because he couldn't face another comeback tour?'

*

In one's and two's the rest of the team drifted outside. After collecting a sandwich, they spread themselves out on the extensive lawns; the warm spring sunshine a welcome relief from the Hall's gloomy interior and the smell of death. Mrs Harris, a small rotund woman with greying hair and a cheerful demeanour, duly appeared with her urn. A picnic on the lawn and tea served from an urn – we could all be on a works outing, mused Tudor, as he enjoyed a post luncheon cigarette.

Dudley had taken Mellor to one side and was briefing her on how he intended to handle the interview with Haymer's widow. A police radio crackled into life. The radio was Maggie Mellor's and she and Dudley listened intently for a moment. The brief conversation galvanised Dudley. Moving briskly to the top of the steps, he addressed the lounging 'picnickers', 'All right, you lot. Back to work. Pronto,' he ordered.

As the other members of the team scurried back into the hall, Tudor conferred with his boss. 'What's up?' he said.

'Crawford just called from the gate – Mrs Haymer is on her way up here.'

Dudley had barely finished speaking before a sleek, blue Jaguar XJ came into view. It swept around the curve, the sun sparkling on its gleaming paintwork, and came to a halt at the foot of the gravel pathway that led up to the house. The driver, a tall, broad shouldered man with slicked-back, black hair and dressed in a dark, single breasted suit, jumped out and went round to the passenger side. Tudor's first impression was of a bodyguard rather than a chauffeur. He opened the door and a slim blonde stepped out. She was wearing dark glasses and a dark two piece suit, which, unless she'd taken it with her, she must have bought for the occasion. She glanced up towards the two detectives and the PC waiting for her at the top of the steps and, turning to her chauffeur, spoke briefly to him. He nodded, then getting back into the

Jaguar, he drove it round to the rear of the house.

Patting a stray lock of hair back into place, Ingrid Sandstrom, looking every inch like the Bond Girl she had once been, strode towards her welcoming committee on 3 inch black stiletto heels. A black shoulder bag completed the ensemble.

'That's quite some widow's weeds she's wearing,' murmured Dudley.

Tudor silently agreed; the outfit the widow was wearing bore all the hallmarks of haute couture. The shoes alone, he reckoned, would have cost him a month's wages. He couldn't help wondering just how cut up the lady could be over the death of her husband as she sashayed down the path like a fashion model on a catwalk.

Dudley stepped forward and introduced himself and his colleagues. 'I'm sorry for your loss,' he said.

'Thank you, Inspector,' she said in a firm voice that retained traces of a Scandinavian accent.

'It's a difficult time, I know,' said Dudley solicitously, 'But if we may, we would like to ask you a few questions…'

'Of course, but first I would like to see my husband.'

Dudley looked uncomfortable. He glanced at his fellow officers and back again. 'I'm sorry,' he said. 'Your husband's body has been taken to a chapel of rest but as soon as we have finished here, I will arrange for one of my officers to take you to him.'

Ingrid Sandstrom stiffened and her lips formed a thin line. People were much harder to read when you couldn't see their eyes, but there was no mistaking the lady's body language; she was about to explode. Tudor braced himself for the inevitable outpouring of grief and anger.

Stepping forward, Maggie Mellor positioned herself at Ingrid

Sandstrom's side and, taking hold of her arm, said, 'Sir, Ms Sandstrom has just spent the last 3 hours in a car, perhaps we could allow her a short break to freshen up first?'

Good call, thought Tudor; though Haymer's widow looked as fresh as a daisy to him, Mellor's intervention had diffused an awkward situation.

'Yes, of course,' agreed Dudley.

The two detectives stood aside to let the women pass.

'I'll let you know when we're ready for you,' Mellor called over her shoulder on the way into the house.

Dudley took out his 'penny whistle' and firing it up, took a long draw on it. 'Smart girl that, should go far,' he said vapour curling about his head like a cloud.

Tudor didn't doubt it; in The Crown and Anchor she'd made no bones about her ambition to become a detective. Was that only two nights ago? It seemed an age away.

'I'm sure you're right, Sir,' he said. Patting his pockets, Tudor located his pack of cigarettes but, when he got it out and looked inside, was annoyed to find he'd smoked the last one.

'None left? Here, have one of mine.' Dudley produced a silver cigarette case and, flipping it open, handed it to Tudor. 'My secret stash. For emergencies only, you understand. Just don't tell the wife.'

'Your secret's safe with me, but what if she goes through your pockets?' Helping himself to a cigarette, Tudor placed it between his lips and lit it.

'All she'd find is the odd parking ticket or petrol receipt,' said Dudley. He snapped the two halves of the cigarette case together. 'This is one case that stays at the office when I go home.'

'You crafty, old fox.' Glancing up at one of the Hall's two towers,

Tudor half expected to see Rapunzel lower her flaxen hair down from its upper window. 'So, what do you reckon – is Mrs Haymer pouring out her heart to PC Mellor or is she pouring herself a large gin and tonic?'

'My money's on the gin and tonic,' said Dudley. 'The lady's probably on the phone to her old man's insurance broker as we speak.'

Tudor grunted. 'Sadly, I think you're probably right.'

The two men fell silent for a moment, each lost in their own thoughts.

Tudor was the first to break the silence. 'Other people's lives, eh?' he said with a shake of his head.

'Well, you know what they say, "there's nowt as queer as folk."'

'I know, but here was a guy who had it all; a legend in his own lifetime, who lived in a castle with a Bond Girl for a wife – what's not to like? And yet,' he continued without pause, the words tumbling out with increasing vehemence, 'and yet, he tops himself just as he's about to record a new album and re-launch his career. It doesn't make sense.'

'All right, Glyn. 'Calm down,' said Dudley. 'He didn't do it just to spite you, you know.'

Tudor wouldn't argue with that, but he felt cheated and didn't understand why. For a moment there, he realised he would have been prepared to swap places with his idol. A part of him still longed to live that same dream, especially on nights like that last one at The Crown and Anchor when he felt at the top of his game. But empty though his own life was, would he be any happier in someone else's skin? After all, the dream appeared to have turned pretty sour for Rik Haymer of late – why else would he have killed himself? And who could really blame the guy? Those closest to him weren't exactly prostrate with grief. Quite the contrary, in fact from what he'd seen of them so far...

'That chauffeur looked a bit useful.'

It was as if Dudley had been following a parallel chain of thought.

'He did, didn't he,' agreed Tudor. 'And I bet he's got a six-pack.'

'Young too,' said Dudley. 'What do you reckon – mid-thirties?'

'Thereabouts. You think he and the merry widow were having it off?'

'Wouldn't be the first time that the young wife of an older man has copped off with the hired help. Assuming the lady is the chief beneficiary of Haymer's will, it would provide us with a motive for his murder, should the coroner decide that that's what we have here.'

'Except that they both have an alibi.' Tudor reminded him.

'Hmmn…,' Dudley conceded. 'As long as their alibis hold water.'

Tudor grinned. 'No pun intended, eh, Sir?'

'Oh yeah, see what you mean?' said Dudley after a moments reflection.

Further speculation was interrupted by the arrival of Maggie Mellor. 'We're ready for you now,' she said from the doorway.

Tudor consulted his watch; 25 minutes had elapsed – time enough for several gin and tonics…

He and Dudley followed Mellor back into the house, the cucumber in the sandwich he'd eaten playing havoc with his digestive system. Tudor had assumed they would be interviewing Ingrid Sandstrom in her office. Instead, Mellor led them across the marbled entrance hall and back through the pillared archway they had passed through on their return from the basement pool. Halting at the first door they came to, Mellor gave it a discreet tap, and showed them into a spacious reception room. Ingrid Sandstrom was curled up on a two-seater sofa, a cup of coffee cradled in her hands. She was still wearing her dark glasses, Tudor noted. A cafetiere of coffee had been placed within easy reach on a small table beside her. On the other side of the table was an empty chair which

Tudor assumed Mellor had been sitting in. As in the offices, there had been concessions to modernity here too; Ingrid Sandstrom's Scandinavian heritage was reflected in the simple lines of the furniture, the woven rugs that covered most of the light oak flooring and the lack of clutter. Soft drapes hung at the windows and colourful abstract pictures decorated the walls. But there was nothing flat-pack about any of it; a cursory glance was enough for the visitor to see that Haymer and his wife didn't shop at Ikea. In contrast to much of what he'd seen of Morecroft Hall, the room had a light, airy feel about it and Tudor found himself wishing he had a room just like it to relax in after a long day at work.

Ingrid Sandstrom invited them all to take a seat. A game of 'musical chairs' followed as Tudor and Dudley went about selecting one from a number that were scattered around the room and seated themselves opposite her sofa. At a nod from Dudley, Mellor took out her notebook and the interview began.

'I'll be as brief as I can, Ms Sandstrom,' said Dudley. We just need to get some idea of your husband's state of mind. Had he seemed depressed at all recently?'

Ingrid Sandstrom placed her empty coffee cup on the table and clasped her hands in her lap. 'Inspector, my husband has suffered from bouts of depression for most of our married life and, like a lot of creatives, he could be very moody. He told me once that he only ever felt truly alive when he was on stage.'

'Is that why he toured so much?' Tudor asked.

'That's one explanation,' she said.

And what might the other one be? Tudor wondered. She had a slightly turned up nose and a pointy chin and reminded him of the blonde one out of ABBA.

'Did you ever join your husband on these tours?' asked Dudley.

'In the early years of our marriage, yes, but it's not much fun being a groupie, you know, you spend most of your time just hanging around waiting for something to happen. Besides, I had my own career commitments to fulfil.'

'Of course, you were in a Bond film, weren't you?'

'Amongst other things,' she said

There was such a stillness about the woman that Tudor wondered what, short of an earthquake, it would take to shake her. Dudley appeared to have dried and Tudor jumped in again.

'Mike Moretti told the Inspector here that he and your husband were working on a new album. How was that going?'

'They were being very secretive about it but they were making progress, I believe.'

It was like throwing a ball to someone and having them lob it straight back at you – only twice as hard. Ingrid Sandstrom's replies were short, sharp and succinct and, it seemed to Tudor, designed to discourage any further probing. Was she afraid she might say too much and let slip some dark secret? Or did she just want to be with her husband? The only time she had displayed any emotion over Haymer's death was when she was told his body had been taken away.

Dudley gamely picked up the ball once more. 'Ms Sandstrom, would your husband have any reason to be worried about money?'

The widow gave a derisive snort. 'Look around you, Inspector – does that seem likely?'

Unabashed, Dudley pressed on. 'I hope you understand that, in the absence of a note, I have to ask these questions...'

There was a polite knock and PC Wharton's head appeared around the door. 'Sorry to disturb you, Inspector, can I have a quick word?'

Dudley got to his feet. 'Excuse me for a moment would you, Ms Sandstrom.'

He followed Wharton into the hallway and closed the door behind him. Tudor could hear their muffled voices but was unable to make out what was being said. Ingrid Sandstrom remained staring fixedly ahead and Tudor took the opportunity to try a slightly different tack.

'What about Mike Moretti's finances?' he asked.

'Mike? The man's had holes in his pockets for as long as I've known him. Rik's always been sensible with his money but Mike has made some bad investments – most of them at the racetrack or the casino. Why do you ask?'

'Just something he said earlier…'

The door opened and Dudley slipped back inside.

'Bad news, I'm afraid. Our friends from the press are at the gates,' he announced, his distaste for their tribe evident in his tone.

Ingrid Sandstrom jumped to her feet. 'The Press!' she said, sounding brighter and brushing at her hair with her fingers. 'Perhaps I should make a brief statement.'

Dudley consulted his watch, 'It's getting late, Ms Sandstrom. If you still wish to visit the Chapel of Rest, we should leave now.'

'I see,' she said icily, clearly annoyed at having to postpone her big entrance till later.

'Is there another gate we can leave by?' asked Dudley.

'There's a service road at the back of the house,' she admitted, following a dramatic pause Harold Pinter would have been proud of.

This then, was the real Ingrid Sandstrom, thought Tudor; the passed over actress eager to raise her profile, however inappropriate the occasion. Because there was no such thing as bad publicity, right? Glyn was prepared to bet his flat on her rushing down to the front gate the second she got back from the mortuary; giving interviews, posing for photographs, talking about her next role. And what better role for her to play, than the part of the beautiful young widow, mourning her much more famous husband, whilst basking in his reflected fame?

CHAPTER ELEVEN

MONDAY MORNING found Tudor in a reflective mood as he sat down to eat his breakfast; two slices of toast and marmalade and a mug of very strong, black coffee. After a disastrous weekend in which work had once more intervened to place obstacles in the way of what he laughingly called his love life, he'd gone on a bender with his bandmates. All but Paul Hudson, who declined to join them; claiming he needed an early night, but it was obvious he was still in a strop over the events at Thursday night's gig in The Crown and Anchor. Tudor, for one, didn't miss the band's resident lothario and his constant boasting about his conquests – he felt bad enough where his love life or, rather the lack of one, was concerned, without having Paul rub his nose in it.

He and Mellor had parted on Saturday evening after what had been a very long day, without arranging another date for the lunch they had been forced to postpone. Maybe it was for the best, he decided; somethings were never meant to be and perhaps this was one of them. Why was he so useless with women, he wondered? It was a question that had kept him awake at night many a time in the years since Sally had run off with her lover. And something he had in common with Conan

Doyle's great detective; Holmes didn't have a clue where women were concerned either. The difference between them being that the fictional detective had no interest in women whatsoever; unlike the hopelessly romantic, Watson, that cold, analytical brain of his was untroubled by the carnal thoughts of lesser men. The only problems women brought to his door were the crimes they wanted him to solve. And he unravelled most of those without even leaving his rooms in Baker Street. Tudor almost envied Holmes and a life that was unfettered by the demands of his libido. His own would be so much simpler without this aching desire to be with a woman. And for him 'the woman' was Maggie Mellor. On reflection, Tudor decided he was much closer to being the hopeless romantic as opposed to the cold, analytical thinker than he cared to admit. Thinking was the last thing he wanted to do, in fact, because at that moment, the dark-eyed PC was all he could think about.

Why was he a detective at all, he wondered? It was a lousy job, clearing up the mess in other people's lives whilst at the same time making a mess of your own. Although Tudor had spent enough years as a young copper on the beat in Birmingham to know that it could be far worse; he didn't see anything like the amount of violence and death that a detective working in a city force encountered. That's why, when he met and married Sally, he'd wanted to move back to Shropshire. When he'd first suggested moving back to the county of his birth, Sally had been enthusiastic, seeing it as an idyllic place in which to raise the children they planned to have, but she'd never really embraced the rural life. It was alien to her. She was always complaining, "It's too quiet. There's nothing to do. I'm bored."

Eventually she had found excitement in the arms of another man. They lived in London now. Lots of diversions there to keep boredom at bay, but it meant he only got to see his kids during school holidays. And now, Gareth and Cerys found the country as boring as their mother had done.

In need of distraction, he reached across the breakfast bar and turned on the small radio he kept in the kitchen.

"Thanks Rob, and now at 29 minutes to eight, it's over to Kathy Clugston in the newsroom for today's headlines..."

The first item about the Prime Minister's latest talks with Angela Merkel drew little interest from Tudor, but the second had him turning up the volume.

"Ingrid Sandstrom, actress and widow of rock guitarist, Rik Haymer, who was found dead at his Shropshire home on Saturday, today announced that she is to set up a fund in her late husband's name, dedicated to discovering and nurturing talented, young British guitarists. In an exclusive interview with the BBC, Ms Sandstrom said she was sure that Rik would have approved; adding that the charitable trust was the most fitting way to honour her husband's memory and his contribution to British popular music."

Tudor found himself applauding. You had to hand it to the woman; she hadn't wasted a moment since her husband's death before stepping into the limelight. And the search for young, British guitarists was a masterstroke; he could already see it becoming another of those tacky TV talent shows and of course, Ingrid Sandstrom would be there as one of the judges. Watch this space he thought; further announcements will be forthcoming.

As he walked into the station, the desk sergeant, Tom Corfield, called him over. 'Message for you from a Mr Paget, wants you to call him.'

Tudor groaned. 'That's all I need,' he said.

Corfield grinned. He was a large man with a nose to match and a bald pate. One of those irrepressibly cheerful individuals, who, no matter what shit life dished out to them, still saw their glass as being half full. Tudor wondered what made the man so annoyingly chirpy at this time of the morning and wondered where he could get some of it.

Corfield leaned in closer to the glass partition that separated them, 'Got that Monday morning feeling, Glyn, have we?' he said with a conspiratorial wink.

'In my case, it's every day,' replied Tudor.

'Like that, is it? Life's a bitch, and then you die? You should take comfort from that, you know...'

'Why's that?'

'Well, look at it this way,' the sergeant explained. 'At least you know that one day all that bloody misery is going to come to an end.'

'What a comforting thought,' said Tudor. 'Your counselling talents are wasted here. You should be working for the Samaritans.'

'I know, little ray of sunshine, me,' he said. 'Inspector Dudley was looking for you earlier, by the way. He didn't look too happy either...'

'It's all that responsibility, I expect,' said Tudor.

'Yeah? So, what's your excuse then?'

Some uncharitable souls amongst his colleagues might dispute the desk sergeant's claim of kinship with the sun, but despite Tudor's best efforts to resist it, Corfield had managed to put a smile on his face.

Pausing at his desk to drape his jacket over the back of his chair, Tudor went to see what Dudley wanted. His office door was open, so Glyn felt able to dispense with the usual formalities.

'Morning Boss. You wanted to see me?' he said, stepping inside. A framed poster for *The Phantom of the Opera* and a photo of his wife were the only personal touches in the otherwise utilitarian office.

'Yes Glyn.' Dudley indicated an empty chair. 'Take a seat.' He laced his hands behind his head and leaned back in his chair. 'How did it go at the mortuary? Did you and Mellor get anything more out of Ingrid Sandstrom?'

Tudor was a little surprised by the question; mortuaries were hardly the place for exchanging confidences – too much of the awful silence and the sickly smell of death hung over them. Most visitors and Tudor included himself, couldn't get away quickly enough.

'No, she didn't say much at all other than to confirm that the guy lying on the slab was her husband. Got a little tearful when they uncovered his face, but that was it.' Her reaction had been very low-key in the circumstances; Rik had not been a pretty sight. Rigor mortis had begun the reverse journey back up the body and the arms were no longer raised in supplication but they hadn't managed to shut that gaping mouth or close those staring eyes. 'Still, by the time we got back to the car she was in control again. Take it from someone who knows, there was very little love left in that marriage. Till death do us do part? I don't reckon the day could have come too soon for Mrs Haymer. You should have heard her on the radio this morning.'

'I did,' said Dudley. 'She doesn't miss a trick, does she? Still, the show must go on, as you showbiz types say.'

That was the problem, thought Tudor; the woman was an actress and that made her tricky. She spent her working life convincing audiences that she was someone other than herself and was therefore much more difficult to read than other people. Liars were easy to spot but an actress could convince herself that she absolutely was that character she was playing. The widow had become quite animated on the drive back to

Morecroft Hall, but was that because she was eagerly anticipating talking to the press or just nervous relief at having left death behind her at the mortuary? Had they even met the real Ingrid Sandstrom yet?

'How's that band of yours doing?'

Still musing over Ingrid Sandstrom's true persona, Tudor wasn't sure he'd heard correctly; Had Dudley just asked him about the band? He'd always had the impression that his boss thought him a little too old to be 'rocking it up,' as he put it. He frequently enquired about the kids – or used to, before he and Sally divorced – but the band, that had to be a first.

'Oh, the band's just a hobby. It's hardly show biz. But we've got a big wedding coming up in a couple of months. They pay well.'

'Oh yeah, how well?'

'The going rate's around a thousand, but you can get two thousand or more for a posh do.'

'As much as that? Well, I hope you're declaring all these extra earnings, Glyn,' said Dudley with a wink.

'Yeah, yeah... It has to be split between four of us, you know. So, when will we get the post mortem results?'

'Should get sight of a preliminary report sometime tomorrow. Thanks to Haymer's high profile and the press speculation surrounding his death, the powers that be want it fast-tracked.'

'Look forward to reading it,' said Tudor.

Dudley slowly sat up and brought his elbows up on to the desk. 'You still think it could be murder, do you?'

'If I had to bet on it, it would still be each way, but it just doesn't feel right.'

'Well, let's see if this will throw any light on the matter.'

Dudley's hand closed over the mouse sat dormant beside his computer's keyboard. He wasn't very adept at using it and it took him some time and much cursing to find the file he wanted. 'Right. Got it,' he announced. 'This is the recording of Alex Rainesford's call to the emergency services.'

Dudley double-clicked on the mouse. There was a brief interval and then the recording began with a beep. The sound quality was reasonably good, but the caller's voice wasn't as clear as the operator's and Tudor asked Dudley to turn up the volume.

Operator: 'Emergency. Which service?'

Caller: 'Ambulance…no… sorry, I mean, yes, ambulance.'

Operator: 'Putting you through.'

Call Handler: 'Ambulance Service. Tell me exactly what's happened?'

Caller: 'I've just found my boss at the bottom of his swimming pool'

Call Handler: How long's he been in there? Do you know?'

Caller: What? No, I think he's dead.'

Call Handler: 'Is he still in the pool?'

Caller: 'Yes.'

Call Handler: Is there someone there who can help you get him out?'

Caller: 'I told you, he's dead!'

Call handler: Try and stay calm. Help is on its way. Where are you?'

Alex Rainesford gives her the address and the call handler asks for the number she is calling from. There followed an exchange between the ambulance service and the police. Both attended the scene. Alex Rainesford's call was timed at 6.59 am. She hadn't lied about phoning from the pool; there was an unmistakable echo even down the phone line. Rainesford sounded far from her cool, imperturbable self, but that was unsurprising given the circumstances.

'Can you play it once more, Boss? I thought I could hear someone else in the background.'

Dudley played the recording again and leaning in closer, Tudor tried to isolate the faint sounds he'd heard; no more than a whisper – three words perhaps, though he couldn't make them out – a male voice?

Dudley thought he could hear something too, but was less convinced it was anything more than background hiss. 'Leave it with me,' he said. 'I'll see if the geeks can do anything with it. You were right about one thing, though…'

'The missing thirty minutes, you mean? Tudor straightened up. 'Yes, why did she take so long to call the emergency services?'

'Moretti told me Alex Rainesford woke him at six forty-five, so they both have time they haven't accounted for.'

'We need to question them both again,' said Tudor. 'I could drive over there this afternoon, if you like.'

Dudley considered this for a moment. 'No. Leave it till we have the autopsy report. If it says Haymer's death was anything other than suicide, we will have a lot more questions to put to those two…'

Back at his desk, Tudor picked up the phone and dialled Paget's number. It was answered after just two rings, as if the man had been standing by the phone all morning just waiting for his call.

'Mr Paget? DS Tudor. Sorry I haven't got back to you before. You're chasing up that crime number I promised you, I expect.'

'Actually I was hoping you could tell me how the investigation is going, only it said in the paper that a man had been arrested,' was the

terse reply.

Tudor silently cursed *The Post* for linking Edkins arrest to the burglary. Had someone on the force been talking to the press? For no reason other than that he disliked the man, Tudor was ready to believe that PC Crawford was responsible for the leak. Thanks to that press report, Paget was convinced that more progress had been made in the investigation than the facts warranted. It was especially galling for Tudor, as he had so far failed to establish any link at all between Paget's burglary and Tomlins or his fence.

'It's true, we did arrest a man, but so far we have been unable to connect him to your burglary. But we are following up several lines of enquiry and I will keep you advised on any progress we make,' he said.

There was an explosive sigh from the other end of the line. 'That sounds to me like police speak for "go away and stop bothering me",' said Paget.

Tudor knew better than to argue that there had been more pressing matters for him to deal with in the last few days; nor that the suicide and/or possible murder of a high profile individual took precedence over an aggravated burglary. Excuses like that, however justified, would only reinforce Paget's already jaundiced view of his local constabulary. Instead, without revealing anything that in the public domain might prejudice their enquiries or any future prosecution, Tudor brought him up to date on the investigation. Paget remained sceptical, but Tudor got the impression that the man was a little happier than he had been at the start of their conversation. Finally, he gave Paget the crime number he would need for his insurance company and assured him once again that he would be in touch if there were any further developments.

It was not a good start to the day and, his head still throbbing, Tudor badly needed a coffee. The muddy looking liquid that came out of the vending machine barely deserved the name, but at least it was hot, wet and sweet. Slumped down in his chair, Tudor pulled up the reports on the house to house that had been conducted amongst Edkins' neighbours. His pulse quickened when he saw Maggie Mellor's name on many of them; the other officer being PC Crawford. The first report he looked at was one of Maggie's. It felt strange to be reading her words and hearing her voice in his head. It quickly became obvious that Mellor had done most of the leg work; Crawford's name appearing at the head of not much more than a third of them. Another reason for Tudor to dislike the man; he hated a lazy copper almost as much as he hated a bent one.

Edkins' neighbours broadly fell into two categories; those who backed up his story almost word for word as if they had been coached and those who, like the three wise monkeys, heard nothing, saw nothing and had nothing to say. Only one interview struck Tudor as falling outside these two camps; a Mrs Welby-Smith who lived at number 82. The numbers being so close there was a strong probability that she lived directly opposite number 79 and he decided to follow it up. She hadn't said much and she hadn't directly contradicted Gary Edkins' assertion that he and his wife had been living apart; just a hint here and a nudge there, but it was enough to make him curious and, with skilful handling, more might be teased out of her. It wasn't much but it was all he had for the moment and he was pretty certain that Shaun Tomlins hadn't stolen those iPhones; breaking into warehouses and hijacking lorries was way out of his league.

Tudor grabbed his jacket and headed for the car park. As he stepped outside, he paused to put it on and saw Mellor and Crawford coming towards him. Walking between them was an impeccably dressed and coiffured, middle-aged woman.

'Hi, can I have a quick word,' he said to Mellor as they drew level.

For one anxious moment Tudor thought she was going to say no, but then turning to Crawford, she said, 'Take Sylvia in would you, I'll be along in a minute.'

The woman appeared troubled by this change of plan and kept turning back to stare at Mellor as Crawford pulled her away.

'Friend of yours?' enquired Tudor.

'Sylvia's one of our regulars – shoplifter – we keep catching her and the court keeps letting her go. Sad really, I think she only does it to get some attention.'

'I know the feeling?' said Tudor.

Maggie laughed.

'Seriously, what do I have to do to get your attention?' he pressed her.

'You could arrest me...' she said, putting her wrists together and holding them out to him.

'I'm not into S & M,' he said.

'Shame,' she said, her dark eyes twinkling mischievously.

This teasing, though pleasant enough in its way, wasn't getting him anywhere. Why couldn't she be serious for a moment? He decided to go ahead and ask her the one question he desperately needed an answer to.

'We...er, didn't arrange another date for that lunch,' he said.

'No, that's right.'

'So...?'

Maggie's gaze slid away towards the door Crawford and their prisoner had not long passed through. 'Can I give you a ring when I finish my shift?' Tudor's face fell. 'I'm really sorry, Glyn, but I'll have to go, Sylvia will be getting anxious. She doesn't like Dave?'

'Dave?'

'Dave Crawford,' she explained.

'That's something your friend Sylvia and I have in common, at any rate,' said Tudor but Mellor had already turned away and was hurrying towards the station entrance.

Mrs Welby-Smith was a small woman in her late-sixties with silvery, grey hair and skin tanned to a deep mahogany. There was at least half a dozen pairs of shoes to be made out of her hide when she dies, thought Tudor.

She showed him into her front room and while she went off to make some tea, Tudor took the opportunity to look out of the window. As he'd confirmed when he pulled up outside, she had an unobstructed view of the Edkins' residence. Today though, there was no sign of Gary or his 4 x 4. No bad thing as it happened, he decided; Gary's car on the drive across the road might well make Mrs Welby-Smith nervous and his trip would be wasted. Tudor heard footsteps in the hall and the tinkling of china cups. Stepping away from the window, he went and stood in front of a coal effect, gas fire and pretended to admire a large, framed print; a florid still-life of a vase overflowing with pink roses.

'Lovely, isn't it?' said Mrs Welby-Smith, placing the tea tray on a Queen Anne style coffee table.

Tudor thought it was bloody awful but politely agreed with her. He had one of Gered Mankowitz's iconic photos of Jimi Hendrix hanging on his living room wall; the one of him blowing cigarette smoke out of the corner of his mouth.

'Milk and sugar?' she said, holding a milk jug aloft.

'Both, please,' said Tudor.

He wondered if Mr Welby-Smith was still around. In an ornate silver picture frame on the mantelpiece, there was a photo of Mrs Welby-Smith with a man whom Tudor assumed must be her husband, but he'd not seen any gent's shoes in the shoe rack that stood just inside the front door, no gent's coats or caps hanging on the coat pegs above it. And only one armchair by the fire, he noted.

She handed him his cup of tea and indicated that that's where he should sit. Mrs Welby-Smith stationed herself next to the tea things on a small two-seater sofa which was upholstered in the same pale green fabric as the armchair.

'Have you and your husband lived here long, Mrs Welby-Smith?' Tudor began.

'I moved here four years ago after my husband passed away,' she said with evident regret. 'We'd lived in our previous house for almost thirty years but it was far too big for me to rattle around in on my own.'

'I'm sorry,' said Tudor and meant it; he'd lived on his own long enough to know how hard it could be.

Tudor took a fresh look at the room; tried to see it through Mrs Welby-Smith's eyes. And from what he'd gathered so far, he suspected that she had been used to better when her husband was alive. But, for some reason, the provisions of his will had fallen short of her expectations and Mrs Welby-Smith had been forced to downsize and move to what she no doubt considered to be a less respectable area.

'Yes, it can be lonely living on your own,' he said. 'Divorced,' he added by way of an explanation. 'Wife ran off with another man and took the kids with her. I live in a flat now – one of half a dozen in the same block – but it's not the same; I hardly ever see the other residents, let alone talk to them. Still, you've got family and friends, I expect, and neighbours too, of course...' He waited expectantly for his host to pick up on his cue.

'We were unable to have children,' she said.

In the awkward silence that followed, Tudor could hear the soft tick of a clock on the mantelpiece and the sound of his own breath going in and out.

'As for the neighbours...' she began but whatever it was she had been about to say, she thought better of it and her voice trailed off.

'Actually, it's your neighbours I wanted to talk to you about.' said Tudor and, taking his tea with him, strolled over to the window. He stared out at the Edkins' house, and said quite casually, 'Have you seen much of Mr. Edkins lately?' He continued to stare out of the window as he waited for her reply.

'N-o, she said, then after a moment's hesitation added, 'Not really...'

Tudor turned back into the room and Mrs Welby-Smith immediately lowered her eyes. Unable to meet his gaze, she stared into her cup as if trying to read the tea leaves. It was obvious to Tudor that the woman had qualified her initial denial because she was reluctant to tell an outright lie. 'You get a pretty good view of the Edkins' house from here. You must have seen quite a bit of what went on out there last Thursday morning. I was there. Did you see me?'

'Yes,' she admitted. 'I just happened to be by the window and wondered what was going on...'

Tudor had suspected all along that Mrs Welby-Smith was a 'curtain twitcher' and now he was sure of it. 'Oh, of course,' he assured her.

'I've never seen anything like it, running around without her knickers on. Hammering on people's doors... it was an affront to public decency,' she said, her voice ringing with righteous indignation.

'Yes, well people do some strange things when they're in a panic.'

Tudor recalled the arrival of his eldest child, Owen. When Sally had announced that her waters had broken and they should go straight to the hospital, Glyn's first thought had been to run upstairs and wash his feet! Afterwards, he was at a loss to explain his irrational behaviour. He smiled to himself at the memory but knew that to linger on it would only bring him down. Back to business then...

'I'd like to concentrate on Mr Edkins for the moment, if you don't mind,' he said. Tudor took his empty cup over to the coffee table and placed it on the tray. As he leaned down he stared straight into Mrs Welby-Smith's pale blue eyes, 'I wonder,' he said. 'Can I rely on you to be discreet?' Mrs Welby-Smith nodded. Tudor straightened up and stepped back a pace or two. 'Fact is,' he went on. 'We found a large quantity of stolen goods in Mr Edkins house. I'd like to charge him with receiving but he claims to have been living apart from his wife and has had nothing to do with the stuff we found. Instead, he's trying to put the blame on a young man his wife has been seeing. I'd hate to see an innocent man do time for that thug, Edkins,' he said with as much sincerity as he could muster.

Tudor almost blushed at making Shaun Tomlins out to be an innocent victim of crime, but salved his conscience somewhat with his conviction that the little scrote was innocent of this particular bit of larceny.

Mrs Welby-Smith considered this for some time. 'He's got a garage,' she blurted finally. 'There are three or four of them behind the houses over there. He's hiding his car in one of them.'

'How do you know this?'

'Smokey went missing. My cat,' she explained, forestalling Tudor's question.

It was then that he recalled seeing a poster attached to one of the lamp posts when he parked his car.

"You see but you do not observe, Watson." as Sherlock Holmes was wont to say.

'I'd searched all the gardens on this side of the road,' Mrs Welby-Smith continued. 'So I decided to look for him over on the other side. There's a narrow drive runs behind the houses. A short way down from number 79 it opens out and there's a block of garages. I saw him coming out of one of them. The door was still up and I saw his car inside.'

'And did you find your cat?'

'Not then, no. I found him yesterday morning. He was lying stiff and cold on the front lawn.' There was a tremor in her voice as she said, 'Someone had tightened a wire noose around his neck.' She took a tissue from her sleeve and dabbed at her eyes with it.

Tudor didn't need to be Sherlock Holmes to work out who had killed Smokey and why. The message was as clear as it was brutal.

Back at the station he contacted the council and obtained a list of those residents currently renting garages in the lane at the rear of number 79. It transpired that Mr Gary Edkins was renting not one but two of the lock-ups. Tudor would need a warrant before he could search them and, eager to get the job done before Gary got wind of his intentions and cleared them out, went straight to Dudley's office. His boss was hunched over his desk leafing through a sheaf of papers.

'Is that what I think it is?' said Tudor.

'Yes, told you they wanted it fast-tracked, didn't I. Seems Haymer was still breathing when he went into the water. Blood alcohol concentration was high but we know he and Moretti had been drinking all evening. No suspicious physical injuries or bruises.' Dudley closed the file. 'And that's all she wrote. The top brass want this one gone, Glyn.'

'Suicide it is then,' said Tudor.

He drove home feeling frustrated and, if he was honest, disappointed that Haymer hadn't been murdered. Murder investigations in the county were relatively rare and therefore generated a great deal of excitement and media interest. Of such cases were careers and promotions made.

Too tired to cook a meal from scratch, he shoved a frozen pizza in the oven and checked his phone. No calls. No messages. He stared at it for some time but it remained stubbornly silent.

When he'd finished eating, he dumped the dirty plate in the sink and in a few paces, moved from the kitchen into his living area; the two separated only by a breakfast bar. Tudor felt the walls close in on him and his spirits sank. He turned on the TV and flicked through the channels; his eyes barely registering the programmes listed and turned it off again. Desolate, he threw himself down on the sofa and stared moodily at the ceiling. He lay there with the phone resting on his chest until long after the room grew dark, but she didn't phone.

CHAPTER TWELVE

HARRY PAGET stared out through the rain-beaded windscreen of his Citroen at the cluster of terraced houses some fifty yards away on the opposite side of the street. Rising up behind them, a mist shrouded Long Mynd was fast disappearing beneath a glowering sky. It was the third time in a week that Harry had stationed himself in Badgers Meadow, a small development of mainly social housing on the edge of the town. Harry very much doubted that badgers could survive there; sandwiched as it was between the railway line and the busy A49. He had come prepared for a long vigil; laid out on the front passenger seat was a packet of cheese sandwiches wrapped in foil, a banana, a large flask of coffee, a well-thumbed paperback and a small pair of binoculars. He was staking out the familial home of Shaun Tomlins.

He'd been sat there for two hours now and hadn't seen so much as a curtain twitch over at the house Shaun lived in with his single mother and two younger siblings. The de-da sound of its horn and a low rumble signalled the imminent arrival of an approaching train. The rumble grew louder, there was a clatter of wheels to his right and moments later he saw it emerge from behind the houses; a diesel unit and two carriages.

He was almost sorry to see it go as it quickly disappeared again behind a curtain of rain and mist. Its appearance had brought an all too brief instant's relief from the tedium of just sitting there, waiting for something to happen.

Harry couldn't help thinking that, even for a so-called petty criminal, Shaun seemed remarkably lazy; which some might regard as sinful but was not in itself a crime. When he wasn't lying in bed, Shaun was in the Jasper Arms drinking lager and playing pool with his mates. Again, neither was a crime. These meagre crumbs of information were all that Harry had gleaned from two days and nights of bum-numbing surveillance of his suspect. Could he be mistaken in thinking Tomlins was the culprit? After all, it had been two months since the burglary and he had only glimpsed his assailant's face for a few seconds and that in the red glow of his alarm clock's digital display. This fixation with Shaun Tomlins had only come about after a chance encounter with the man outside *Sandfords* Café Bar. As the rain which had seemed to be easing off lashed his windscreen with renewed ferocity and obliterated his view, Harry's mind drifted back to the previous Tuesday when the seeds of his suspicion had been planted.

He had been feeling anxious on and off all day about venturing out in public for the first time. As he buttoned up his shirt, he caught his reflection in the mirror. The face that stared back at him was his own, thank God, and not the swollen gargoyle that had gurned at him from his shaving mirror every morning for the past two months. Though the physical injuries he'd sustained at the hands of the young burglar had healed, the mental scars still lingered. They had always been less visible but had caused just as much, if not more pain, than the damage done to mere flesh and bone. Those blows from his assailant's fists and feet had gone much deeper than the skin, deeper than the bone, to the very marrow of him.

There had been a dark period when, with his features showing little sign of returning to normal and the balance of his mind as skewed as his face, Harry had doubted if he would ever be anything like his usual self again. Worse, that his agoraphobia would prevent him from attending Julia's graduation ceremony. But, just as an abandoned balloon slowly loses its air, the swelling went down, the bruising faded and his mood lightened.

Julia's graduation and her first class honours degree had provided a further boost. What a memorable day that had been; the weather was perfect, Julia had looked wonderful, if a little self-conscious in her cap and gown, and his heart had been fit to burst as she stepped up to receive her diploma. If only her mother had been there to see it.

Harry smiled at the memory as the rain continued to turn the world around him into a living, breathing watercolour.

In the event, when Harry and his two friends walked into *Sandfords*, it was virtually empty. None of the handful of punters looked up as they approached the bar and when they got there, there was no one waiting at the pumps to serve them.

'Bit quiet in here tonight, isn't it?' said Alan, peering over his bifocals. Alan Halliwell was a retired schoolmaster. Short and plump, he had a bald pate and the wispy strands of hair at the sides stood up like feathery ears, giving him an owlish appearance.

'It's early yet,' Colin reminded him and, going to the top of the steps that led down to the bar's kitchens, shouted, 'Oi, can we have some service up here?' At 58, Colin Turner was the youngest of the trio. Before moving to Shropshire, he had run a small engineering company in

Bedford. Physically he was the exact opposite of Alan; tall and broad-shouldered, he had retained his dark hair but had gained quite a bit of extra weight around his midriff recently, Harry noted.

While they waited, Harry cast an eye over some of the new paintings that had appeared on the walls since he had last been in. The landlady, Jackie Walters, an enthusiastic supporter of the town's annual arts festival, encouraged local artists to display their work in her bar. It was an arrangement that benefited both parties; the paintings lent *Sandfords* a cool, arthouse feel and she provided the artists with an audience for their work.

Presently the lady herself appeared; pushing 50 with short cropped, straw blonde hair atop a permanently furrowed brow, she had what Harry would politely describe as a full figure.

'Oh, I might have known it was YOU,' she said to Colin with a touch of the old-time schoolmarm in her voice, then spotting Harry at the far end of the bar, let out a little cry of delight. 'Now *you*, I am pleased to see,' she exclaimed rushing towards him and Harry was enveloped in a rib crushing embrace. He was in danger of suffocating by the time she let go and stepping back, said, 'You look well enough anyway. How are you now?'

'Got my own face back, at least,' Harry said and showed her both profiles.

The furrows on Jackie's brow deepened, 'Yes, I heard it was absolutely horrific,' she said with a shudder.

Harry flicked an accusing glance at his two companions but they both looked away and suddenly seemed very interested in the specials board. Still, there was no doubting the sincerity of Jackie's concern and, in a small town like Stretton Spa, an incident like the one Harry had been involved in, was bound to arouse a great deal of interest. We were at our most vulnerable when sleeping, thought Harry, and the fear of finding an intruder in the house was pretty much universal.

Jackie gave Harry another hug, this time it was mercifully brief and bustled off to take up her station behind the bar. 'Right, what are you boys going to have?' she said, gripping one of the pumps in a podgy hand. 'First round's on the house,' she added, bestowing a beaming smile on Harry.

An offer like that always brought the same response from Colin, 'Champagne!' he'd cry to groans from his companions, but turning to them both he simply said, 'I think we'll have the usual please, Jackie.' He smiled broadly. 'Back to normal, eh?'

They carried their drinks over to their customary table. Propped up against the condiments was a handwritten card – *"Reserved for the old gits"* – it read. Harry chuckled; it was a nickname they had given themselves which had then been enthusiastically adopted by the *Sandfords* landlady and bar staff.

Alan settled himself down and raised his pint of bitter, 'Here's to the old gits,' he said, 'Good to have you back, Harry. We've missed him, haven't we, Colin?'

They touched glasses together and after a few sips of his beer, Harry began to relax. He really valued these convivial evenings in the company of Colin and Alan. Their long term friendship was as easy to slip back into as a comfortable pair of slippers.

'Cheers! I've missed you too, you old reprobates,' he said.

'Not badly enough to leave some money behind the bar, it seems', said Colin, reproachfully. 'We were very disappointed weren't we, Alan?'

'What? Oh, yes, very,' he said, catching on a fraction too late.

It was another of Colin's standing jokes; one he trotted out any time one of them had been absent from their regular Tuesday night gatherings.

'You've got a lot of catching up to do, Harry, I'm afraid,' he said, then turned to Alan. 'What do you reckon? He buys every round for the next two weeks?'

'Sounds fair enough to me,' said Alan dutifully.

Harry readily agreed knowing that it was all in fun and they didn't intend holding him to it.

'Anyway, that's enough about you,' said Colin. 'When are we going to see the lovely Julia?'

'You're going to have to wait a bit longer, I'm afraid; she's in Barcelona at the moment. She's having a well-earned holiday with a couple of the girls she shared a house with in Leeds.'

'God, I could do with going on holiday with a couple of girls myself,' joked Colin.

'You,' said Harry, 'on a ten day holiday with a couple of twenty-three year olds? They'd bring you home in a body bag!'

'Oh, I'm more or less harmless where women are concerned these days,' said Colin.

'Harmless and at least forty years too old,' said Alan.

The rest of the evening followed the long established pattern; the conversation flowing back and forth between them; a bit of politics, a bit of gossip, some harmless flirtation with Jackie and the young women she employed as bar staff, the occasional heated discussion on an issue of the day and all of it leavened with a bit of good-natured banter. Male banter can easily slip into bullying, even cruelty sometimes, but they were well enough aware of each other's sensibilities to know where the boundaries were and so avoid stepping over the line.

Harry was taken by surprise when Colin stood up and announced it was time to go. He couldn't believe how quickly the evening had gone. All that worrying beforehand had been groundless and he had thoroughly enjoyed himself. So it was with renewed confidence that he stepped out into the street.

Dusk was falling and the street lamps were lit. Alan's car was parked a little way down the road and, as they began walking towards it, Harry saw a figure coming towards them on the opposite pavement. The man was walking head down, puffing on a cigarette. As they drew level, the man raised his head and his face was caught in the glow of a street light. With a cursory glance at the trio, he tossed the butt end into the gutter.

In that moment, Harry felt his heart stop. His knees buckled and he staggered back against a shop window. Fearing Harry was about to collapse, his two friends caught hold of him and held him up.

'Harry, are you all right, mate?' said Alan, the tremor in his voice betraying his alarm.

Harry's mouth was so dry it was like chewing on cotton wool balls as he tried to get the words out.

'Colin, run back to *Sandfords* and get him a glass of water, will you,' urged Alan.

As Colin hurried back to the bar, Alan began fishing in his pockets for his mobile. 'Hang on Harry, I'm going to call an ambulance.'

Harry shook his head vigorously. Taking deep breathes of air, he let them out slowly; tried to bring his ragged breathing under control. His tongue found some saliva and he ran it over his dry lips. He swallowed hard and said, 'Don't need an ambulance.' Another deep breath then, 'It was him!' he gasped.

'Who? You're not making any sense.'

'The guy who just walked past – he's the one who kicked the shit out of me!'

'Who… Shaun?'

'You know him?'

'Shaun Tomlins? I taught him… tried to anyway, for a few years. Bit of a tearaway, but he was never violent. You look very pale Harry, are you sure you don't need an ambulance.'

'Yes, yes. Just tell me what you know about Shaun Tomlins…'

*

Of course his friends had advised him to let the police deal with him, but Harry wasn't prepared to do that. He'd since found out that the man DS Tudor had arrested the day after the burglary had been charged with assaulting this same Shaun Tomlins after catching him in bed with his wife. The man, Gary Edkins, was a receiver of stolen goods and Tomlins had a conviction for burglary, but DS Tudor had been unable to establish a link between the two men other than the affair between Shaun and Edkins' wife. The only good news to come out of it was that Shaun had got the hiding he deserved. There was a poetic justice in that at least, thought Harry.

He flicked the windscreen wipers on; still no sign of any movement over the road and it was looking as if the rain was set to last the rest of the day. The afternoon was drawing on, he was cold and his right leg was beginning to feel numb. Clearly, the life of a private detective was nothing like as glamourous or as exciting as it was portrayed in books and films. Still, despite the lack of progress or perhaps because of it, he was determined to continue; his resolve fuelled by a simmering anger at the failure of the police to bring Tomlins to book, and at himself for allowing the young swine to get away from him that night.

If only the lazy burglar would get out of bed and get back to work. It was vital he got something on him soon. In four days from now Julia would return home from her post-graduation holiday and his surveillance activities would be seriously curtailed, particularly the night-time vigils.

What Shaun lacked, Harry decided, was motivation. Perhaps he could provide some? But what motivates a thief, he wondered; money, presumably or the lack of it. It followed that if Shaun needed money badly enough, he would soon resort to thieving. All he had to do was create that need for cash. Harry began to sift through the possibilities. What would a young man like Shaun need money for, apart from beer, that is... the answer was staring him in the face but it was several minutes before Harry realised it; Shaun's pride and joy, the orange Fiesta with the 'go faster stripes' along the side. Now, if that should need repairing...

CHAPTER THIRTEEN

GLYN TUDOR stared at the man sat in front of him with open incredulity. He was about 50yrs old, had grizzled grey hair, a boozer's nose and three days stubble growth on his chin. He was wearing an ancient brown suit that even the most desperate of charity shops would refuse to take off him and smelled strongly of the farmyard.

'Mr Landsdale, do you seriously expect me to believe that you just happened to come across those fifty sheep wandering in the lane and out of the goodness of your heart, offered them a home with you on your farm?

'Couldn't leave 'em there, could I?' said the man.

'What were you doing there at one o'clock in the morning, anyway?'

'I'd been to the pub. There was a lock-in.' he said, with a sly smile. He had been doing a lot of smiling but he was no village idiot, though he seemed to think Tudor was.

'The pub? You drove to the pub in your sheep transporter?' Tudor had had enough. The man was getting up his nose, quite literally; for half an hour now Tudor's nostrils had been assaulted by his malodorous odour while he listened to this fairy tale of lost sheep. He pushed his

122

chair back and stood up. 'I think we'll take a break there gentlemen.' He turned to Lansdale's solicitor. 'I suggest you have a serious talk with your client. That story of his is a load of bollocks and you know it.'

The sheep belonged to a Mr Llewellen whose farm was situated about 5 miles away from Lansdale's own. There was a history of trouble between the two men; a running feud that had been going on for years, whose origins had long been forgotten.

Returning to his desk, Tudor slumped down in his chair and, tilting his head back, stared at the ceiling. He stared at it for some time; wondered what he had done to deserve a morning like this one.

Straightening up, he became aware of an unpleasant smell. He sniffed the air several times then, raising his arm, sniffed his sleeve.

'Bloody sheep shaggers,' he roared. Jumping to his feet, he whipped off his jacket and, holding it like a matador's cape, wafted it back and forth.

At the desk across from his, Detective Constable Ferrars popped up from behind his computer screen. 'Taken up bullfighting have you, Sarge?'

Tudor glared at him and Ferrars immediately popped back down again. Moments later, he heard the young, detective constable making sniffing sounds. He was trying to decide if there would be time to nip home and change his jacket when he was called back to the interview room. This time Glyn kept as much distance between himself and Landsdale as the restrictions of the recording equipment would allow. The man now claimed he had been merely playing a practical joke on his neighbour and had no intention of permanently depriving him of his sheep.

Landsdale was charged and released on bail pending an appearance at the Magistrate's court. Tudor was glad to see the back of him. He was not alone; the Custody Sergeant looked as though he had swallowed something particularly nasty.

'Dear oh dear, dunno about his sheep, I reckon *he* needs to be dipped,' he said. The Custody Sergeant wrinkled his nose then shook his head as if trying to shake off the offensive smell that clung to him.

Although the remark had not been aimed at him, Glyn still felt like a man who has farted and not owned up to it. He took his smelly jacket out into the car park and wafted it about some more. After some prolonged and vigorous shaking, the farmyard odours lost their pungency, though faint traces of the sheep shit or whatever it was that that dirty dog Landsdale had been rolling in, clung to him for a further hour or so.

It was a bit early for lunch but, keen to remain a while longer in the fresh air, Tudor drove into town. He parked his car in St Julian's Friars, and walked back up into Wyle Cop where he bought a sandwich and a coffee to go. Heading back towards the river, he passed the open door of a pub and froze; arrested by the sight of Ingrid Sandstrom on a TV screen inside. The sound was turned down but he gathered from the on-screen text that the broadcast was coming live from outside Hereford Cathedral, where the great and the not-so-good were gathering for a memorial service to honour her late husband. Tudor was thoughtful as he took the steps down to the river at the side of Greyfriars bridge which linked this side of Shrewsbury with Longdon Coleham and strolled along the riverbank towards Quarry Park. He hadn't thought much about the events at Morecroft Hall in recent weeks; his interest in the case had soon faded once it had been decided that Rik Haymer had taken his own life. Still he regretted not being there to hear his widow make her eulogy speech. He expected it would be another Oscar winning performance.

He found a bench, sat down and breathed in deeply. The air tasted sweet, reminding him of those summer mornings of his boyhood when he couldn't wait to go out and play, when the dew still lay on the grass and the air was cool. He watched a team of rowers from Shrewsbury School emerge from the boathouse on the opposite bank and carry their boat down to the water. The school itself stood higher up on the bank; a red brick pile with a green cupola that dominated the skyline. Tudor often came here to eat his lunch; it provided a still point in a busy day; put him back in touch with normal everyday life and gave him a chance to collect his thoughts. This last was particularly useful when he was struggling to make sense of a complex case. But as he so often did lately, he found himself trying to understand what it was that Maggie Mellor wanted from him.

He had been out with her just three times in two months and their relationship didn't seem to be going anywhere. It was like trying to get off with Joan of Arc. He had asked her to join him when he and the band played at this posh wedding at the end of the month. The wedding was being held at a Palladian mansion in Wiltshire and the band would be playing later than evening in a huge marquee to be set up in the mansion's extensive grounds. Ever hopeful, Tudor had pushed the boat out and booked a room with a four-poster bed in a four star hotel in nearby Salisbury. Maggie was thinking about it, but had yet to get back to him and, with the gig looming, he was more or less resigned to the prospect of sleeping alone.

The rowers were on the water now, their oars held vertically aloft. At a command from the cox they lowered them into the river and began pulling away; skimming across the water like a giant water boatman towards Kingsland Bridge. Tudor watched them until they passed under it and out of sight then, downing the last of his coffee, walked back to the car. As he inserted the key in the ignition, he noted the time on the dashboard clock, he would have to get a move on, he was due in court in 20 minutes.

*

Tudor felt like a stalker as he waited in his car for Maggie Mellor to emerge from the station. It was 8.20 pm. Her shift had ended twenty minutes ago. Crawford had gone in and come back out again in ten. What was keeping her? It was the eternal question that every man asks himself at some time or another. For Tudor it remained something of a mystery.

A further five minutes dragged by and he began to wonder if a she was ever coming out. By now he was having trouble keeping his eyes open; it had been a long day and his court appearance had left him drained. On entering the witness box he had been dismayed to find the smug face of Gerald Bullstrode glowering at him from the defence benches. The barrister was as bullish as his name implied and his courtroom technique was to verbally batter witnesses into submission. He and Tudor had had several run-ins on previous occasions and Glyn had good reason to believe he would be in for a roughing up when it was Bullstrode's turn to ask questions. As he had learned to his cost, the barrister was no friend of the police.

Meanwhile the defendant, Gary Edkins, sat in the dock, his face as expressionless as a slab of granite; a picture of sobriety in a charcoal grey suit, a white button-down shirt and a pale blue tie.

When the prosecuting barrister, Joycelin Denton, a young female lawyer Tudor hadn't come across before, rose hesitantly to her feet, he realised they were in trouble. Pale-faced and petite, she didn't look tough enough or experienced enough to handle a man like Bullstrode. She wasn't and he proceeded to make mincemeat of them both.

It had all begun well enough.

'Detective Sergeant Tudor, for the benefit of the court, would you please recount the events that led to you entering the home of Mr Edkins on the ninth of April last,' she said.

Turning to the jury, Tudor had proceeded to take them through each step of the events of that day in some detail. When he had finished, Ms Denton thanked him and sat down.

In stark contrast to Ms Denton, Bullstrode jumped to his feet with the suddenness of a jack-in-the-box, and, in the best theatrical traditions of court room drama, tugged at his gown.

'You have something of reputation in the West Mercia force, don't you Sergeant? Bit of a maverick, are you not?'

'No sir.'

'No sir?' Bullstrode had boomed. 'Did you have a warrant to enter and search Mr Edkins home?'

'I didn't need one.'

'You didn't need one?' Bullstrode raised his bushy, black eyebrows like a man who couldn't believe what he was hearing. 'Isn't it usual on these occasions to let a magistrate decide if you need a warrant or not?'

Bullstrode continued in this vein, vociferously challenging each point, as he tried to make the clear appear opaque and cast doubt in the minds of the jury. Tudor wondered how some of these defence lawyers managed to sleep at night; knowing the people they were defending were guilty but doing their damndest to get them off anyway. He'd seen it all before. The trial was continuing, but unless Ms Denton upped her game, Glyn couldn't see her getting a conviction for anything other than the assault on Tomlins.

At long last the station door opened and Maggie stepped out onto the car park, dressed in skinny black jeans and a coral pink T shirt. With her dark hair down around her shoulders, she was breathtakingly attractive. Glyn nervously fingered the handcuffs in his pocket. This could all go so horribly wrong, he thought. As she drew closer, a warning voice in Tudor's head screamed, *'Abort, abort!'* But his heart overruled it. With the flat of his free hand, he sounded the car's horn and lowered the window on his side.

With a smile of recognition, Maggie swerved in his direction and, coming to the driver's window, placed a hand on the sill and leaned in.

'Hi Glyn, you're working late tonight,' she said.

'I'm not officially working. It's more of a pet project really.'

Her brown eyes narrowed and she looked quizzical. 'Sounds intriguing…'

It was now or never, he thought. In one swift movement his right hand shot up out of his pocket and he snapped the open end of the handcuffs he was wearing around Mellor's slim wrist.

Instinctively she pulled away, but Tudor gently pulled her back.

'Glyn, what the hell are doing?' she said, with a mixture of anger and alarm in her voice.

'Just what you told me to do. When I asked you what it would take to get your attention, you said, "Arrest me." He gave her a sheepish grin. 'Consider yourself arrested.'

'You idiot!' she fumed A roll of her eyes, a sigh, then, 'OK, you've got my attention. Now release me.'

'Oh no, you don't get off as easily as that. I want a yes or no on this wedding gig first. And before you say anything, I feel it's only fair to warn you I've booked a room; a double, in fact.'

'Oh, have you? That was very presumptuous…'

Tudor rattled the chain that connected them. 'Yes or no?' he said and held his breath.

'I suppose it will have to be a yes, if you've booked a room. It had better be a nice hotel, mind. I'm not slumming it in some back street B & B.'

'It's a four star hotel and we'll be sleeping in a four-poster,' he assured her.

'And that's all we will be doing in it,' she said firmly.

'Y-e-a-h, that's fine,' said Tudor, his enthusiasm only slightly dampened by this proviso. 'How about we go for a little drink to celebrate?'

'Oh, you're really pushing your luck tonight, aren't you?' It sounded like a rebuke, but there was a smile on her lips as she said it.

Tudor was feeling elated as he fished in his pocket for the key to the handcuffs. But this elation quickly turned to alarm and then embarrassment after several sweeps of his hand failed to make contact with that vital piece of cold metal.

'You do have the key?' Her tone was sharpened by anxiety.

'Y-E-S, I had it here a minute ago, must be in the other pocket.' He reached across and with some difficulty inserted his hand in the pocket on the other side.

Out of the corner of her eye, Maggie saw the station door swing open. Turning, she saw Dudley lean out. He stared across the car park and, spotting Maggie at the window of Glyn's Mondeo, began walking towards them.

'Please hurry Glyn, Dudley's heading this way.' In her agitation,

Maggie was almost dancing at the side of the car.

'Pull the other one, and for God's sake, stand still,' said Glyn irritably. This is difficult enough as it is, without you prancing up and down.'

'Glyn, I'm not pulling your leg, he's…' With a loud slap, Maggie cupped her free hand over her manacled wrist, '…here!' she announced and moved to one side to let Dudley in.

'Got it!' shouted Glyn triumphantly. His head came up just as his boss peered into the car and he promptly dropped the key. 'Oh, hello, Boss,' he said and fervently wished he could dematerialise and be transported out of this embarrassing situation.

'Evening Glyn, I'm glad you're still here…' Dudley's eyes widened as they fell upon the handcuff Glyn was wearing then followed the short length of chain up to PC Mellor's wrist.

'We were just…' Tudor began.

'Never mind, it will keep for now,' said Dudley, eyebrow raised. 'Just unhitch yourself and come with me. There's been another incident at Morecroft Hall. This time it's a stabbing.'

CHAPTER FOURTEEN

MIKE MORETTI didn't look angry anymore; in fact, given the circumstances, he looked remarkably relaxed, thought Tudor. Rik Haymer's former sidesman lay spread-eagled on his back like a sunbather. The only jarring note in this otherwise tranquil scene was the stiletto-thin blade of the paper knife that stuck out like an exclamation mark from the socket of his right eye.

They were in Rik Haymer's office cum study; a much larger and more luxuriously appointed room than that of Ingrid Sandstrom or Alex Rainesford. In addition to the usual office furniture, there was a dark red leather Chesterfield and a big flat screen TV along with a blu-ray player. An entire wall was ablaze with the gold discs that Rik had garnered during his long career; and in one corner, a Taylor acoustic guitar gleamed on its stand. Moretti was sprawled across a Persian rug, his one surviving eye staring blankly at the tungsten light from a cluster of spotlights in the ceiling above him.

'Ms Rainesford must be a mean darts player,' observed Dudley. 'Look at that, scored a bullseye first go.'

Tudor had already seen as much of the wrecked eyeball as he wanted to but despite his queasiness, took another look. Dudley was right; the tip of the blade had gone in close to the centre of the pupil – what were the odds of that happening, he wondered.

'Hum, there's a touch of Christopher Marlowe about this…' Dudley mused.

'Who?' queried Tudor.

Dudley looked up sharply, 'I forgot, you don't go to the theatre, do you?'

'I can't afford to go to the theatre on my salary,' said Tudor.

Dudley ignored the jibe. 'He was a contemporary of Shakespeare – you have heard of him, I take it?'

Tudor nodded his assent. 'Did him at school.'

'Marlowe got stabbed in the eye with his own dagger. It was claimed in a dispute over the reckoning – the bill,' he explained for Tudor's benefit. 'But he was rumoured to be one of Walsingham's spies and it's believed he was bumped off in order to ensure his silence. He was a bolshie bastard by all accounts, just like our friend Moretti here.'

'So, you're thinking what I'm thinking then? It looks staged, just like the last one. And that's another thing; two suspicious deaths in as many months, involving the same people, at the same location? Bit of a coincidence, don't you think?'

'I agree, it's stretching it, but lightning does sometimes strike twice in the same place.'

'I don't know, Boss. My gut reaction to this one is the same as it was last time – it just doesn't feel right.'

'That's as maybe, but the same rules apply. We're dealing with high profile people here and we need to tread carefully.'

'Rank hath its privileges, is that it?' sneered Tudor.

Dudley sprang to his feet. 'Oh grow up, Glyn, for God's sake, that chip on your shoulder is showing again.' Turning his back on his sergeant, he strode over to the filing cabinet.

Tudor was surprised by Dudley's outburst; it was so unlike him to raise his voice let alone lose his temper. An edgy silence ensued which was eventually broken by Dudley.

'Look, Glyn, don't get me wrong, you may well be right and I understand your frustration, but cases like this can break careers as well as make them. You'd do well to remember that.' Dudley fell silent again and appeared to be mulling something over. 'OK, this is what we're going to do. I want you to take Ms Rainesford back to the station, but do it quietly. We've got a roomful of some of the biggest names in show biz and the press are at the gates. Go out through the back lanes like we did last time. Try and get as much out of her as you can before some high-powered brief turns up to spring her. I'll handle the celebs and the press. Go, go,' he said.

Alex Rainesford raised a mascara-streaked face as Tudor entered the same reception room, where only two months ago they had interviewed Ingrid Sandstrom. The ice maiden looked as though she had melted; the perfectly coiffed hair was in disarray and her white blouse was blood spattered. Glyn nodded to the female officer who had been guarding her and she moved closer to stand beside the sofa on which her charge was sitting.

'Ms Rainesford, would you stand up please?'

After a moment's hesitation, she meekly complied and the female officer took hold of her left arm.

'Alex Rainesford, I'm arresting you in connection with the manslaughter of Michael Moretti,' said Tudor. 'You do not have to say anything. But it may harm your defence if you do not mention, when questioned, something which you later rely on in court. Anything you do say may be given in evidence.'

Alex Rainesford's mood was subdued but she remained unbowed and a touch of the Alex that Tudor remembered returned, when the officer went to handcuff her.

'Is that really necessary?' she said, fixing Tudor with an icy stare.

The constable looked to Tudor for guidance and, after a moment's consideration, he nodded his agreement. Rainesford seemed prepared to cooperate and he needed her to go quietly. No point then, for the moment, in being unnecessarily heavy-handed.

'There's a pack of newshounds and TV cameramen waiting for us at the front gates, so we'll be going out through the back lanes,' Tudor explained, as much for the benefit of the constable as for Alex Rainesford. The female constable was an experienced officer, but even Tudor had found the attentions of the press unsettling when he and Dudley had been forced to run the gauntlet on their arrival at the Hall.

Tudor opened the door and, stepping into the corridor, checked the way was clear. 'Right, come on,' he said and led them off at a brisk pace.

In the entrance hall, he paused beneath the vaulted atrium to give his final instructions. The last rays of the setting sun streaming through the glass filled the large space with a mosaic of fiery red, orange and purple light.

'We'll take my car,' said Tudor. 'Be less conspicuous.'

A shadow passed across the glass dome above their heads and the light falling on the marbled floor flickered as if someone had thrown a switch. Tudor glanced up, but saw only burning sky. Then he heard it; the distinctive clatter of rotor blades.

'Shit!' he said. 'The bastards have got a helicopter.'

The drive back to Shrewsbury was hair-raising; Tudor threw the Mondeo around the twisting lanes with the helicopter, buzzing like an angry hornet, in hot pursuit. He had little doubt that the occupants of the machine hired by the TV company were in contact with the TV van he had seen parked outside the Hall's gates and it was just a question now of who got back to the station first. As they approached the junction with the A49, his suspicions were confirmed, as a white van with the tell-tale satellite dish on its rooftop flashed past. Unless he could overtake them, a camera crew would be waiting for them when they arrived at the station. At the junction he endured an agonising wait for a break in the traffic before he could pull out onto the main carriageway and he began to regret not having taken a patrol car; at least then he could have used the 'blues and two's' to force his way through the clogging traffic. Tudor glanced in his rear view mirror; Alex Rainesford had her face turned away from the window, away from the prying eyes of the occupants of oncoming vehicles. He'd taken the precaution of handing the constable a tartan picnic blanket before setting off; not because he thought they might be cold sat in the rear seats, but because they would need to cover Rainesford's head when they transferred her from the car to the station.

Tudor turned his attention back to the road, saw a gap in the traffic and gunned the engine. Their prisoner gave a startled cry and he eased his foot off the accelerator, decided there was little point in trying to overtake the TV company's van after all; they would be well ahead of them by now. The drive through the lanes had been alarming enough and he hadn't the stomach for another reckless pursuit like the one with Shaun Tomlins, which had so nearly ended in a head-on collision. And you didn't need to be a police officer to know that there was at least one of those every week on the A49; it was notorious for them.

Darkness was falling as they approached the lights at Monkmoor Road. Waiting for the lights to change, Tudor said, 'Blanket please, Constable.' But Ms Rainesford, it seemed, was not anxious to cover her face and she pushed the proffered blanket away.

'I strongly advise it, Ms Rainesford,' warned Tudor, 'Unless that's the face you want people to see on tonight's news bulletins or splashed all over the front pages of tomorrow's tabloids.'

Vanity or the desire to protect her identity – perhaps both – got the better of her and she allowed the constable to place the blanket over her head.

Dudley had phoned ahead and advised the station of their coming and so there was a strong police presence ready to fend off the gathered newsmen with their intrusive cameras and TV lights. Despite these precautions, for a few tense moments the car was surrounded before a way was cleared for them and Tudor drove in through the station's security gates, which were firmly shut behind them.

Once inside, Alex Rainesford's bloodstained clothes were removed and placed in evidence bags and she was given a pair of coveralls. But the legal formalities didn't end there, and by the time Tudor had got her into the interview room, he was anxiously glancing at his watch. The soft whir of the tape passing through the recording head filled the silence as Tudor and Alex Rainesford stared at each other across the desk. In stark contrast to the smudged mascara that ringed them, her eyes were deep pools of cerulean blue, as clear and cold as a mountain lake.

'I never intended to kill him,' she said in a firm voice.

Tudor was surprised by this unsolicited admission – without even asking so much as one question, he'd already got a confession from her.

'So, you admit you stabbed Mr Moretti in the eye with the paperknife?'

'Yes, but he had his hands around my throat and was trying to strangle me. I believed my life was in imminent danger.'

An interesting phrase that, thought Tudor; almost as though she was quoting the legal definition of self defence; hardly the words of a distraught woman who thought she was about to die…

'OK, we'll come back to that,' he said. 'Let's rewind a bit. 'You and Mike Moretti hated each other's guts – he attacked you in front of the Inspector and myself – so why would you risk shutting yourself away alone with him?' She didn't bat an eyelid, Tudor noticed; she was a cool one all right, that or a much better actress than Ingrid Sandstrom had been in that Bond movie.

'Ingrid asked me to fetch something from Rik's study. I found Moretti in there. One of the filing cabinet drawers was open and he had a file in his hand. I asked him what he was doing and he told me in no uncertain terms to mind my own business. When I tried to take the file off him, he lost it, I mean, completely. Well, you saw what he was like that day…'

Tudor remembered it only too well; Moretti's pent up fury had boiled over and translated into violence in a matter of seconds. But for Dudley's intervention, he might well have throttled Rainesford that day. And yet, Tudor had had the impression that it was largely posturing of that peculiarly Italian kind, nothing more than empty machismo.

'Go on,' he said.

'Moretti was raving. He grabbed me by the throat and pushed me back onto the desk. He had me pinned down and was squeezing the life out of me.' She gave an involuntary shudder and there was a catch in her throat. 'I'll never forget the look on his face… such hatred. Everything was going dim and I knew I was about to pass out. I was scrabbling about on the desk, desperately searching for something to hit him with. My fingers found the paperknife and, with my last ounce of strength, I lashed out at him with it. I didn't think about it, I didn't have time. It was simply an instinctive reaction to the realisation that he was going to kill me if I didn't do something to stop him.'

She'd done that all right; stopped him for good. What had happened to the file, Tudor wondered. Moretti couldn't have put both hands around the woman's neck with it in his hand. In the heat of the moment would he have bothered to put it back in the filing cabinet before attacking her or just dropped it on the floor? He couldn't remember seeing one lying around. He was about to ask Alex Rainesford when there was a knock on the door and the constable stood just inside opened it to admit a tall, distinguished looking gentleman in a well cut suit – Rainesford's high-powered lawyer had arrived.

CHAPTER FIFTEEN

HARRY TURNED the thin-bladed screwdriver over in his hands; it was a blunt instrument compared to some of the kitchen knives he had at home but he was confident that, driven into the side-wall of the Fiesta's tyres with enough force, it would do the job just as well. Yet he hesitated, even as the rain continued to beat out its staccato rhythm on the Citroen's roof like a drum beat urging him into action. It wasn't the foul weather that held him back but his conscience – that and the fear of being caught in the act. Throughout his adult life, Harry had seen himself as a law abiding citizen, so what he was about to do went against the grain of everything he believed to be true about himself. A nagging doubt slowly wormed its way into the labyrinth of his brain; how sure was he that this Shaun Tomlins was the young man who had invaded his home? Was the fleeting glance he'd caught of a face in his darkened bedroom, or his gut reaction on seeing Tomlins as he passed under the light of a street lamp, good enough to be certain? If he was wrong about the lad then it would only compound this act of criminal damage.

What to do? Time was pressing; another few days and Julia would be living back at home again. Her presence, though most welcome, would inevitably seriously curtail his surveillance activities. Harry could well imagine what his daughter would have to say were she to find out what he was up to – the very same reaction, he suspected, as his friends had had – *leave it to the police*...

But he couldn't do that, could he; they had already proved that they weren't up to the task. No, this was the only way, he decided. Besides, he told himself, even if Tomlins hadn't trespassed against him personally, he had trespassed against plenty of others, as his criminal record clearly demonstrated.

As he got out of the car, he could hear his mother's voice saying, "Two wrongs don't make a right" but the older Harry was prepared to ignore advice that his boyhood self would have heeded. He had little argument with the sentiment, but this quest of his to retrieve Annie's jewellery had become something of an obsession and he couldn't just sit there and do nothing. Harry pulled his flat cap down low over his brow, pulled his coat collar up around his ears and, head down, shoulders hunched, walked towards the orange Fiesta. And still the raindrops managed to sting his eyes, to invade even the smallest opening and fold in his clothing. In seconds, coat and trousers were saturated and he became a drowned man walking. Discomfort aside, Harry was grateful for the cover the deluge provided; it cascaded down windows, blotting out the world beyond the glass and ensured that Tomlins and his neighbours remained indoors and unaware of his presence.

Harry crouched down beside the Fiesta's offside front wheel and glanced up and down the rain-swept street. Satisfied he was unobserved; he brought out the screwdriver and thrust it into the side wall of the tyre with the deftness of an Italian assassin. It went in much deeper than he would have thought possible and he was frantically trying to free it, when he heard a woman's voice call out Shaun's name – Tomlins' mother? Harry pictured her standing in the doorway as he cowered back against the Fiesta's wing. His fevered imagination didn't stop there, but conjured up a whole series of increasingly unpleasant images as it played out the likely sequence of events.

'Fuck's sake! What now?' a male voice.

Christ, he sounded so close – just the other side of the car. Harry now faced his worst-case scenario and his options were minimal – stay or run. Not much of a choice when he considered it, as he couldn't hope to outrun the much younger man. How ironic, that he should be caught in a trap of his own devising, he thought. Though he did have one advantage over Tomlins and that was the element of surprise; Shaun wouldn't be expecting a rain-sodden scarecrow to jump up from behind his car and run off – it could just give him the edge he needed. But this one ray of hope was immediately dashed by the jangling of the mobile in his pocket.

Harry let it ring; he felt like the driver of a run-away car who, seeing no way out, takes his hands off the wheel and, covering his face, surrenders himself to his fate. It continued to ring for some time. He'd expected Shaun to appear at any moment and so was most surprised that, when the phone finally stopped ringing, there was still no sign of him. Slowly uncurling his cramped limbs, Harry peered over the Fiesta's bonnet. Shaun and his mother had apparently taken their argument back into the house; he could hear their angry voices above the hammering of the rain on the car's bodywork.

Harry was more than happy to leave them to it. Seizing the screwdriver's handle in both hands, he wrenched it from its temporary sheath and was rewarded with the satisfying hiss of escaping air. Despite his stiff joints, Harry was skipping through the puddles as he made his way back to his own car and home with the prospect of a warm bath and a mug of hot, sweet tea.

CHAPTER SIXTEEN

TUDOR HAD BEEN too restless to sleep; instead he'd stayed up late, drinking whisky into the small hours. Moretti's death at the hands of Alex Rainesford had re-kindled the suspicions he'd harboured over Rik Haymer's demise. He found it hard to believe that the two events were simply the random acts of desperate people; the one of self-destruction, the other of self-defence. That was just too neat and tidy for Tudor's suspicious mind to accept. Life and death might be at the opposite ends of the spectrum but, in Tudor's experience, both were a messy business. The two events had to be connected, but how – apart from the superficial links, that is? In the final analysis, all crimes could be boiled down to just two factors; motive and opportunity. So that was where he would start…

Several hours and half a bottle of whisky later, he still had his suspicions and a theory of sorts, but he knew it would not be enough to convince Dudley. They already had a confession from Alex Rainesford – so, it would be a case of job done, as far as he was concerned; a pat on the back all round and a booze-up to celebrate. Why waste precious resources on further fruitless investigation? And up to a point Dudley would be right, but what if somebody was getting away with murder –

could they, should they, allow that to happen?

Before retiring for the night, Tudor checked his mobile phone; there was just one message – it was from Maggie; *your turn next,* it read above a photo of a naked man with his hands manacled behind his back. It was a lighter note to end the day on and Glyn was smiling as he made his way to a cold, empty bed.

The following morning he and Dudley were alone in the incident room; the briefing over, the rest of the inquiry team had returned to their desks and the tasks that had been assigned to them. Tudor was propped up against a filing cabinet, a cup of black coffee (two shots, the strongest available from the station's vending machine) in his hand. Last night's drinking and the resulting lack of sleep had taken their toll. Dudley had his back to him and was studying the montage of photographs and other documents displayed on a large whiteboard which covered a significant part of one wall. As yet it was a relatively small collection, but it would grow larger as the case progressed.

'Something on your mind, Glyn?' he said, without turning round. That was the trouble with working with Dudley, for as long as Tudor had, he could read him like a book. 'Nice work by the way,' he added.

'I'm sorry, Boss… what?' Tudor's tired brain was taking much longer than usual to process information and he was experiencing a time delay; it was like conducting a conversation over a long distance satellite link.

'Rainesford's confession…'

'Oh that, it wasn't too difficult, to be honest,' admitted Tudor. 'I didn't even get to show her the thumbscrews…' he joked. Dangerous ground, bearing in mind yesterday's incident with the handcuffs, he realised, and quickly moved on. 'All the same, I would have expected her to hold out until Sandstrom's hot-shot brief arrived. She must have known he was on his way.'

Dudley turned then and, stepping away from the whiteboard, said, 'Your modesty is refreshing but don't undersell yourself, Sergeant.'

Sergeant? A few minutes ago it had been Glyn – was Dudley pulling rank on him? He noted his boss had folded his arms across his chest. Not a good sign, as Tudor knew only too well from past encounters.

Glyn found himself hesitating; late last night he believed he'd had something of an epiphany, but now, in the harsher light of day, or more accurately the incident room's fluorescent tubes, his lightbulb moment didn't appear to add up to much.

'Well, out with it, man.'

Dudley sounded impatient and Tudor knew better than to keep him waiting, it would only increase his irritation and undermine his case.

'Look, Boss, I know you think I'm seeing murder where there is none, but I still don't buy Rik Haymer's suicide…'

Dudley's lips were pencil-thin, bloodless. 'That case is closed,' he said, and his lips barely moved.

It was like watching a ventriloquist, thought Tudor. 'And your mind with it, by the sounds of it,' he replied sharply.

'Tread carefully, Sergeant…'

'All right, but at least hear me out,' he said, adopting a more conciliatory tone.

'Fair enough.' Dudley glanced at his watch. 'You've got two minutes.'

'OK, I can't prove it, not yet anyway, but it's my belief that Moretti killed Rik…'

'Let me stop you right there,' Dudley cut in. 'What did Moretti stand to gain from killing Haymer? Ingrid Sandstrom was the chief beneficiary of her husband's will.'

'Have you looked at the album charts recently?' said Tudor. 'Sorry, of course you haven't, rock music's not your thing.' He took a small square of paper out of his pocket, unfolded it and handed it to Dudley. 'Five of Haymer's old albums are in the top fifty – two of them in the top ten; including the number one and number three best sellers. Every CD or download sold is a double payday for Moretti; there's his royalty as a band member and another as co-writer of the songs. The back catalogue, undoubtedly an asset while Haymer was alive, is the goose that lays the golden egg now he's dead. His career had been in the doldrums for years and was all but over when his record label dropped him eighteen months ago. Both men enjoyed a lavish lifestyle and were no doubt piling up debts. My guess is that Moretti, who had a long standing love-hate relationship with Haymer, saw the way the wind was blowing, realised this new album wasn't going to reboot Rik's career and decided he was worth more to him dead than he was alive.'

Dudley looked thoughtful. 'And where does Alex Rainesford fit into this theory of yours?' he said.

'Truthfully? I'm not sure. Maybe she found Rik in the pool like she said and worked out what Moretti had done – she already suspected him of stealing from Rik... she began blackmailing him, got too greedy and Moretti decided to kill her but she got in first...'

Dudley stroked his chin, took a deep breath and blew it out. 'I don't know, Glyn, it's all a bit flimsy. I can't see it holding together.'

'So give me a few more days, let me dig a little deeper...'

There was a talent show moment's hesitation before Dudley announced his decision. 'All right, you've got 48 hours to come up with something concrete enough for me to take upstairs but softly, softly,

146

Glyn; there were more high profile public figures at that memorial service yesterday than you could shake a stick at – one of them a cabinet minister – we can't afford to tread on anybody's toes.'

'Don't worry, Boss, I'll be wearing my brothel creepers.' His boss gave him a sideways look. What's wrong with me, Tudor asked himself; every time I open my mouth, I say something inappropriate. It's like I've got Tourette's. Now I've got Dudley thinking I'm some kind of sex addict. As if to confirm this, he had a flash image of himself standing naked with his hands handcuffed behind him like the ripped guy in the photo Maggie Mellor had sent him. Tudor patted his stomach and wondered if he should join a gym; he'd developed a small paunch in recent months and worried that Maggie would be less than impressed when the time came to reveal his flabby torso. This inevitably led to thoughts of what she might look like without her clothes. It didn't require a great leap of the imagination on his part to picture the young, toned body that lay beneath the spray-on jeans and tight fitting top, but it left him with even more reason to be worried about his own physique.

He heard his name and it broke his reverie; he looked up to see Dudley staring at him through narrowed eyes. 'Sorry, Boss – what was that? I didn't catch all of it.'

'I said, I've got to pop out for an hour so. The wife's got a hospital appointment, said I'd take her.'

'Nothing serious, I hope?'

'No, no, just a… check-up, nothing to worry about,' he said as if to reassure himself, but sounded distinctly anxious.

Tudor wondered if there was more to the hospital visit than this boss was letting on – he and his wife were very close – it would explain Dudley's uncharacteristic outburst up at the Hall the other day.

'You don't look so good yourself,' observed Dudley. 'Late night, was it?'

Tudor managed a weak smile. 'Yes, but not the way you mean.' He approached the whiteboard and tapped a crime scene photo of Moretti's skewered eyeball. 'I couldn't sleep, so I stayed up half the night trying to work out what's really been going on in Haymer's fairy-tale castle.' He decided not to mention drinking half a bottle of scotch in the process; he didn't want his boss thinking he was an alcoholic as well as a sexual deviant.

'You've got nothing else to think about, that's your trouble. You need to get yourself a girlfriend, mate. Failing that, I suggest you have another coffee and get digging because there will be no extension beyond the forty-eight hours, unless you come up with some supporting evidence for your theory.' Dudley consulted his watch. 'Right, I've got to go, the wife's nervous enough as it is, without me making her late for her appointment.'

Tudor decided to work on in the incident room; it was quieter in there, but first he dialled Ferrars' extension – the young detective constable was the team's computer whiz-kid – and asked him to get as much financial information as he could on both Moretti and Rainesford, along with their phone records for the past few months. That done, he got himself a fresh cup of coffee and settled down to read the witness statements taken from the VIP's, who had gone back to the Hall after the memorial service. The names read like a Who's Who of showbiz; there were actors, musicians, film stars, TV celebs and a smattering of leading businessmen and politicians. It must have been an autograph hunter's idea of paradise and, if you hadn't got a collection, you could have started one, thought Tudor. Scanning down the list, he spotted another of his heroes; a man regularly voted the world's best rock guitarist. Once the young pretender to Rik Haymer's throne, he now wore his crown as the undisputed king of the axemen.

None of those present had witnessed the killing, of course, and reading through their statements it became increasingly clear that the majority of them had been too busy promoting themselves and their latest pet project to notice anybody else. Less than a handful of them had seen Alex Rainesford leave the room. But that was all they had seen, except for one Chris Currie, a leading music journalist, who said that an argument had broken out between Moretti and Rainesford and that Ingrid Sandstrom had immediately stepped in to silence them and usher them out of the room.

Suddenly alert, Tudor eagerly flicked back to Rainesford's confession. No, he wasn't mistaken – there it was in black and white – *"'Ingrid asked me to fetch something from Rik's study.'"* No mention of an argument; Currie's statement directly contradicted her, but was Alex lying or had the journalist embellished the truth a little in order to create a better story? If nothing else, Currie's statement introduced an element of doubt. By itself it wasn't enough to undermine Rainesford's plea of self-defence, but a small lie was often used to cover up an even bigger one.

The phone rang and he reached for it. 'Tudor,' he said, absently; his mind still on the matter at hand.

It was Ferrars. 'Oh, hello Sarge, is Mr Dudley still with you?'

'No, he's had to go out, won't be back for a couple of hours. Why?' he said, without any real interest.

I've got a Mr Mayfield on the line for him, says he's Mike Moretti's solicitor...'

That got his attention. 'Now, that is interesting…' he mused.

'Sarge?'

'Never mind, just put him through,' he said. There was a short delay, then a click as the call was transferred.

'Good morning, Mr Mayfield. I'm sorry, but Inspector Dudley isn't here at the moment. You're speaking to Glyn Tudor. I'm his sergeant, I understand you have some information regarding Mr Moretti?'

'Yes. Indeed.' The voice on the other end of the line was public school with just the hint of a West Midlands accent – a grammar school boy, perhaps? 'Heretofore, Mr Moretti's affairs have been handled by one of my colleagues at our London office, but, some months ago he came to see me here in Birmingham and left a small package in my care with instructions that, in the event of his death, it should be placed in the hands of Detective Inspector Dudley.'

Why did lawyers insist on using archaic words and phrases like *heretofore* and *hereinafter*, he wondered? It just confused matters. 'And he gave you no indication of what was in the package?'

'No, none at all.'

'Intriguing… can you get it biked over to us today?'

'Yes, of course, if you consider it that important.'

'Yes, Mr Mayfield. I do.'

Tudor was thoughtful as he replaced the phone; could this be the breakthrough he was looking for? Was it possible that a dead man could provide the answer to the questions that had been nagging at him for the past two months? Thankfully, he'd have the answer to that question before the day was out.

CHAPTER SEVENTEEN

HARRY LAY BACK in his bath and luxuriated in its warm, soapy embrace. Funny, he thought how, despite getting soaked to the skin earlier, he'd sought solace in doing exactly the same thing when he got home. The difference being the warmth, he supposed – that and the fact that he'd taken the precaution of removing his clothes beforehand. Raising himself up, he reached for the steaming mug of tea perched precariously on the bath's rim. He sipped it slowly, savouring each mouthful as if it were a glass of oak-aged brandy.

The warm water and the hot tea revived him and he felt the tension drain from his body. It had been a close call – far too close and he had been lucky to get away with nothing more serious than a good soaking. Harry shuddered at the thought of what might have happened if Shaun's mother hadn't called him back into the house. And that phone call... what a time for his mobile to ring. What had surprised him more was why he hadn't immediately shut it off and why he'd just sat there; abandoned himself to fate like that. It wasn't like him to give up so easily, or was it simply another indication of how reckless he'd become in his pursuit of the young burglar? He resolved to be a lot more cautious in the future; *softly, softly, catchee monkey...*

Harry lay in the bath until the water began to cool and emerged pink and shiny as a prawn. He dried himself thoroughly and, pulling on a dressing gown, padded across the landing into his bedroom. The mobile lay on the bed where he'd tossed it and picking it up, he checked for missed calls. There was just one; from his old friend, Colin Turner, accompanied by a voicemail message inviting Harry to join him and Sue for a meal at *Sandfords* that evening. Harry's initial reaction was to politely decline the invitation, but the long soak in the bath had revived his spirits, and on reflection he decided to celebrate his lucky escape. Yes, why not? It would do him good. He had nothing better to do, in any case; to go anywhere near Shaun Tomlins tonight would be foolhardy in the extreme, he told himself.

In stark contrast to the last time Harry had been there, *Sandfords* was busy with half a dozen tables already occupied. Colin stopped at one of them on the way in to speak to some people he knew. It was the same wherever they went; there would always be someone there that Colin was acquainted with, however tenuously. Harry's circle of friends and acquaintances was tiny – the social equivalent of a capsule wardrobe by comparison, and he experienced a tinge of envy. The emotion was misplaced, however, for, as he would readily admit, the reason he didn't have a large number of friends was because he preferred it that way. Other people meant work and, in any case, for most of his life Annie had been all the company he needed. No, the few close friends he had gathered around him were as much as he could cope with. He had no need of any more.

They ordered drinks at the bar and were shown to their table where they were handed some menus. Harry was trying to decide whether to have the pan fried sea bass or the home-made steak and ale pie when Colin demanded to know where he'd been lately.

'Me?' Harry stalled, while he tried to come up with a convincing reason for his many absences from home in the past couple of weeks.

'Yes you, I've called round several times recently – you're never in,' said Colin accusingly. 'Been seeing someone, have you?'

'Col!' Sue admonished him. 'That's none of our business…'

'OK. I'm sorry, that was out of order but I was worried about you, mate,' offered Colin by way of an apology.

'Well, I'm here now and, as you can see, I'm fine,' said Harry, hoping this would be enough to head off any further questioning, but Colin, it seemed, wasn't prepared to be put off that easily.

'So, where were you then?' he persisted.

Lost for an explanation, Harry said the first thing that came into his head. 'Oh, you know, been doing a lot of walking, trying to get myself fit.'

Colin looked hurt. 'You should have said, I'd have come with you.'

Sue rolled her eyes at him. 'Perhaps he wanted to be alone,' she said, placing heavy emphasis on the last word. 'Darling, an experience like that affects people in different ways…' her voice dropped to a whisper, 'and I don't just mean physically.' She gave Harry an apologetic smile. 'Insensitive as ever,' she said, her tone conveying her exasperation.

Unabashed, Colin looked as if he was about to press on regardless when, thankfully, the waitress appeared and enquired if they were ready to order; this refocused everyone's mind on the food and put an end to further questioning on the subject of Harry's recent whereabouts. The food ordered, the conversation turned to other matters and Harry began to relax. Colin and Sue, as always, were good company and kept him entertained throughout the meal with a host of stories about the weird and wonderful people who had passed through their B & B over the years.

'You'd be amazed at the stuff we find in their rooms after they've gone,' said Colin.

'And we're not just talking about paperbacks, are we, Col?' said Sue gleefully; knowing what was coming.

'If only, we've had some very interesting sex toys, haven't we? More like instruments of torture some of 'em. They never phone and ask us to send those back, funny that … There's the usual shoes and various items of clothing, of course – Oh, and pets!' he cried, warming to his theme. 'We had a tarantula spider once – bloody great hairy thing it was – safely locked up in its cage, thank goodness…'

'And, what about the man who left his artificial leg behind? I mean, how could you forget something like that?' Sue prompted.

'It was a spare, apparently,' Colin explained. 'Which was why he hadn't missed it. We had to parcel it up and post it back to him. Have you ever tried wrapping up an artificial leg? It's not easy, I can tell you. Got some funny looks when I took it to the post office – think they thought I'd chopped the wife up and was posting the bits back to her family.' He grinned widely. 'You couldn't make it up, mate.'

Harry, who had of course heard most of these stories several times before, strongly suspected that Colin had most likely made up some of the more outlandish of them. Not that this knowledge spoiled his enjoyment of them in any way; true or not, they *were* funny and Colin told them so well, aided by his equally talented stooge, Sue, who fed him the lines.

An excellent meal and, at Colin's insistence, several large glasses of

Pinot Noir had left Harry feeling decidedly mellow. For the first time in months, he felt at one with his world; this bar and these people, the hills around the town that he loved so much. He was contentedly sipping at an *Americano* when the door at the far end of the bar opened and Shaun Tomlins, no less, walked in. He was accompanied by a small but shapely blonde a good ten years his senior. Harry was so shocked by this surprise appearance of the very man he was doing his best to avoid, that he came close to dropping the cup of coffee into his lap. Somehow he managed to bring the cup down where it was intended to go, but it was a crash landing that sent enough coffee spilling out over the rim to fill the saucer.

Harry's new-found sense of well-being dissolved in a heartbeat and he watched with growing trepidation as Tomlins and his companion came towards him. Had Shaun come back out of the house and seen him running away from the Fiesta with the screwdriver in his hand? Was he about to confront him and accuse him of piercing his tyre?

'Woah, steady on Harry – bit of a hand-eye coordination malfunction there, mate,' Colin observed wryly.

Sue, who had pushed her chair back fearing the coffee was about to land in her lap, now came to Harry's aid. She jumped up and, moving round to his side of the table, she poured the coffee back out of the saucer into his cup. Then, snatching up Colin's discarded paper napkin, she proceeded to mop up any of the liquid which had splashed onto the table.

When she had finished, she gently placed a hand on his shoulder. 'Are you feeling all right, Harry? You're looking rather pale.'

Harry didn't answer right away; his attention totally taken up with keeping an eye on Tomlins and what he was doing. And at that very moment he and his lady friend were being shown to a table uncomfortably close to his own.

'Harry?' Sue repeated.

'It's OK, I'm fine,' he assured her, when he could tear his eyes away from the unlikely couple. 'Just wasn't looking where I was putting my cup, that's all.'

'What *were* you looking at that was so interesting,' Colin enquired. He whirled round and craned his neck to see what had so captured his friend's attention. When his gaze fell upon Tomlins' blonde companion, he turned back to Harry and raised his eyebrows in mock reproof. Colin always had an eye for an attractive woman and had wrongly assumed that she and, from his perspective, her low cut neckline, was the cause of Harry's momentary confusion.

Harry didn't disabuse him of this notion; thankfully Colin hadn't recognised the young burglar and pretending to perve at the blonde gave him a reason, at least as far as Colin was concerned, for glancing over at her table at regular intervals. He examined her properly now for the first time. She looked to be somewhere around her mid-thirties but could pass for younger, Harry decided. She had a slightly pinched face which made her look a little petulant but, when she smiled, she became captivatingly attractive. She glanced up, caught him staring at her and Harry quickly turned away. He made a conscious effort not to look at them after that, deciding that as long as they remained at their table, he had nothing to fear from Tomlins who, in any case, had shown no interest in him.

But a little later, when an ice bucket containing a bottle of Champagne was delivered to their table, Harry couldn't help but wonder at the cause for their celebration. He stared fascinated as Shaun took a heart-shaped ring box from his pocket and, opening it up, revealed its contents to the blonde. The lady beamed at him and gave a little squeal of delight. Looking very earnest, Shaun placed the heart-shaped box on the table and extracted a ring. His lady friend offered up her left hand. He took hold of her wrist and, with his right hand, slid the ring onto her ring finger; one large diamond, flanked by two smaller diamonds, set on a white gold shank. She dipped her hand the better for him to see it and the diamonds sparkled in the bright spotlights that dotted *Sandfords'* ceiling.

Harry went through a series of emotions in rapid succession; first joy, then anger and finally disgust. That ring rightly belonged to Annie – it was the ring that he had given her when they had become engaged and that scum bag, Shaun Tomlins, had just bestowed it on his what – partner in crime? It was then that Harry recalled something he'd read in the paper during the trial of the man Sergeant Tudor had arrested – Elkins or Edkins – something like that. Wasn't it his wife that Shaun had been having an affair with and her husband, a receiver of stolen goods, had given Tomlins a good hiding?

His head swam and the room became a blur. He was dimly aware of the sound of a chair falling over and Colin calling after him as he jumped up and charged towards Shaun's table. The couple's heads came up at the sound of Harry's chair hitting the floor to find Harry bearing down on them. The woman's face registered her alarm but Shaun, resentful of this noisy interruption of his romantic proposal, looked angry. He sprang to his feet just as Harry launched himself at him and knocked him down with a right to the chin.

'You thieving bastard!' Harry bellowed at him. 'That's my wife's engagement ring.'

There was a collective gasp of dismay from the other diners as Harry turned his attention to Shaun's companion and, grabbing her hand, attempted to prise the ring from her finger. The diminutive blonde screamed at him to get off her, and when he didn't, she appealed to the other diners around her for help. But they sat there as immobile as manikins in a department store's window display. Then Colin appeared at Harry's side and threw an arm around his shoulders.

'Harry... HARRY,' he repeated, louder this time. 'It's me, Col, What are you doing, mate? Let go of her.'

Harry turned and stared at his friend as if he'd never seen him before in his life. A sudden hush fell over the room, which was almost immediately broken by the sound of water or some other liquid splattering onto a hard surface.

Unnoticed by the other protagonists, Shaun had staggered to his feet and was brandishing the Champagne bottle aloft like a club, as the equivalent of a large wine glassful of *Sandfords'* house Champagne poured out onto the bar's scrubbed wooden floor.

'Get your filthy hands off my fiancée, you crazy bastard, or I'll smash this bottle over your fucking head!' he screeched.

'Do as he says, Harry. And you,' Colin told Shaun, 'Put that bottle down and let's sort this out in a civilised manner.'

'I'll put it down when that lunatic lets go of her.'

'Come away now, Harry,' Colin pleaded.

As quickly as it had descended, the red mist which had veiled Harry's vision lifted and his friend's familiar face came into sharp focus. He felt a tug at his wrist and glanced down at the small hand he held in his. Took a closer look at the diamond engagement ring that adorned it; one large diamond, flanked by two smaller diamonds, set on a white gold shank, except that now he could see that the setting wasn't the same and it was not the ring he had placed on Annie's fingers all those years ago.

'The police are on their way,' the young waitress piped up from behind the bar.

Colin spun round, threw his hands up in the air in a despairing gesture. 'Oh, brilliant, just what we didn't need!' He turned back to Harry and said, 'I'm not asking now, Harry. I'm telling you – let go of the lady's hand.'

But Harry was still staring, stupefied, at the ring, as the full horror of what he'd done sank in. He'd been so sure that it was Annie's.

'NOW, Harry,' Colin insisted, speaking in clipped tones.

Harry opened his fingers and the blonde snatched her hand away. Interlacing it with her right, she placed them in her lap. Colin took hold of his friend's arm and pulled him away.

'I'm so sorry,' Harry called back over his shoulder.

When they reached their table, Colin righted the fallen chair and sat Harry down. 'Can you fetch Harry a brandy please, Sue,' he said. But Harry didn't want a brandy. Harry just wanted the earth to open up and swallow him. He shook his head and waved the suggestion away, but Colin insisted he have one. 'It will settle your nerves,' he assured him.

Sue went off to fetch the brandy and Shaun came striding towards them. Colin had his back to him but, at the sound of his footsteps, he turned and moved quickly to intercept him before he could get to his friend.

'Your mate belongs in the loony bin,' he told him and, leaning around Colin's bulky figure, pointed an accusing finger at Harry, then drew circles in the air with it at the side of his head. 'You're crazy, old man,' he shouted.'D'ya hear me? Madder than a box of fuckin' frogs, you are.'

Colin remembered the young man now; a petty criminal, Alan had said. He drew Shaun to one side. 'My friend's not been very well lately. He made a genuine mistake. There's no need to take this any further, is there?'

'I was proposing to my girlfriend and that nutjob,' he glared at Harry, 'totally ruined it.'

'Well look, how about I buy you and your… fiancée, another bottle of bubbly and pay for your meal, hum? Harry's had enough grief lately. He doesn't need any hassle. And do you really want the police poking their noses in?' he added pointedly.

Shaun's eyes narrowed and he gave Colin a searching look. Colin stared back at him, the embodiment of guileless affability. Shaun turned away and glanced back at his fiancée, who was happily engrossed in admiring her newly acquired engagement ring.

'OK, but I don't want none of that cheap stuff. Only the best is good enough for my fiancée,' he said fiercely.

It was turning out to be an expensive evening, but Colin felt it would be well worth it to keep Harry out of trouble. 'Fine,' he said. 'The best *Sandfords* have to offer. Order whatever you want and I'll make sure the bar staff know that I'll be settling your bill.'

He watched Shaun swagger back to his table to rejoin his fiancée who, in his absence, had acquired a small group of admirers, among them the young waitress, all of them keen to view her engagement ring. Colin allowed himself a thin smile of satisfaction; it hadn't taken that much to put things right with them. But a glance at his old friend told a very different story; though he lacked the physical injuries, Harry looked like a man who had had the stuffing beaten out of him. Head down, he was staring into the brandy glass he had cupped between both hands on the table in front of him.

Harry barely looked up as Colin slipped into a chair beside him. 'Colin, I'm so sorry, I really am,' he said. 'I've completely spoiled what had been a really enjoyable evening.'

'Oh, come on, mate, you don't have to apologise to us...'

'But I do, I don't know what came over me...'

'I've told you, forget it.'

'I saw him give her that ring and I just snapped. I was convinced it was Annie's, you see.'

'Yeah we got that.' said Colin, 'Anyway, the good news is, I've had a quiet word with our friend over there and he's agreed not to press charges.'

Harry found himself welling up inside. Moments ago, he'd been close to the edge again and could see nothing but dark clouds. Now, thanks to Colin, things were looking a little brighter. 'Really?' He still couldn't quite believe it.

Colin nodded, then sat there beaming at them both.

Sue was impressed; her husband wasn't exactly renowned for his diplomatic skills. 'How did you manage that?' she asked incredulously.

'I'll tell you later,' he said and emptied the last of the Pinot Noir into his glass. He took a generous slurp, settled back in his chair and stretched his legs out under the table. 'The main thing is... Harry is off the hook.'

A buzz of excitement went around the room. All three turned to see what was going on, saw the flashing blue light outside.

'Let's hope you're right,' said Sue, sounding a little less convinced now than she had a moment before.

Harry's mouth felt as dry as a man who has just swallowed a mouthful of sawdust. He took a quick sip of brandy, swilled it round his parched mouth. 'Oh, my God,' he said, 'what do I tell them?'

'Don't panic,' said Colin.' He leaned in closer, and lowered his voice. 'You tell them the truth. OK? But you keep it simple. Just stick to the bare facts and, whatever you do, don't volunteer information. Got it?'

'I think so, but you know what I'm like when I'm nervous, my tongue runs away with me.'

'I know but try not to worry, you'll be all right.'

But Harry couldn't help worrying; he always felt guilty when being questioned by the police, even when he had done nothing to feel guilty about. As the police patrol car continued to splash its garish blue light across *Sandford*s' windows, he took another tot of brandy to steady his nerves. Seconds later the door opened and the young, dark-haired policewoman who had been so kind to him after the burglary stepped inside.

CHAPTER EIGHTEEN

A YOUNG GIRL, 14 or 15 at most, swims the width of a pool. The unseen cameraman zooms out to reveal the Roman pillars and statuary of Rick Haymer's basement swimming pool. The girl bends at the waist, her bottom comes up and she slips beneath the surface in a trail of bubbles. Moments later she bobs up again and, standing waist deep in the water, shakes out her dark, brown hair. Someone calls to her; a male voice and the cameraman zooms out again. The voice belongs to Rik Haymer; clad in a pair of trunks, he is kneeling at the poolside. Smiling, he gestures to the girl to join him. The camera follows her as she wades over to the side of the pool. She raises her face to him. Haymer leans down and kisses her on the forehead. At Haymer's urging, the girl raises her arms and, scrambling to his feet, he pulls her out of the pool and deposits her, water dripping off her costume, onto the tiled poolside.

Rik Haymer runs a hand over the girl's wet hair as if to stroke it, but then, gathering up a large clump in his fist, he places a hand on her left shoulder and pushes her roughly to her knees. The girl begins to sob. Haymer ignores her cries and, yanking her head back, pulls his trunks down over his thighs with his free hand.

Tudor couldn't bear to watch another second of it and turned his face away; clearly this was a movie that would not have a happy ending. He couldn't shut out the sound, however; distorted though it was by the poor acoustics in the cavernous pool, it was, if anything, more disturbing than the pictures had been. Beside him, a grim-faced Dudley continued to watch until the climactic moaning from Haymer and the choking sobs of the girl proved too much for him and he ejected the DVD.

The stunned silence that followed was eventually broken by Tudor, who said, 'Well, to paraphrase John Lennon, that's thrown a bloody great Spaniard in the works.'

'I won't ask you why you took the trouble to commit those immortal words to memory, but I have to agree, this does rather bugger up your theory.'

Tudor looked rueful. 'Yes and no... I've no doubt Moretti used this DVD to blackmail Rik and he was making regular payments to him... remember what Ms Rainesford said about unaccounted for sums being taken out of a bank account Rik had set up to finance the new album?'

'Yes, I do remember. But don't you see?' said Dudley, 'All this DVD does is give Rik a motive for murdering Moretti not t'other way round.'

Tudor sucked air through his teeth. 'Well... perhaps Rik called his bluff; refused to hand over any more money and Moretti decided to go for the nuclear option.'

'Umm, perhaps...but that's not really the issue here.'

'What do you mean?'

'The girl, sergeant... the girl! It's pretty clear from the video that she was raped. Added to which, she appears to be below the age of consent.

164

And, unless this was Haymer's first offence, God knows how many other under-age girls he's put to the sword in that subterranean Roman baths of his.'

The full implications of Dudley's words became horribly clear. 'And we haven't got the manpower to investigate historical sex abuse on that scale,' observed Tudor glumly.

'Nothing like enough, we'd have to hand it over to a team from a larger force – our friends in Birmingham probably.'

'Ssh-it!' hissed Tudor.

He got up and went over to the window, stared out at an unexpectedly clear blue sky in a month that had been notable for its unusually high rainfall. *Damn you*, Haymer, he thought. *Perhaps you deserved to die after all*. But was he angry, he wondered, because he felt let down by his hero or because the axeman's sexual proclivities threatened to jeopardise his murder investigation? It didn't take him long to realise that such thoughts were unworthy of him and to understand that the frightened young girl in the video was the real victim in all this. Her violation at the hands of the rock star cried out for justice and, although she might not get the redress she deserved now that her violator was dead, he felt duty-bound to see to it that her voice did not go unheard.

'Couldn't we at least try and identify this poor girl, before we call anybody else in? It shouldn't be too difficult – someone at the Hall must know who she is. After all, as things stand, we've no evidence that this was anything other than a single incident.'

'And if we find there were others?'

'Then we hand it over to the Brummies… come on, Boss, we're close to cracking this case, I know it.'

'I didn't have you down as an ambitious man, Glyn. What's brought this on, I wonder?'

Dudley gave him a knowing little smile and Tudor coloured. So, his school boy antics with the handcuffs had registered as something more than just a silly prank and Dudley had been busy joining up the dots.

'All right, your 48hrs grace isn't up yet in any case, but that's it, Glyn. I mean it. We can't afford to be seen to be ignoring sex abuse cases – historical or otherwise.'

'I know. I've got a daughter who's not much younger than her, remember?' Tudor picked up the DVD and put it back in its plastic case. 'I'll just get the techies to do me a print of the girl's face and I'll be on my way.'

'While you're doing that, I'll see about getting a warrant to seize Haymer's computers in case he did a bit of filming of his own, Moretti's too. If your hero was a serial abuser then that,' he indicated the DVD Tudor was holding, 'might not be the only time Moretti secretly filmed him. I'll send a team over as soon as I've got the warrants.'

Despite his Italian name, Moretti, like Haymer, had been born and brought up in Birmingham. Having made their fortunes in London, first Haymer, then Moretti, had returned to their Midlands roots; Haymer to South Shropshire whilst Moretti had based himself closer to Birmingham in South Worcestershire. His country residence was a modest affair compared to Rik's castellated pile, though still impressive. The timber-framed, manor house not far from the market town of Evesham stood in several acres of gardens and paddocks which gave onto the river Avon. He also retained a small apartment in London.

'What about his London flat? We'll need the Met's co-operation to raid that,' Tudor pointed out.

'We'll leave that for another day. Let's see what we turn up at his

Shropshire residence first.'

Good call, thought Tudor; if that lot down south were to get so much as a sniff of this, they'd go in mob-handed and with a TV crew in tow. He was on his way out of the door when he remembered he'd forgotten to ask Dudley about his wife's tests. Stepping back inside, he pulled the door to behind him.

'How did it go at the hospital this morning, everything all right?' he asked.

'Oh, you know how these things go, Glyn, the people who do the tests can't tell you anything until the specialist has taken a look at them. Then he's got to write to her GP.' He let out a dispirited sigh. 'It could be weeks before we get a diagnosis.'

For the first time, Tudor noticed the dark shadows underlining his boss's eyes. They spoke of sleepless nights so, whatever was ailing Dudley's wife, it had to be serious and Tudor could only imagine what he was going through. Waiting weeks for a diagnosis would, he knew, be hard to bear for Dudley, who would be lost without Mary if anything were to happen to her. And, in the absence of certainty, his troubled mind would be prey to a thousand terrors.

'I know… anyway, give her my best, won't you?'

'I will, and thanks, Glyn, it's much appreciated.'

It was one of those rare moments; a glimpse into someone else's life that puts your own and its little problems into perspective, thought Tudor. Didn't we all need to love someone and be loved in return – what else was life about, if not that? He made a mental note to phone his kids; he hadn't spoken to them for a week, he realised.

'Right. Well, I'd better get moving, the clock's ticking and all that,' he said and for the second time made for the door.

'Oh, and Glyn,' Dudley called after him. 'You'd better take a female officer with you. See if Mellor's available – smart girl that – she showed great sensitivity in the way she handled Ingrid Sandstrom, I thought...'

Tudor was surprised by the suggestion and it showed on his face. His boss's face, on the other hand, remained deadpan. It wasn't that he questioned the wisdom of having a female officer with him when dealing with a sensitive issue like sexual assault but that Dudley should be playing matchmaker. In his confusion he forgot that the door was closed and walked straight into it.

*

Happily, as it turned out, Mellor was in the building; she and Crawford had just brought a young tearaway in for violating his parole conditions. She jumped at the chance to escape and join the detective force for a few hours. Facing the prospect of having to work the remainder of the shift on his own, PC Crawford looked decidedly unhappy.

'So, what's this about? Mellor asked, once they were in the car.

'I'm not trying to abduct you again, if that's what you're thinking.'

'I think we're past that stage, aren't we?' she said. 'I've agreed to come quietly.'

'Oh, I won't mind if you groan a bit,' he said and laughed nervously; a man had to be so careful what he said to a woman these days, especially if that man happened to be her superior officer. Sexual harassment, which had for so long been part of the canteen culture in the service, was no longer tolerated.

'I've agreed to share a four-poster bed with you, nothing more,' she reminded him rather more sharply than she had intended. And, adopting a softer tone, added, 'Let's not get ahead of ourselves. I'm not frigid or anything. I just think we should get to know each other a bit better first, that's all.'

'Yeah, I know,' he said, 'Though, I have to admit, when I saw that photo you sent me, I did wonder if I'm the type you go for.'

'Mr Muscles? He was *very* fit, wasn't he,' she recalled with evident relish.

Glyn felt a sudden rush of jealousy. He did his best to hide it but his face was an open book.

'Glyn, it was a joke. I don't want to go out with some guy who spends more time looking at himself in the mirror than I do!' She gave him a reassuring smile, 'Now, forget about it and tell me what I'm doing here. We're supposed to be working, remember?' She became more business-like. 'So, I assume it's got something to do with Mike Moretti's stabbing, but why do you need me to go with you? Those two cold-hearted bitches at The Hall don't need any emotional support from me.'

This drew a wry smile from Tudor. 'What – Cruella and Morticia? No, you've got them all wrong. Beneath that frosty exterior beats a heart of gold – just takes a pickaxe to find it,'

'Hope you brought one with you,' she said.

Feeling happier than he felt he had any right to be, Glyn spent the remainder of the journey briefing her on the reason for their visit to Morecroft Hall. By the time he was finished, a grim-faced Maggie was staring mutely at the road ahead as it rushed to meet them.

*

Arriving at the Hall's main gate, Tudor pressed the intercom and announced himself. There was no reply from the other end, but moments later the gates opened soundlessly; moving as if by magic rather than electricity.

He pulled onto an empty parking area. All weekend it had been packed with police vehicles and the SOCO team's vans, but they had completed their work, packed up and gone. The Hall looked similarly deserted. Then he remembered that Alex Rainesford was in court this morning. Her lawyer would be seeking bail for his client and in all probability would get it. Tudor began to wonder if Ingrid Sandstrom would be at home or if she too would be at the Magistrates' court supporting her PA's application and on hand to bring her back with her. If so, he would have a much freer hand to question her employees about the young girl in Moretti's video. There was only one way to find out. Tudor got out of the car and, accompanied by Mellor, approached the front door.

'By the way,' she said, as they ascended the short flight of steps that led up to the house. 'I got called out to a bit of bother in Stretton Spa the other night, that Mr Paget – remember him?'

'Sure. Please don't tell me he's been burgled again...' said Tudor.

'No, listen to this; he was having a drink in *Sandfords* bar when in walks your friend, Tomlins, with a tiny blonde cougar.'

'That would be Gary Edkins's missus, Karen.'

'That's right. Tomlins orders champagne and is about to slip an engagement ring on her finger...'

'Whoa, hold on. They were getting engaged? Tomlins must have a death wish. I'd love to be a fly on the wall when Karen gives her banged-up hubby that bit of news!'

'Must be love... Anyway, Mr Paget thought it was his late wife's engagement ring Tomlins was giving her; accuses him of stealing it and socks him on the jaw.'

'And was it?' he asked. They were at the door now and Tudor gave the wrought-iron bell-pull a tug. It sounded faintly from somewhere deep within the house.

'A case of mistaken identity, I'm afraid.'

'I had a feeling that one would take the law into his own hands – just what we don't need, a flaming vigilante pensioner – bloody fool.'

'The man's still grieving, Glyn; he saw what he wanted to see. And the ring did pretty much match the description he gave us of the one that was stolen. Three diamonds; one large with two smaller ones either side…'

'I suppose that bastard Tomlins insisted on pressing charges…'

'Quite the opposite; he made it very clear from the outset that he didn't want to take it any further. So, I let Mr Paget go with a stiff warning. He was very apologetic. I don't think he'll be playing detective again.'

'For his sake, I hope you're right.' Tudor gave the bell-pull another tug. 'Is anybody going to answer this bloody door-bell?'

Mellor stepped back and stared up at the windows, but the front of the house was lit up by the bright morning sunlight and all she could see at the windows was the sun's glare reflected back at her. She shaded her eyes and cast them over the façade's stonework. 'You'd think they'd have CCTV,' she said.

'Yes, I found myself wondering that the first time I was here, but that footage of Moretti's would explain why Mr Haymer was camera shy.' He joined her in staring up at the building then, impatient to get on, he said, 'Stay here in case somebody does come to the door, while I go and see if there's anybody round the back there.' He indicated the right-hand corner of the building.

Set well back at the side of the house, the original stable block had been converted into a row of garages that housed the rock star's collection of cars. In any other setting they would have seemed showy, grandiose even, but in direct comparison with the Hall and its architectural extravagancies, they looked plain, almost nondescript. One of the garage's doors was open. Standing just inside and partly hidden in shadow, Ingrid Sandstrom and her beefcake chauffeur were deep in conversation. The man had rolled up his sleeves at some point, perhaps while he polished the gleaming Jaguar XJ that stood outside. As Tudor watched, Ingrid stroked his muscular forearm. The intimacy of the gesture hinted at a relationship that was more than just that of master and servant – but how much more, Tudor wondered. It could be something and it could be nothing, but both he and Dudley had considered the possibility of their being in a relationship.

Tudor hadn't moved since spotting them but now, as he tried to get closer in the hope of overhearing their conversation, the crunch of gravel under his feet alerted them to his presence. As one they turned and, seeing him there, Ingrid quickly withdrew her hand from the chauffeur's arm and with a muttered aside, came striding towards him. Tudor stayed where he was and let her come to him. He could tell by the look on her face as she bore down on him, hips flicking rapidly back and forth, that she was not pleased to see him. He was used to that – it came with the territory in his line of work – people who had something to hide rarely welcomed his intrusion into their private lives.

'Looking for the tradesmen's entrance, Inspector?' she said, in a tone which managed to convey disdain as well as a sense of righteous indignation at his invasion of her domain.

Ingrid Sandstrom, it seemed, liked to play the same silly games as Alex Rainesford, or perhaps she had learnt them from her employer. 'It's

Sergeant,' Tudor pointed out with deliberate politeness. 'And no one's answering the front door.'

'The bell-pull sticks sometimes; perhaps you didn't pull it hard enough,' she said, her ice-blue eyes almost crystalline. Anyway, you've found me, what can I do for you, but you will have to be quick – I was just telling Walker there the good news – Alex got bail and as soon as he's ready we'll be off to Shrewsbury to bring her home.' She sounded triumphant.

'In that case, if you let me in, I won't trouble you any further,' said Tudor affably.

It was testimony to the actress's icy self-control that, despite the tendency amongst members of her profession to assume the world revolved around them, she appeared unsurprised to learn he was not there to interview her.

'By all means,' she said and beckoned him to follow her.

'Glyn, we can get…' Mellor's voice trailed off as she stepped around the corner of the building to discover that Tudor was not alone.

'Your constable appears to have more pull than you do, Sergeant,' said Ingrid, looking Mellor up and down.

'So it would seem,' said Tudor, his discomfort evident; he and Maggie had agreed that she would address him as Sarge or Sergeant whenever they were working together. He turned on his heel and was walking away but, as if as an afterthought, turned back again. Pulling the print taken from Moretti's video from the inside pocket of his jacket, he handed it to the one-time Bond Girl.

'Have you seen her at all?' he asked casually, as if not expecting anything to come of his enquiry. Ingrid's clear, blue eyes narrowed as she studied the grainy print. Tudor watched her closely; her expression didn't change but he thought he detected a slight twitch at the corner of one eye.

After a moment's study, she handed it back to him. 'No, sorry... why, who is she?'

'What about your chauffeur?' he said, sidestepping the question.

She studied Tudor's face intently, far more intently than she had the photo and without turning, called to her chauffeur, 'Walker, would you come here for a moment please?'

Tudor found her stare unsettling; perhaps that had been her intention. If so, it had worked. He looked away, watched Walker instead. The chauffeur dropped the damp cloth into a plastic bucket and, moving on feet as light as a dancer's, crossed the yard, unrolling his shirtsleeves as he did so. He had slicked back, black hair, smoke grey eyes and a hard stare that would have a Rottweiler cowering. He gave the photo a cursory glance, shook his head and handed it back. But Tudor wasn't buying his strong, silent type act.

'Take another look,' he suggested. 'A *good, long* look this time.' He was getting tired of treating these people with kid gloves.

Tudor detected a flash of anger in the man's eyes but he accepted the photo and went through the motions of studying it at least, before shaking his head once more.

'Thank you for your co-operation,' said Tudor pleasantly.

The chauffeur smiled or was it a smirk? He couldn't be sure, but Glyn resolved to run a criminal records check on Mr Walker when he got back to the station.

Though Tudor hadn't seen her go, at some point in the proceedings, Maggie had made a diplomatic retreat and he found her waiting for him at the front door. 'Thank you, *Constable*,' he said as she stepped aside to let him through.

'Sorry about that,' she said, once they were both inside. She lowered her voice, 'This work/relationship thing messes with my head. Forgot where I was for a moment.'

Worried that she was having second thoughts, Tudor was quick to reassure her. 'One small slip, that's all.'

'The Sandstrom woman picked up on it though, didn't she?'

'It was all an act. She was lying about the girl – they both were.' He took a few steps across the marbled floor of the entrance hall, his footsteps echoing beneath its high ceilinged atrium. He glanced up, remembered the last time he stood there; the helicopter hovering above him and the mad dash along narrow country lanes that followed. Momentarily lost in the past, he thought he saw the flicker of rotor blades in a shaft of sunlight that pierced the glass roof. The sound of a door slamming somewhere in the house brought him back to the present and the matters at hand.

'Who was it let you in?' he asked.

'The housekeeper – Mrs Harris, is it?'

'Damn! We need to speak to her.'

'It's all right, she's coming back. Some disaster in the kitchen which she couldn't leave – that's why she took so long to answer the door.'

'Sounds like my last attempt at a Sunday roast.'

Maggie laughed. 'Didn't your mother teach you to cook?'

'I come from a mining family,' and switching to a Welsh accent he said, 'Women cook, men work.'

'You're not a *New Man*, then?'

'I'm trying to be. I'm just not very good at it. Or hadn't you noticed?'

The crime scene tape was still in place across the door of the late Rik Haymer's study. Tudor carefully pulled it to one side before opening the door and going in. The room was much as it had been the last time he was here, except for the absence of Moretti's body; a dark stain on the carpet the only sign of the violent act that had taken his life. Deep in thought he stared at the stain for a while. Such a small amount of blood, he thought, considering a man has died here. He glanced up to find Mellor staring at him.

'Not much of a bleeder was he?' he told her. 'You tend to associate violent death with lots of blood, but there's barely a cupful there. Given his temperament, I imagine Mr Moretti would have preferred to go out with a bigger splash.'

'Like Rik Haymer, you mean?'

'Yes. I wonder...'

The crunch of gravel killed the thought and Tudor went rushing to the window. He got there in time to see the gleaming Jaguar sweep past with the blonde at the wheel and her chauffeur, Walker, sat in the passenger seat.

'Why employ a chauffeur then drive yourself?' he mused aloud.

'I presume we're talking about Ingrid Sandstrom?' said Mellor. 'It's a lovely day, perhaps she fancied a drive.' She suggested.

'I suppose... all the same, be worth checking if he's had his licence pulled.' Tudor turned his attention to the filing cabinet and tugged at the top drawer. It was locked but the key was in it. Unlocking it, he flicked through the tightly packed files, but none of the titles written on the tabs jumped out at him.

'One thing has always puzzled me about Rainesford's statement,' he said, one arm leant across top of the open drawer. 'She claims that when she found Moretti in here that day, he had a file in his hand. And when she tried to take it off him, he flew into a rage and tried to strangle her. Yet when we arrived, the filing cabinet drawers were closed and there was no sign of a file.'

'Perhaps Moretti put it back before attacking her, so she wouldn't know what he'd been looking at...'

'Oh, come on, he lost it completely.' she said, "He grabbed me by the throat and pushed me back onto the desk. He had me pinned down and was squeezing the life out of me". If he was that angry, he would have dropped the file and rushed at her. No, Rainesford or Sandstrom must have put it back after Alex had stabbed Moretti.'

'Or Rainesford is lying about the file,' Maggie suggested.

'That's a distinct possibility...'

There was a tap on the half-open door and the rotund form of Mrs Harris peered round it.

'Ah, come in Mrs Harris. Crisis over, is it?' Tudor closed the filing cabinet drawer and produced the photo of the girl in the pool.

'Yes sir,' said Mrs Harris brushing her hands down the front of her apron. She looked hot and flustered and there was a film of perspiration on her wrinkled brow. 'Will you be requiring tea, sir?'

'No, I think we're all right,' he said with an enquiring glance at Mellor who nodded her agreement.

'How can I help you then, sir?'

'We're trying to identify the girl in this photo,' he said, stepping forward and handing it to her. 'Have you seen her before, do you know who she is?'

Mrs Harris took the photo from him, 'I'm going to need my glasses for this,' she said and, scrabbling amongst her grey curls, pulled them down from their perch on top of her head. 'Umm,' she mused. 'It's hard to be sure from this but I think she was here last summer...'

Tudor and Mellor exchanged glances. 'Do you know her name?' he pressed.

Mrs Harris put a hand to her brow and closed her eyes. 'Oh dear, my memory...' she said. 'She's the daughter – no, the niece I think, of one of the casuals.' She continued to search her memory but the girl's name eluded her. Finally, with an exasperated sigh she admitted defeat. 'No, I can't recall the name but my husband will know.'

'Is he about?'

'Yes he's in the walled garden. If you follow me, I'll take you to 'im. It's time he came in for his lunch anyway.'

'Let's hope it wasn't his lunch that she burnt,' Tudor muttered to Mellor under his breath, as they trailed along behind the bustling housekeeper.

CHAPTER NINETEEN

JULIA HAD ONLY been home for a few hours, but in that time she must have mentioned the young man's name a dozen times; Adam said this and Adam did that and Adam is so good at… well, just about everything it seemed. Apparently she had met this paragon of young British manhood in a tapas bar in Barcelona, following a hot afternoon spent trudging round some of the city's most famous museums. One of the girls Julia had gone on holiday with was an arts graduate and had insisted they couldn't leave the city without visiting at least some of them. Bored and exhausted, Julia and her other friend, Katie, had managed to escape and had sought refuge and refreshment in the first bar they had come to.

'So what does this Adam do for a living?' Harry asked when, he could get a word in.

'He's a technician,' Julia announced proudly.

It sounded rather vague, 'A technician? Doing what exactly?' Harry pressed her.

'Oh Dad, don't start grilling me. It was a holiday romance. I'll probably never hear from him again.'

Harry doubted that somehow and was proved right when, a day or two later, Julia took a call on her mobile and, with a little shriek of delight, took herself and her phone upstairs where she could conduct the rest of the conversation in the privacy of her bedroom.

Harry was washing up the breakfast things when Julia came downstairs half an hour later. She looked a little flushed and was clearly happy about something.

'Who was that?' he asked.

As if he couldn't have guessed.

Julia's roseate glow increased. 'Oh, it was that er, guy I met on holiday,' she said, the petulance that had peppered many of their recent conversations now absent.

Dangling a soapy wet plate over the washing-up bowl, Harry pretended to search his memory. 'Ah yes,' he mused. 'I vaguely remember you mentioning someone. Now, what was his name?'

Julia snatched up the tea towel and, taking the plate from him, began to dry it. 'All right, I admit I did go on about him a bit, but I really like him Dad, and I'm sure you will too.'

Harry gave his daughter an indulgent smile. 'I see, and when am I going to meet this Mr Wonderful?'

'Not just yet and not at all if you're going to be sarky about it,' she scolded him.

Harry held up his hands in mock surrender and, soap suds dripping from his fingers onto the tiled floor, said, 'Okay, okay. No more inquisitions, no more sarky comments, I promise.'

'You'd better,' she said then, balled the tea-towel, threw it at him and ran off giggling. Harry caught it and hurled it at her retreating back, but he was too slow; Julia was already through the doorway and, hitting the wall with a damp slap, the tea-towel flopped onto the floor. Harry retrieved it and placed it back on the rail to the sound of his daughter's mocking laughter as she ran up the stairs.

It was good to have her home again, he thought. But his joy was tinged by concern; he hadn't seen her like this over a member of the opposite sex for a while, not since she went off to Uni, in fact. What bothered him most was that Julia fell in love at the drop of a hat and he wasn't sure he could cope with a lovesick daughter moping about the house if she got her heart broken. He reminded himself that she was a grown woman and he couldn't protect her from the vagaries of love. All he could do was provide a shoulder for her to cry on and a sympathetic ear if it didn't work out with this Adam. For the moment she was happy and he welcomed that; her mother's death had been no less traumatic for Julia than it had been for himself and she deserved a little happiness. No point in worrying over something that might not happen, he decided.

On the down side, with Julia at home he had been forced to abandon his surveillance activities. He told himself it was just a temporary measure; that once Julia had moved on, he would pick up where he left off, but in his heart of hearts he knew he no longer had the stomach for it. The embarrassing debacle in *Sandfords* had left Harry swinging in the wind without a compass. He had been so certain Shaun was responsible for stealing Annie's jewellery box and yet, despite this conviction, he had managed to get it so spectacularly wrong. And having made such a calamitous mistake in front of all those people, he was reluctant to risk making a fool of himself all over again by pointing the finger at someone else. Besides, he had no idea who that someone else could be. If that wasn't disincentive enough, PC Mellor had made it abundantly clear that she and her colleagues would take a very dim view of any further breach of the peace, as she put it, and next time he would find himself standing on the wrong side of a cell door.

Harry didn't feel good about giving up and letting Annie down in this way, but what else could he do? He had already discredited himself in the eyes of his friends, his neighbours and the West Mercia Police Force – why risk further humiliation and a possible prison sentence? He imagined himself sat opposite a tearful Julia in a prison visiting room. The mere thought of it was unbearable.

No, he couldn't put her or himself through that. Hard though it was for him to accept defeat, he must let it go, unless and until he had some real evidence he could take to the police.

CHAPTER TWENTY

IT WAS LATE AFTERNOON and Tudor was in Dudley's office. The sun slanting through the window at Dudley's back was dazzling. Noting his sergeant's discomfort, Dudley got up from his desk and closed the blinds. Having briefed the team first thing they were reviewing the various nuggets of information they had garnered during a day of fevered activity and attempting to pull it all together.

'So, what do you want to look at first?' asked Tudor.

'Let's start with the girl in Moretti's video.'

Glyn opened the file, extracted a recent photograph of the girl and passed it to his boss. 'Rosie Goddard, now sixteen, but at the time of the offence she was still below the age of consent. Her uncle, Tom Brandon, took her to Morecroft Hall with him on two occasions last summer whilst working there as a casual gardener. He's worked there most summers for the past ten years.'

'But this was the first time he'd taken Rosie with him?'

'That's right. You think that's significant?'

'Maybe, I don't know. Was Rosie Goddard a fan of Haymer's?'

'No, just curious; she'd heard about his fairy-tale castle from her uncle and wanted to see it for herself.'

'This uncle of hers – what do we know about him?'

'We're running a background check but there are no red flags so far.' Tudor knew where Dudley was going with this; the very idea was distasteful but he had learned in his brief stint with the vice squad that where human sexuality was concerned, there were few depths some people were not prepared to sink to. 'You're thinking Brandon pimped his niece to Haymer?'

'I think we have to consider it as a possibility, no more. That summer job at The Hall must represent a large chunk of his annual earnings – he's a casual gardener, I doubt if he could manage without it.'

Dudley picked up a stapler, moved it to the other side of his desk then put it back again. Next he fiddled with a pencil sharpener, turning it end over end in his fingers. Tudor recognised the signs – his boss needed a smoke. Dudley caught him watching him and put it down. 'What about Rosie's parents?' he asked. 'Do you think they knew?'

Tudor's mind went back to the neat cottage in Leominster and the long afternoon spent with Rosie's parents; the fear that appeared in her mother's eyes the moment she answered the door and saw Maggie Mellor's uniform. Her first thought, like any parent on finding the police on their doorstep; has my daughter, son, husband been in an accident? Her anguished cry when they had explained the purpose of their visit. The tears, the numerous cups of tea which he had made, leaving Mellor to supply the sympathy; only to put her through it all over again when her husband, summoned home early from work, came in.

'I don't believe so. The news seemed to come as a complete shock to them. Either that or they're very good actors. But no, I'm as certain as I can be that they knew nothing about it. They've been worried about her;

said she'd been a bit tearful lately, but they had put that down to her age and worrying over her upcoming exams – the usual teenage angst.'

'Umm, they must be a constant worry, kids – I'm so glad I haven't got any.'

He didn't sound that glad about it and Tudor thought he detected a hint of wistfulness in Dudley's voice, wondered if his boss ever regretted not having had a family of his own. Still, people made choices or they were forced upon them by circumstance. His only regret was that he didn't get to spend enough time with his own two, but apart from moving back to London, there wasn't much he could do about that. For the first time in some while, Tudor found himself hating his ex-wife for taking them away from him.

'What about the girl?' Dudley asked and Tudor was pulled back to the present and matters at hand.

'Nice kid. Quiet sort; bit shy, according to her mother.'

He pictured Rosie Goddard framed in the doorway of her parents' lounge. In her green school uniform and with her long, dark hair scraped back into a ponytail, she had looked much younger than her sixteen years. Was that resignation or relief he saw on her face? Relief, he'd decided, as she stepped into the room and, without a word, sat down beside her mother on the sofa. She and Mellor exchanged glances and from then on the girl would only speak to her. Encouraged by Mellor's gentle probing, slowly and hesitantly at first, Rosie began to open up.

'It was a warm summer's day. Remember those? Rosie was sunbathing in the orchard. Haymer comes out of the house with a beer in his hand, sees her there and says something like, "You look hot – how would you like to cool down in my swimming pool?"'

'And she fell for that corny line?'

'She's just a young girl and he's a legendary rock star; old enough to be her granddad maybe but, there's something about the guy, she's never met anybody like him before. So, of course she says yes. Why not? She'd been sunbathing in her bikini, so she jumps straight in. He doesn't get in the water with her, just stands at the side of the pool sipping his beer. After a while he says something about getting changed and disappears leaving her alone in the pool.'

'But he came back?'

'Yeah, only now he's wearing swimming trunks, but he still doesn't get in the water with her. Just hangs around at the poolside and watches *her* swim. She was a little bit nervous about being alone with him at first, but now she's feeling a lot more relaxed. Rosie's not much of a talker, but that's not a problem because Haymer never stops talking. And he's funny; he has forty years' worth of amusing stories from his time on the road to call on and he has a captive audience.'

Tudor picked up the bottle of Evian he had brought with him and took a swig. Dudley pulled a face. He didn't agree with drinking water, beer or any other substance straight from the bottle. He considered it uncouth. Dudley was invariably the only one with a glass in his hand when the team adjourned to the pub to celebrate a successful end to a particularly difficult case.

Another big swig and then Tudor carried on. 'So, when Haymer calls her over and kisses her on the forehead, Rosie doesn't wonder what he's after - she just thinks how sweet. And alarm bells still don't ring when Haymer says, "Come on out of there, I've got something to show you..."'

'Yes, well I think we both know what happens next,' Dudley cut in. 'Is the girl up to making a statement yet?'

'I've spoken to the FLO and Rosie's parents have agreed to bring her in tomorrow morning.' The arrival of the Family Liaison Officer had been something of a release for Tudor. Watching the Goddard's as their world fell apart had been too close to home for him, reviving as it did, memories of his own which were still raw, despite the two years that had elapsed since his wife's bombshell disclosure that she was leaving him and taking the kids with her.

'Glyn?'

'Sorry, what?' Tudor had been so wrapped up in his own thoughts he'd failed to take in what Dudley had just said.

'I was saying, you'll be relieved to hear that so far, we haven't found anything on either Moretti's or Haymer's computers that would lead us to believe that the assault on the Goddard girl was anything more than a one-off, opportunistic encounter.'

'No pre-pubescent porn? No history of visits to dodgy web sites?' Tudor queried. Despite feeling relieved to learn that they were unlikely to have a massive historic sex abuse inquiry on their hands and the implications that would have for his murder inquiry, he couldn't quite believe it.

'Nothing, that is, that you wouldn't find on the laptops of a large proportion of the male population, anyway. Cheer up. I thought you'd be pleased.'

'Oh, I am. Just surprised, that's all.'

'Anything you want to add?' asked Dudley, set to close the file and move on.

'Not at the moment,' said Tudor.

'Which brings us to Mr Walker – what put you onto him?'

'It just struck me as odd that Ingrid Sandstrom should choose to chauffeur her driver around.'

'Why buy a dog and bark yourself?' Dudley observed dryly.

'Precisely. So I checked out his driving licence status and found it had recently been pulled. Seems our friend, Walker is a lover of fast cars and, no doubt, fast women too; Seeing him and Ingrid together yesterday I got the impression there's something going on between them.'

'That wouldn't surprise me,' observed Dudley.

'Maybe not, but this will,' said Tudor, pushing the file across the desk.

It was a moment or two before the significance of the details Tudor had highlighted on the copy of the speeding summons sank in, but when it did, Dudley's eyebrows shot up. 'I see what you mean. This places him within...what – an hour's drive from Morecroft Hall?'

'Less probably AND, two hours later, Haymer was dead...'

Dudley swivelled round in his chair and, getting to his feet, walked over to the window. From there he could look down on the sparse patch of lawn at the back of the station where the nicotine addicts gathered to get their fix. He gazed at it longingly for a moment then, turning back to Glyn, said, 'OK, we've got opportunity and, by the sounds of it, a motive... what was it they were doing?'

'She was stroking his arm...' explained Tudor. 'Affectionately,' he added for extra emphasis.

'Affectionately? That's one of those tricky words whose meaning is open to interpretation.'

'Meaningfully then, she was stroking his arm meaningfully...'

'That's a better one. Still not enough though... Sandstrom could claim that what you saw was no more than her trying to console Walker, who had just received some bad news about his dear old mum or some such tale. We're going to need more than that. Let's backtrack a bit.

We've established Walker was within an hour's drive of Morecroft Hall at 10.15pm on the night Haymer died; which means he must have left London around…'

Tudor was already Googling it on his mobile, '…according to this, it would take him a little over 3hrs to make that journey, so we're talking 7pm or thereabouts at the latest.'

'And remind me, where was Sandstrom staying?' Tudor named a well-known, West End hotel. 'Not quite the Ritz maybe, but still ritzy enough. Did Walker stay there too? If so, I doubt if the widow would risk booking a double room, but adjoining rooms might appear respectable enough. Get onto them and find out. Go down there if you have to. And we're going to need Sandstrom and Walker's phone records – put our technical genius onto that, will you?'

Tudor smiled. Dudley could never remember DC Ferrars name and habitually referred to him as the resident techie or computer bod. Technical genius was simply the latest in a long line of nicknames he had coined for the young detective constable.

'It's Ferrars, Sir.'

Dudley looked bemused, 'What? Yes, yes. I know,' he said with a flash of irritation; his craving for nicotine fast approaching the point beyond which he could not go. 'How's it going with PC Mellor?' he enquired in a clumsy attempt to cover for his tetchy manner of a moment ago.

'Ask me again, the weekend after next,' said Tudor.

'Why, what's happening then?'

'That posh wedding gig I told you about. I've booked a room.'

'A double room, I take it?'

Tudor grinned. 'A four-poster…'

'Lucky man,' said Dudley. He got up and, slipping his jacket off the back of his chair, pulled it on. 'Right, off you go then,' he said, ushering Tudor out of his office. 'I've just got to pop out for a moment.'

Tudor didn't have to ask why or what for; Dudley was reaching for his vaping device before he'd reached the office door.

CHAPTER TWENTY-ONE

TUDOR TOOK a traditional black cab to Covent Garden and The Garden House Hotel, where Ingrid Sandstrom had stayed the night she'd attended the Bond film premier. The driver had been disappointingly taciturn and not a bit like the legendary chirpy cockney portrayed on TV and in films; the born raconteur who engages his passengers in lively discourse or regales them with tales of the famous people who have sat in the back of their cab. But, he supposed, even the chirpiest of cabbies had their off days.

Keen to stretch his legs after his train journey, Tudor got the driver to drop him off at the end of the street and walked the rest of the way. He was immediately struck by the absence of CCTV cameras. Surprising, he considered, for a busy thoroughfare with delivery vans and trucks arriving at all hours of the day to service the hotels and restaurants that catered for its tourists and theatre goers. As he strolled along the pavement, Tudor spotted French, Italian, even Moroccan cuisine on offer.

He found The Garden House Hotel easily enough; a red brick art nouveau building with gaily striped awnings that extended out over the pavement and contrived to give the hotel a continental air. The aroma of fresh roasted coffee tempted Tudor to sit down at one of the pavement tables and order an Americano, but he decided to keep walking. He wanted to get a feel for the area first, to explore the streets surrounding the building, in particular those at the rear of the hotel, before he met with the manager of The Garden House.

A little further down the street, he spotted his first CCTV cameras; three in all above a French restaurant. One of them pointed towards The Garden House and may well have captured Sandstrom's arrival and Walker's too, if he had stayed there with her. Taking out his note book, Tudor jotted down the restaurant's name with a view to following it up later.

He walked on until he came to the famous Seven Dials Clock immortalised by Agatha Christie in her mystery of the same name. Clustered around the base of the monument, a group of tourists rested their aching feet and picnicked on packed lunches, seemingly oblivious of the traffic that swirled around them. Beyond them, the Cambridge Theatre's billboards proudly proclaimed the arrival of yet another new musical. And everywhere he looked there were more posters advertising hit shows with titles that even he had heard of. This would be Dudley's idea of heaven – it should be him standing here, not me, thought Tudor. It was doubtful, however, if either of them would have the time see a show nor, as he would have preferred, to call in and see his children.

Turning the corner, he walked round the block and into Shaftesbury Avenue. It was busier here with two-way traffic and a greater number of pedestrians. There were a lot more cameras too and, faced with having to note them all down, Tudor instead used his mobile's camera to record their locations. He had expected the rear of the hotel to back onto

Shaftesbury Avenue but found that this part of the building was occupied by a firm of accountants. This meant that Walker could only have come and gone by way of the hotel's front entrance. Nor was there any provision for parking at the hotel and once again, Tudor turned to his mobile to find the nearest car park. This, he learnt was an NCP multi-storey located in the aptly named Parker Street and just a 6 minute walk away. They were bound to have CCTV there and he made a note to call on them after his meeting with The Garden House's manager.

*

Jonathon Hadley turned out to be a dapper young man with dark, wavy hair and a serious manner which belied his schoolboy looks. He met Tudor in the lobby and, after ordering coffee for them both, they adjourned to his office.

The manager waved Tudor to a chair. 'I understood from your phone call that you require some information about one of our guests,' he said, when they were both seated. 'May I ask why?'

'At this stage it's just a case of establishing her whereabouts on these particular dates,' Tudor told him and handed over a slip of paper on which he'd written Sandstrom's name and the dates in question.

The young man looked concerned, 'I can check the bookings register for you but, before I do, I need to see your warrant card.'

Tudor duly produced the card and held it up for Hadley's inspection.

'West Mercia... where's that?' he asked after studying it carefully. 'I've not heard of it.'

Tudor had been expecting the question; Hadley had no doubt assumed that he would be from The Met. And of course, as protocol demanded, they had been informed of his visit and its purpose.

'It's the old English word for what we now call the West Midlands,' he explained. 'I'm based in Shrewsbury – that's in Shropshire – The Marches area, on the border with Wales; perhaps you've heard of it?'

He hadn't. 'I see, sounds... lovely,' said the young man without enthusiasm.

Tudor suspected that in truth, Hadley was appalled at the idea of living at the arse-end of nowhere, as he saw it, without access to the sophisticated pleasures to be found in the nation's capital.

'Well now, let's see...' Hadley pulled a keyboard towards him and his fingers, moved rapidly over the keys. 'Ah, yes, here we are... Ms Sandstrom booked one of our smaller suites plus a single. Both were for two nights.'

Tudor leaned forward eagerly. 'And the name of the person who occupied the single?' he asked.

The manager took another look at the screen. 'That would be... a Mr Roderick Walker. Her chauffeur, I believe.'

The way it had been said left Tudor with the impression that Hadley hadn't believed it for one minute. But on reflection, decided it was probably just his manner; the presence of an archness verging on the camp in the man's tone.

'And has Ms Sandstrom stayed with you before?'

'No, this is the first time we have had that pleasure.' Again that implied disapproval was evident in the manager's voice.

'To the best of your knowledge, did Walker sleep in that single room?'

'One would assume so... why book it otherwise?'

Tudor could have pointed out that as a recently widowed celebrity, Ingrid Sandstrom might well have booked a separate room for her Chauffeur lover, if that was what Walker was, in order to protect her reputation, but he decided not to pursue the point. Instead he asked, 'May I see the rooms?'

Mr Hadley seemed to take the suggestion as a personal affront. 'To what purpose?' he asked indignantly. 'The rooms are cleaned and the bedding changed every day. There will be absolutely no trace of your actress and her chauffeur this long after their stay with us.'

'I'm aware of that,' said Tudor patiently. 'I would expect nothing else from a four star establishment like yours,' he added in an effort to smooth the manager's ruffled feathers. 'But it would be useful if I could see the rooms and get a firm idea of where they are in relation to one another. So if you could just get someone to take me to them, I needn't take up any more of your valuable time.'

The manager was still considering Tudor's request when his deliberations were interrupted by the arrival of a young, blonde-haired waitress. Placing a silver tray on the desk she proceeded to lay out cups and saucers, milk jug, sugar bowl and a cafetiere of richly aromatic, dark coffee.

'Enjoy,' she said to Tudor with a bright smile. She spoke with a slight, Eastern European accent.

Hadley thanked the girl and, turning to Tudor, said, 'If you would like to help yourself to coffee, I'll just make sure the rooms aren't occupied at the moment.'

*

The polite young man, who had been deputed to show Tudor to the rooms was also from Eastern Europe. He hovered in the open doorway as Glyn inspected the small suite which Ingrid Sandstrom had occupied on the night of the premier. Unable to avoid comparisons with his own tiny, one bedroom flat, Tudor found the accommodation surprisingly spacious.

If this was a small suite of rooms – how much bigger must the large suites be, he wondered.

Still, Hadley had been right about one thing; there was little to be learned from the room itself. Despite this, Tudor felt obliged to make a show of examining each of the spotlessly clean rooms in turn; starting with the bedroom cum sitting room which was decorated in the Regency style with pale blue, vertical striped wallpaper and swagged curtains in a delicate floral print. The bed was a large king-size affair big enough for a family of four never mind a couple and at its head was a canopy with more swagged drapes, which hung down on either side. Set beneath one of the tall, vertical windows was a small table and two chairs, and directly opposite the foot of the bed, a two-seater sofa and a low-level coffee table. On the walls, framed prints of ladies dressed in period costume provided the hotel's guests with fake ancestral portraits.

It was all fake really, thought Tudor and, as Dudley would no doubt have said had he been there, "looks like a tart's boudoir".

He stepped over to the window and peered down into the street. Below him people went about their daily lives for the most part unaware of the killers, thieves and other assorted villains they shared their city with. In truth, few of them wanted to know about the less than savoury underworld to be found just below the surface of any major town or city, any more than they wanted to know about the rats that lived only feet away from them, wherever they lived. Ignorance was bliss and these inconvenient truths could be pushed to the back of their minds until, that is, they jumped out and confronted them.

What exactly had been going on in this room two months ago? Were Sandstrom and Walker lovers? Did he kill Rik Haymer? And was it at Sandstrom's bidding?

196

"Please Rod, will you kill my husband for me? I'll make it worth your while".

Was that how it had been? Was that the deal – share her bed and share Rik's estate?

He moved on to the bathroom which was considerably larger than his bedroom at home and which contained the deepest bath tub he had ever seen. It stood alone in an alcove surrounded by mirrors. Staring into the tub, he saw himself and Maggie sharing it, the warm, soapy water lapping against her pale breasts. The thought was an extremely pleasant one and he hoped the room in the hotel he'd booked for the wedding gig had a bath just like it. Whether he could persuade her to get into it with him was another matter. He pushed the thought to the back of his mind; just thinking about it, he decided, was enough to put a jinx on it.

Walker's room was tucked away on the floor below Sandstrom's suite; a cramped box-room of a bedroom in which most of the floor space was taken up by a double bed. Opening the door, Tudor had just about enough room to squeeze in past it. Closing it behind him, he moved to the foot of the bed where there was a little more room. Here there was a tub chair and a small table. On it was a tray set with kettle, cup and saucer and the ingredients required to make tea or coffee. To the right of the bed, another door gave access to a small en-suite bathroom with wash-hand basin, wc and shower. Looking around, Tudor decided it was just as well Walker hadn't had to spend too much time in here, but then it was never intended that he should; his dash to Ludlow and back had seen to that. Satisfied that he had seen enough, Tudor returned to Hadley's office where he arranged to come back later and speak to the night manager when he came on duty at six.

After a late lunch in a pub (Tudor couldn't afford the prices in the hotel's brasserie, though both establishments were shockingly expensive compared to what he would have paid in Shropshire) he chased up the CCTV. First stop was the French restaurant. At the *La Petite Rose* the lunchtime rush had ended and most customers were only ordering coffee. Tudor approached the bar counter and, flashing his warrant, asked to speak with the owner. The young man behind the bar – everyone seemed to be young in the hospitality business, thought Tudor – sent one of the waitresses off to fetch him and then offered Tudor a coffee. Sensing this could mean he might have a long wait, he accepted the offer and asked for an espresso. He was still sipping it, however, when a small, dark, man with a bald pate and a neatly trimmed beard, shot through with grey, approached him.

'You wanted to see me?' the man enquired a little warily, as if he suspected that a booted and suited Tudor might be a salesman of some kind.

'Yes sir, Detective Sergeant Tudor.' He produced his warrant card.

'Phillipe Gaston, co-owner and chef.' A brief handshake then, 'what can I do for you Sergeant? I'm not in any trouble, I hope?'

Despite his French name, Gaston had a North London accent; the English born son of a French father, perhaps?

'No sir. Not with me, anyway…'

Gaston gave a nervous laugh.

'We're interested in the movements of two people who were staying at The Garden House Hotel on the 23rd and 24th of May and I'd like to see any CCTV recordings you have from that period.'

'Ah, in that case it's my son you need to speak to,' he indicated the tall, gangly looking fair-haired young man Tudor had spoken to earlier. 'He's our resident expert on all things electronic... PAUL,' he called. The young man glanced up and Gaston beckoned him over.

Father and son were as different as chalk and cheese and Tudor decided that the lad must take after his mother's side of the family.

'Paul, Detective Sergeant Tudor here would like to take a look at some of our CCTV footage. I suspect he will want to take a copy away with him. We can do that can't we?'

His son rolled his eyes. 'Yes, Dad, of course we can,'

'My son despairs of me.' Gaston gave a Gallic shrug. 'I'm absolutely hopeless when it comes to computers.'

'It's not a computer, Dad – it's a camera' The upward inflection at the end of the sentence, habitual these days amongst the young, made his reply sound like a question.

'See what I mean?' said Gaston senior. 'Well, I'll leave you in Paul's capable hands.'

Tudor knew just how Gaston senior was feeling as he watched the chef make his way back to the kitchen; Glyn's own children were on the cusp of their teenage years and already they treated him with the same casual disdain, when his inability to master modern technology drove him to seek their help. But even the young have to grow old eventually and one day, they too would feel the sting of their offspring's disdain. It was a comforting thought and hopefully he would live long enough to see it.

The images flicked across the screen in a dizzying blur as Paul rewound the recording.

'The feed from the cameras is stored on that recorder there,' Paul explained. 'At the end of each week, I transfer the previous week's recordings onto this external hard drive,' he indicated the small, black box which he had just connected to his laptop. 'When it's full, I delete all the recordings and begin again; record, transfer, delete. It's all rather boring really.'

Tudor wasn't entirely sure if the lad was referring to the CCTV recordings or working in his dad's restaurant. Following in a father's footsteps must be hard, he thought; especially so if you are only doing it out of a sense of duty, as this lad seemed to be. Tudor had had no intention of following his father down the mine and fortunately he hadn't had to; the mine had closed before he left school and his father had been thrown out of work.

Paul's hands, which had been hovering over the keyboard, came down on the spacebar and the images on the screen stopped moving. He pointed to the timestamp at the foot of the screen.

'Here we are; 23rd May, 10am. Do I need to go back any earlier than that?'

'No, that's fine. They didn't check in until one-thirty.'

'OK, I'll take it forward a bit, then.'

The images began moving across the screen again but slower this time which animated them in much the same jerky way as flicking through the images in a flip book.

'Stop!' shouted Tudor a few minutes later.

He peered at the frozen image. The hotel entrance was some distance away but there was no mistaking the dark blue Jaguar XJ nor the short, blonde hair and slim figure of Ingrid Sandstrom, who had just stepped out of it.

'That's them,' he told Paul Gaston. 'OK. Keep going'

They watched the pair enter the hotel, Walker carrying the bags. Five minutes later he came out again, got back in the car and drove off, presumably to take it to the NCP multi-storey in Parker Street. Sure enough, fifteen minutes later, as recorded by the timestamp, Walker returned to the hotel. People came and went but of Sandstrom and Walker there was no further sign until at 2.20pm, when the pair stepped out into the street and walked towards the restaurant's camera; Ingrid Sandstrom in a figure-hugging, white dress and Walker in open-necked shirt and dark slacks. As they drew level with the doorway of *La Petite Rose*, Tudor ordered Paul to freeze-frame and zoom in. And there they were in close-up, Ingrid in dark glasses smiling as if for the camera; Walker with his head turned towards her. If only we had audio, thought Tudor, it would be interesting to know what he had just said to make her smile; particularly so, if he had made any reference to their plan to murder her rock star husband.

'I could do with a print of that,' said Tudor. 'Could you do one for me?'

'I can grab a screen shot and print it off on our inkjet printer. I haven't got any photographic paper so it won't be best quality...'

'That's OK, it doesn't have to be. They're clearly recognisable and that's all that matters for my purposes.'

*

It was well after six when Tudor returned to The Garden House Hotel to interview the night manager. In the meantime, he had trudged round Covent Garden trying to find someone, anyone, who remembered seeing the couple. Quite a lot of those he had spoken to remembered Ingrid but that was only to be expected; her face had stared out from the pages of the nation's newspapers on at least three occasions in recent months; first at the Bond premiere and, hot on the heels of that event, when Rik's death was announced. She had barely been out of the news in the ensuing weeks when, at the reception that followed Rik's memorial service, Alex Rainesford had stabbed Mike Moretti in the eye with a paper knife and killed him. By anybody's standards, it was sensational stuff.

So far, only one person had remembered seeing Walker and that was the guy in the booth at the NCP car park.

'"Something about the eyes", he had said, "No life in 'em, like a dead man's eyes they wos. Proper put the wind up me, 'e did'"'.

The Night Manager, Mr Roper, greeted Tudor with a beaming smile and a painfully firm handshake. Custody of the hotel was now in his hands until Hadley came back on in the morning and, having made the necessary introductions, the latter was eager to get off home. So with a curt goodbye to both men, he left them to it and hurried away.

Wasting no time on unnecessary preamble, Tudor produced the screen shot of Sandstrom and Walker and handed it to Roper.

'Can you remember much about these two, at all? he asked.

'I remember *her* of course,' he said, tapping the print. 'I'm a big Bond movie fan, you see. She was in *'To Die Is Never Enough'*. Not the best Bond film ever made, but it has that nude scene in it where her character, Fanny Fairbright, has to seduce the Chinese girl cryptographer...'

'I must confess, I've not seen that one,' Tudor quickly interjected, afraid that, given the chance the man would go on to list his favourite moments from all the other Bond films. 'It's their comings and goings I'm interested in and particularly, those of Mr Walker on the night of the twenty-third.'

'Oh, yes of course,' said Roper, unable to hide his disappointment that Tudor was not a fan. 'Well, it wasn't an evening I could easily forget; I'd just phoned Ms Sandstrom's room and advised her that her limo had arrived...'

'What time was that?' Tudor interrupted him and took out his notebook.

'Around six-thirty. A few minutes later she came down with Mr. Walker. She looked absolutely stunning in a clingy red dress and he wore a dark blue jacket, tweed maybe, and black trousers. We had a brief conversation; I told her I was a big Bond fan and she said she'd get me Daniel Craig's autograph.'

'And did she?'

'Yeah, she did. I didn't for one minute expect she would. I thought she was just being a luvvie. You know the way they talk; Dar-ling this and Dar-ling that, but I have to say, what a sweet lady.'

It didn't sound much like the Ingrid Sandstrom Tudor had come to know, and sweet wouldn't be the first adjective to spring to mind if he were to be asked to describe her nature.

'And what time did they return to the hotel?' he continued.

'The lady came back just after midnight. I'd just made myself some coffee and she asked if she could have some. We chatted for a while about the première, and just as she was about to go up to her suite, she takes a programme out of her evening bag and hands it to me. '"Here," she says, "I always keep my promises"'. And there it was on the inside front cover, '"Best wishes, Daniel Craig"'. Then she kisses me on the cheek! What a night...' His face took on a wistful expression.

You don't know the half of it, Tudor thought to himself.

And as for Sandstrom's antics, it was so out of character for her that it was suspicious. It was almost as though she had been going out of her way to make sure the Night Manager remembered her.

'She came back alone, you say? So, what time did Walker turn up?'

'Oh *him*, he turned up looking very much the worst for wear about four and a half hours later.'

'You didn't like him?'

'Not much, if I'm honest. A hard man in every sense of the word and scary with it; those eyes of his made the hairs on the back of my neck stand up, I can tell you.'

'Yeah, I know what you mean. You say he looked the worst for wear – in what way, exactly?'

'His clothes were crumpled and it looked like he'd spilt some red wine down the front of his shirt. Said he'd been to a casino with an old friend of his and had a big win on the roulette.'

'Did he indeed,' mused Tudor, who considered that Walker's cash windfall was more likely to be a down payment for bumping Haymer off. 'You've been most helpful,' he told Roper and handed him his card. 'If you think of anything else, give me a ring.'

Walking out of the hotel, he decided he would have more chance of hailing a cab in Shaftsbury Avenue and began walking in that direction. The sun was lower in the sky now, throwing long shadows, and his side of the pavement was in shade, so he decided to cross over to the sunny side. The road was clear, but before he'd taken more than two or three paces, he heard the snarl of a high-powered motorcycle engine being gunned. He turned to find the bike and its black leather-clad rider almost on top of him. A shouted warning from a bystander, a flash of silver and black, and Tudor was sent flying through the air.

CHAPTER TWENTY-TWO

WITH JULIA BACK at home and his physical injuries behind him, life for Harry had settled back into something approaching normality. Domestically, at least, he felt content and although Julia had not so far managed to find a job commensurate with her degree, this new boyfriend of hers seemed to be making her happy. And if his daughter was happy then, as night followed day, Harry was happy too.

One thing, or rather two things – though the two were linked – threatened this satisfactory state of affairs and they were; his attacker remained at large and, more importantly, Annie's jewellery had not been recovered. The insurance company had paid up at last, but no amount of money could compensate for the hurt their loss had inflicted.

Much to his surprise, however, Harry had found his attitude softening of late and he had begun take a more positive view of these contentious issues. An idea had been forming in his mind to use the insurance money to purchase a nice piece of jewellery, made to his own design perhaps, which could replace the stolen items as the family heirloom. A unique piece that Julia could one day hand on to her daughter, if she had one, and so on down the generations of female Pagets to come. He hadn't yet discussed the idea with Julia, but he was sure it would meet with her approval.

Harry stifled a yawn and, for the third time in as many minutes, he eyed the mantle clock. He would normally be in bed by now, but he was waiting up for Julia who was out again with her new boyfriend. He was hoping that this time she would bring him in with her and he would finally get to meet this paragon who so enthralled his daughter that she could talk of nothing else. For, aside from gushing admiration, Julia had not been very forthcoming when it came to detail and all Harry's enquiries about the young man's background had been met with a coy smile and, "It's early days yet, Dad".

He had just dozed off when he was roused from his shallow slumber by the sound of a key being inserted in the front door lock. As he listened, the door swung open with a protesting creak, heeled shoes clicked upon the tiled floor, and then the door was gently closed again. This was followed by the jangle of keys as Julia returned them to her handbag and the tread of muffled footsteps on the stairs. Harry jumped up out of his chair and, running to the door, flung it open.

'Julia, is that you?' he called, as he stepped into the hallway.

His daughter came back down and stood at the foot of the stairs. 'Sorry Dad,' she said. 'I thought you'd be in bed.'

'I fell asleep,' he explained, rather than admit he had stayed up in order to interrogate her elusive boyfriend; so elusive he was beginning to wonder if he actually existed. His explanation for not being tucked up in his bed was in any case partly true, so strictly speaking, it wasn't a lie. 'Did you have a nice time with a…'

'Adam,' she supplied.

'Yes, of course, Adam…'

'Lovely, thanks.'

Why was she being so reticent about him, Harry wondered. 'Did you go anywhere special?' he probed.

'Oh, we drove into town to see the new Woody Allen film and then we had a meal in a lovely Thai restaurant that's just opened.'

'Any good?'

'The film or the meal?'

The conversation was following the usual ping pong trajectory, where every question he put to her was batted straight back into the net. There was nothing for it but to be direct.

'So, when am I going to meet this new man of yours, then?'

By way of a reply he got the usual coy smile and that thing she did where she brushed her hair back from her right ear. As she did so, Harry caught a glimpse of her earring before the strands fell back into place. The sighting had been brief and the light in the hall wasn't particularly bright, but he was convinced his eyes had not deceived him.

But certainty was quickly replaced by doubt, as Harry remembered the trouble and embarrassment he had brought upon himself the last time he had made wild accusations based on rash assumptions. He needed to tread carefully if he was to avoid making a fool of himself all over again and, more importantly, not alienate his daughter's affections.

'Are those earrings new?' he asked. 'Let me see...' He had sounded calm enough, but suddenly there was knot in his stomach and the throbbing of blood at his temples.

Julia dutifully pushed her blonde hair back off her ears so that he could see them clearly. Harry peered at them for a second or two, but it took a lot less time than that to confirm what, in his heart, he already knew, these were indeed Annie's missing earrings. His head reeled at the implications of this discovery and he fought to calm the turmoil inside him before he said something that might give him cause for regret. Subtlety was what was needed now, if he was to avoid an angry confrontation with his daughter. There would be no point in regaining one treasure only to lose an even greater one. In any case, he had already decided he would not be playing the amateur sleuth this time but would pass the information on to the police and let them deal with it.

'They're lovely, darling,' he said. 'Where did you get them?'

'Adam bought them for me,' Julia said, her eyes shining as bright as the diamonds on her earrings.

'You were with him, were you, when he bought them?'

'No... Why, what are you suggesting?' she asked, the colour rising in her cheeks.

'Nothing, darling, they look expensive, that's all.'

She laughed at the suggestion. 'DAD! They won't be *real* diamonds. He hasn't got that sort of money.'

'No, of course not,' Harry hastily conceded, aware that he had come perilously close to provoking the very outcome he was desperate to avoid. 'Well, it's very late,' he said. 'Time I was in bed.' He leaned forward and kissed his daughter goodnight. 'What did you say your boyfriend's name is?'

'A sigh. 'You know very well what it is...'

'I know it's Adam but what's his surname?'

Her eyes narrowed with suspicion. 'Why do you want to know?' she asked,

'Why don't you want me to know?' he countered.

The name she gave him meant nothing to Harry, but he knew a man who might be able to enlighten him.

CHAPTER TWENTY-THREE

TUDOR PLACED two Codeine tablets on his tongue and washed them down with a mouthful of black coffee. He had been trying to manage without taking the painkillers for hours now because the damned things 'bunged him up', but the pain had steadily increased to the point where he couldn't take it anymore. He carefully adjusted the sling on his left arm in the vain hope that it might bring a little relief until the Codeine kicked in. His one consolation was that Maggie Mellor had displayed a gratifying concern for his welfare and only that morning had sent him an affectionately worded text that had ended with three capital x's.

'That looks painful – accident, was it?'

Tudor looked up to be met by Walker's dead-eyed stare. The man's face, like his eyes, was expressionless, leaving Tudor wondering what had prompted his enquiry. He found it hard to believe the chauffeur felt any sympathy for him and he doubted if such feelings troubled him overmuch.

Schadenfreude then, or was there more to it than that; something rather more sinister – a connection between what was now almost certainly a murder investigation and his hit and run accident in the West

End? But if it had been a deliberate attempt to injure him, why use a motorcycle when a car would have made a much better weapon? As it was, the powerful bike had struck him a glancing blow and his injuries, although painful, had not been serious; he'd sat in A & E for more than three hours to learn he hadn't any broken bones, just heavy bruising on the left side of his body and some minor cuts and grazes. The injured arm worried him most as it threatened his ability to perform at the wedding gig, and not just on stage…

'I think you know how this works by now, Mr Walker. I ask the questions and you answer them.'

Walker's lips widened a little to form a thin smile.

'Now, I'll ask you again, what were you doing until 5 o'clock in the morning on the night of the Bond film premier?'

'I told you, I met up with an old friend of mine. We went for a meal, had a few drinks and finished up at a casino.'

'In that case, how do you explain this?' Tudor slid a copy of the Notice of Intended Prosecution for speeding out of the file he had in front of him and pushed it across the desk.

'I'm showing Mr Walker a copy of a 'Notice of Intended Prosecution' issued on the 2nd of June' He allowed the chauffeur time to read it before continuing. 'That is the vehicle you drove to London earlier that day, is it not?'

'It is, but I wasn't driving it at the time of the offence.'

'Oh no, that's right. You told Worcester Magistrates that the car had to have been taken without your permission. Who do you reckon took it then?'

'I dunno, joyriders, I suppose.'

'I don't know how many cars you've had taken without your

permission, Mr Walker, but I've been a policeman for more years than I care to remember and I've never known any of 'em to bring the car back and park it exactly were their owners had left them. Frankly, your explanation is laughable.'

Walker was about to say something but his solicitor, a senior partner in the same law firm who were representing Alex Rainesford, pre-empted him.

'You asked my client for an explanation, Sergeant Tudor, and he has given you one and, despite you're undoubted experience, there is always the exception that proves the rule.'

They had been in Interview Room 1 for just under an hour now and so far Walker had proved to be as intractable as a brick wall. Earlier, Tudor had questioned him about the nature of his relationship with Ingrid Sandstrom. The chauffeur had replied with just one word – 'friendly'. Friendly was another of those tricky words, as Dudley called them, those which had so many shades that they could just as easily signify something meaningful as nothing much at all.

The real problem was that they had yet to find anything on the CCTV they had so far examined, that proved conclusively that Walker was driving the Jaguar that night. They had him leaving the hotel just after 6.30pm and walking away in the general direction of the Parker Street car park. And they had a figure that could be Walker approaching the car park just minutes before the Jaguar was driven out, but that was all they had.

'It's still a bit of a coincidence, don't you think, that with any number of possible destinations to choose from, these joyriders decided to take the car back up the exact route that had brought you to London earlier in the day?'

'The route was in the Sat Nav. It's common knowledge that when criminals steal a car they often use the Sat Nav to take them back to the owner's home and rob them.'

'Got an answer for everything, haven't you, Mr Walker?' He wasn't under arrest but he was being interviewed under caution. Tudor retrieved the copy of the Notice of Intended Prosecution and slipped it back into the file. 'All right, that will be all for the moment, you can go, but before you do, I'm going to need the name of your friend and the casino you say you went to.'

'Got a piece of paper? I'll write them down for you.' Walker offered.

'Very obliging of you, I'm sure, but I need you to say them out loud for the benefit of the recording.'

'No problemo.' He was sounding really cocky now. 'Her name's Eleanor, Eleanor Fox-Stuart; we go back a long way, she's my ex, in fact, and we were in *The Hippodrome*.'

A woman friend… did this mean he was wrong in thinking Walker was Sandstrom's lover? Tudor could almost hear the crash as another brick fell out of the wall he'd been trying to build around Walker. If the chauffeur's alibi proved to be kosher, he might actually have to start looking for those unbelievably considerate joyriders of his.

'Did you win anything?' Tudor asked as he rose to his feet.

A smile from Walker, a wider one this time, 'You won't believe me, I know, but yes, I did. Quite a substantial sum it was too.'

'You're right, I don't, so you'd better hope Lady Luck doesn't run out on you. Good day, Mr Walker, we'll be in touch.'

*

Tudor was thoughtful as he returned to his desk, to be greeted by a jangling telephone. He snatched it up expectantly with one thought in his head, that it heralded a breakthrough in the case that would wipe that thin smile off Walker's inscrutable visage. This hope was quickly dispelled; it was the desk-sergeant, Tom Corfield, who, in his usual droll manner, informed Tudor that a Mr Paget was downstairs and was seeking an audience with him.

'I think you're confusing me with that other Welshman, Owen Glendower. Couldn't you have told him I was out?' Tudor protested.

'Can't do that, sir,' said Corfield. 'It's our job to serve and protect from harm,' he reminded him, quoting from the force's motto.

'All right, tell him I'll be down in ten minutes or so,' said Tudor, with a sigh. Paget seemed to be making a habit of popping up at the most inconvenient of moments. As he replaced the phone on the receiver, Tudor sincerely hoped that he hadn't been trying to do his job for him again and got himself into another bit of bother. He blamed his misguided attempt at crime solving on the plethora of police procedurals on TV. Would-be vigilantes like Paget seemed to think that watching one series of DCI Banks equipped them with all the investigative skills they needed to bring their transgressors to justice.

Tudor picked up the phone again and dialled Eleanor Fox-Stuart's mobile. Within five rings, he was transferred to her voicemail service. He decided not to forewarn her of his reasons for phoning by leaving a message and made a note to phone her later. He really needed to speak to Ferrars about obtaining CCTV footage from *The Hippodrome,* but he wasn't at his desk so, with some reluctance, Tudor made his way downstairs.

The last time Tudor had seen Harry Paget his face had been badly disfigured by the beating he had received at the hands of his intruder, so he didn't immediately recognise the figure he found waiting for him in reception. Paget recognised *him,* of course, and was on his feet and moving towards him the moment Tudor appeared in the doorway.

Tudor braced himself and put on a smile. 'If you would like to follow me, Mister Paget…' He held the door open for him and allowed him to pass through, then led the way to a vacant interview room. 'You're looking a great deal better than the last time I saw you, I must say,' he said as they shook hands. He indicated Paget should sit. 'Well now, what can I do for you?' he asked, once they were both seated.

Tired and emotional though he was after a restless night, Harry barely paused for breath as he proceeded to describe in some detail the events of the previous evening and those that had led up to it. Throughout this lengthy outpouring of Harry's, Tudor did his best to appear attentive, but by the end of it, the strain was beginning to show. He wasn't unsympathetic; the man had been through a lot, but clearly the recovery of his late wife's jewellery had become an obsession and sadly, one that was predicated on an unrealistic expectation. Tudor doubted that this 'new lead' would be anything more than another case of mistaken identity and a waste of his valuable time. How many more of these interventions would he have to endure before the poor man came to his senses and accepted the reality of the situation, however harsh it might seem? Even so, he felt he owed it to the aggrieved man to let him down gently…

'The thing is Mister Paget, we've been here before,' he began.

One look at Harry's expectant face and he could see that this wasn't going to be easy; the pensioner was as excitable as a young dog who's owner is about to throw him a bone.

Paget ploughed on as if he hadn't heard him. 'So, is he known to you?' he asked.

This threw Tudor, who had been about to deliver a short homily on the realities of a real detective's work as opposed to their fictitious counterparts, who always got their man…

'I'm sorry…'

'Adam Barclay – do you know him?'

'No, I don't believe so. As I was saying, we have been here before, Mr Paget and you can't keep…'

Tudor's voice trailed off in mid-sentence as he made the connection; he had completely forgotten about young Barclay, but then he hadn't figured heavily in the original investigation into Haymer's death.

'Adam Barclay… are you sure? Only there was a *Jack* Barclay working up at Morecroft Hall.'

'I'm absolutely certain,' Paget affirmed. 'My daughter hasn't stopped going on about him since she got back off holiday.'

'I see,' said Tudor who wondered how he would feel when his own daughter started dating. It must be hard for a father living with the knowledge that most men were just like him, he thought. 'What's he look like, this Adam Barclay, then?'

Paget's face clouded and for the first time since his arrival he seemed unsure of himself.

'I don't know – I've not met him yet,' he admitted and looked sheepish.

Tudor, who was on a short fuse thanks to the nagging ache in his left arm and the pressure of the investigation, had to make a superhuman effort to control his exasperation.

'You've not met him?' he said, each word punctuated by a pause.

'No, my daughter is being rather secretive about him, but I got a good look at the earrings he gave her and I am prepared to swear on the bible –

on my daughter's life – they are my wife's!'

His voice breaking with emotion, Paget spoke with such conviction, such undeniable passion, that Tudor found it hard not to believe him.

'You said she met this guy on holiday. She's bound to have some pictures of him on her phone or her camera. Have you got access to these devices?'

Paget was visibly distressed by the suggestion that he should go poking through his daughter's things. 'I'm not very comfortable with the idea,' he said.

'I can understand your discomfort, Mr Paget, but you're going to feel a damned sight more uncomfortable if I come barging in and falsely accuse your daughter's precious boyfriend of stealing her mother's earrings.' Tudor thought for a moment. 'OK, forget the photo for now. We need to confirm that the stones in those earrings are real diamonds and not cubic zirconia. So, here's what you do. You tell your daughter you have to get them valued for your contents insurance.'

'But she's convinced they're just cheap imitations.'

'And your answer to that is that she can't be sure without a valuation and it's better to be safe than sorry.' Harry still looked doubtful. 'Come on, Mr Paget, you don't want to embarrass yourself again, do you? In the meantime, I'll find out what I can about this Adam Barclay.'

In the end, Harry had reluctantly agreed to at least try and get the earrings valued and Tudor had sent him on his way with a parting assurance that he would keep his part of the bargain.

*

Returning to his desk, Tudor was about to sit down when Ferrars popped up from behind his computer console. 'Ah, there you are, Sarge, I've been looking for you.'

'Snap,' said Tudor.

'What?'

'Never mind, what have you got for me?'

'I've been taking another look at the CCTV footage we have of Walker...' he began a little hesitantly, 'and there's something I think you should see...'

It sounded like bad news and Tudor wondered if another spanner was about to be lobbed into the workings of his case.

Ferrars sat down in front of his computer monitor and, with a few clicks of a mouse, the chauffer appeared on the screen, clearly identifiable as he walked towards the camera. 'Right,' said Ferrars. 'This is Walker just after he came out of the hotel – OK?' Tudor leaned in over his shoulder. 'And this, we think...' he clicked the mouse several times, 'is him again approaching the car park.'

A rear view this time. Tudor stared at the figure on the screen; it was the man who had entered the car park not long before the jag had been driven out.

'He's wearing a hat.'

Ferrars leaned back in his chair and folded his arms across his chest, his face a picture of smug satisfaction. 'I know, but where did it come from? He wasn't wearing a hat when he came out of the hotel and he wasn't carrying one.'

'And the night manager made no mention of him wearing a hat when he came down from his room ... damn!' said Tudor. 'So it can't be Walker.

He walked away from Ferrars' desk, spun on his heel and came back again to peer at the screen, as if unable to believe the evidence of his own eyes. 'That's great, just great,' he groaned and threw his hands up in the air. He was still staring at the frozen image of the unknown man in the black fedora when his phone began to ring. Still cursing whichever gods had conspired against him, he walked round to his own desk and picked up the phone.

'YES!' he barked into the mouth piece.

'Charming!' A woman's voice; she was well-spoken and sounded more amused than offended by Tudor's bad-tempered tone. 'Someone phoned me earlier from this number. Who am I speaking to?'

It could only be Walker's friend and alibi, Ms Fox-Stuart.

'Sorry about that, I was expecting it to be someone else.'

'Someone who got on the wrong side of you, by the sounds of it,' she suggested.

'Something like that. Perhaps we could start again. I'm Detective Sergeant Glyn Tudor of West Mercia police and you must be Ms Eleanor Fox-Stuart.'

'The one and only,' she said, yet despite the flippant reply, her tone was noticeably more guarded now. 'To what do I owe the pleasure?'

It was obvious to Tudor, even over the phone, that it was no longer a pleasure. To begin with her manner had been teasing, almost flirtatious, but a sudden chill had set in when he had identified himself. He tried to picture the woman on the other end of the line. Voices, he knew, could be deceptive, but he imagined she was attractive – Walker was a tough looking 'bad boy' – a type that many women, even intelligent, well-spoken women like Fox-Stuart, found desirable, despite the many drawbacks of being in such a relationship.

'Would you mind telling me where you were on the night of the twenty-third of May, Ms Fox-Stuart?'

Silence and then... 'Is Roddy connected with this in any way?' she asked. 'Has he got himself into some kind of trouble?'

'If you could just answer the question,' Tudor insisted.

A sigh, 'Hang on a sec, I'll have to check my diary,' she said and put him on hold.

She was back on the line in less than a minute. 'Sorry about the delay; I just wanted to be sure of my facts before I said anything – I *was* with Rod that night. I hadn't seen or heard from him in over a year then, typical of Rod, he phones me – says he's in London – can we meet up. I'd nothing better to do, so I said yes. We had a lovely meal at the Hawksmoor and afterwards he took me to a casino.'

'Which one?'

'The Hippodrome.'

'I see. And did you have any luck at the tables?' Tudor certainly wasn't having any; his case against Walker was, like the Berlin Wall, being dismantled brick by brick.

'I didn't, but Roddy had a big win on the roulette wheel.'

'I see. All right, Ms Fox-Stuart, thank you for your co-operation. We'll need to get a written statement from you, but I can arrange for you to do that at your local police station. Someone will be in touch to make the necessary arrangements.'

In an untypical display of bad temper, Tudor slammed the phone down, but only after he was sure Ms Fox-Stuart was off the line.

'Ferrars!' he bellowed, even though the young DC was just the other side of the desk. 'What's happening with the CCTV from the Hippodrome?'

'On its way, Sarge...'

'On its way? That's no good to me. I need it here now! Chase 'em up, will you.'

Ferrars wondered what part of "on its way", his sergeant didn't fully understand, but let it go.

'Yes, Sarge,' he said dutifully.

'And when you've done that, see what you can dig up on this guy...'

Ferrars read the name on the slip of paper Tudor had just handed to him. 'Adam Barclay... isn't that the kid who was working up at Rik Haymer's place?' he asked.

'That was Jack Barclay, but they may be related.'

*

Tudor drove home in high dudgeon, the sling lying on the passenger seat; an empty noose which, in his present mood, he was tempted to slip around his neck, when he got home. It was only when he pulled up outside his flat that he remembered Maggie Mellor was coming round that evening. His heart lightened at the prospect, but then he remembered that she was bringing an Indian take-away with her and he was supposed to be getting a nice bottle of wine to go with it. Cursing all the while, he performed an embarrassing 5 point turn and, his injured arm protesting violently, drove to the nearest off-licence. There he wasted no time in grabbing what he hoped was a reasonably decent bottle of wine and rushed back to the flat to find her waiting on the doorstep for him.

She looked wonderful in a pale blue summer dress; belted at the waist, it accentuated her trim, shapely figure and with a hemline several inches above the knee, those fabulous legs of hers. Entranced by this vision, Tudor found himself wishing he had left work early enough to have got changed and at least made himself look presentable.

She waved the carrier bag of food at him. 'Come on, you old fart, this is getting cold. I was beginning to think you'd stood me up. Another five minutes and you would have been eating baked beans and pasta.'

Foolishly, he had once admitted that, when he couldn't be bothered to cook a proper meal, he simply boiled some pasta and then poured a tin of baked beans over it. She wasn't angry with him; since getting to know each other a bit better, they had fallen into this easy going, slightly blokey, banter.

'Sorry, it's just been one of those days,' he explained, as he reached past her and tapped in the code that opened the communal front door. She led the way upstairs, leaving a trail of lightly scented perfume in her wake.

'Case not going well?' she said over her shoulder.

'You could say that,' he replied glumly.

She waited for him at the top of the stairs. 'Sounds like you need some cheering up,' she said. 'And I've got just the thing.' Dipping her hand into a smaller carrier bag that Tudor hadn't noticed before, she pulled out a DVD. 'TA-Da!' she announced with a grin.

It wasn't quite the sort of cheering up that Tudor had had in mind, but he did his best to look pleased. *To Die is not Enough*, it said on the cover in large, blood red letters. Below the title there was a shot of Bond, gun in hand, and behind him, the scantily-clad figure of Ingrid Sandstrom.

'Great…' said Tudor. 'Just what I needed…'

'I thought so too,' she said beaming. 'Especially as it stars one of your favourite suspects…'

She leaned into him and pressed her lips against his. The kiss seemed to go on for a long time and, just like that, the disappointments and frustrations of his day from hell evaporated in a moment.

'Umm, I feel quite a lot better already,' he said pressing himself against her.

'Yes, I can tell,' she said, disentangling herself. Maggie took the few steps across the hallway to stand beside the door to his flat. 'Come on, Tiger – it's feeding time,' she held the bag of Indian food aloft and beckoned him over.

She is going to tease me to death, he thought, but he went to her anyway for, like some ancient mariner lured onto the rocks by the siren's call, he was unable to resist.

*

'Do you want to talk about it?' she asked.

They were sat at the breakfast bar in the flat's cramped kitchenette, a large plate of Chicken Biryani and a glass of white wine in front of them.

'My day from hell, you mean? Tudor put his fork down and took a sip of wine. Earlier in the day perhaps, but not now – not with the memory of that kiss still fresh in his mind. Why spoil what promised to be a delightful evening... 'Do you really want to talk shop – it's the same old, same old ... just as I'm about to close the cell door shut on our friend, Walker, out of the blue, he produces a get out of jail card.'

'Ah...'

'Ha, ha – is more like it. You should have seen the smug bastard; he was just loving it...'

She reached over and placed a hand on his. 'You think he set you up?'

'Maybe... I don't know. All I do know for certain is, I just lost my prime suspect.'

'But if he wasn't driving the car, who else could it have been?'

'The only other possible candidate I can see is Ingrid Sandstrom, and she was attending the Bond Premiere.'

'Speaking of which...' she said.

To Die is not Enough was a mediocre example of the usual Bond film nonsense in which an arch villain with an extremely rare medical affliction planned to take over the world. Only one man stands in his way - the indestructible James Bond. Enter a beautiful but deadly femme fatale, who is tasked with the job of eliminating him. Along the way, Bond meets and has sex with, a string of aspiring young actresses who naively think the movie will be their ticket into the big time; among them, Ingrid Sandstrom. Tudor had seen it all before but, snuggled up on the sofa with Maggie Mellor and a bottle of wine, he was more than happy to let it wash over him. It was only when the end credits began to roll that he sat up and took any real interest...

CHAPTER TWENTY-FOUR

HARRY HESITATED before the door to Julia's bedroom. From the bathroom came the sound of cascading water, as she turned on the shower. This was his chance, but he was reluctant to take it because the action he was considering represented a huge breach of trust.

Last night he had proposed that he get Julia's new earrings valued and added to the contents insurance, as a named item of value. His daughter's reaction had been immediate and volcanic.

'I knew it,' she'd shrieked. This isn't about insurance – you still think he stole Mum's earrings. Just like you thought that poor guy in *Sandfords* had stolen Mum's ring! How many more times do I have to tell you? Adam can't afford to buy me diamonds!'

'All the more reason...'

'All the more reason to what? Steal them!' Her eyes blazed into his and the disgust he saw reflected in them was crushing. Lost for words, all she could add was, 'Unbelievable!' and, banging the living room door behind her, his daughter had flounced off to her bedroom.

Once there, she'd begun to cry, but for the first time in her life Harry made no attempt to comfort her. What would be the point? Given the circumstances there was nothing he could say; nothing, anyway, that she would be prepared to listen to. Not now...

It was these considerations that troubled Harry as he stood with his hand on the door-handle. From one point of view, he had already spectacularly messed up and therefore had little to lose and a lot to gain, if he obtained the proof he needed to convince Julia that he was right to suspect her boyfriend. Conversely, if he was wrong about the earrings, his daughter might never speak to him again.

Harry's fingers tightened around the door-handle. He took another glance towards the bathroom and pushed down. As he stepped inside the darkened room, a further wave of doubt swept over him; this felt so wrong – like swearing in church, it was almost sacrilegious. He was ready to run back to his room, when he spotted the small, dark blue jewellery box which Julia had placed next to her watch, on the bedside table nearest the window. He cocked an ear towards the bathroom and was reassured to hear that Julia's showering continued. In that moment, Harry determined to go through with his plan. Planting one knee on the bed and supporting himself with his left hand, he reached across with his right and snatched up the case; blue velvet, he noted, not blue leather like the original. A resurgence of doubt; didn't it follow that he could be just as mistaken about the earrings it contained, or had Adam simply switched boxes?

Harry was feeling a little less confident as he backed off the bed and stood up, but when he opened the lid and, stepping out onto the landing, viewed the earrings in the daylight, any remaining doubts he had evaporated.

"You slept in your earrings? You've never done that before."

"You've never bought me diamonds before. I love them so much, I'm

never going to take them out. "

These words came echoing back to him from across the years and with them the love-making that had followed; the remembrance still as vivid as if it had been yesterday. Harry gazed fascinated at the two diamond droppers nestled on their cushion of blue velvet; just two polished pieces of compressed carbon, but what joyful memories they could conjure. Lost in his past life, it was a while before he became aware that the shower had stopped running. Realising that Julia might appear at any moment, Harry snapped the lid of the box shut and hurried downstairs. Grabbing his coat from the hall stand, he let himself out and, closing the door quietly behind him, almost ran to his car.

The 'loot', as it were, safely stowed in the glove compartment, Harry drove into Shrewsbury and the small, independent jeweller from whom he had purchased his late wife's earrings.

CHAPTER TWENTY-FIVE

INGRID SANDSTROM posed for photographers on the red carpet in a stunning red dress that clung to her like a second skin. It was as if the designer had taken liquid silk and poured it over her naked body; every curve, every contour was on show along with an impressive amount of bare flesh. The neck-line plunged dramatically in a deep V that reached almost to her navel, whilst slits from hip to hem showcased her long, slim legs. Red stilettos completed the attention-grabbing ensemble.

Next came an interview she had done for the ITN ten o'clock news broadcast. Ingrid Sandstrom's only connection with the new film was that she had once been a Bond girl herself. That alone wouldn't necessarily guarantee her a place on the red carpet – after so many movies, there were plenty of ex-Bond girls to choose from – a few of them indeed had gone on to make other movies and therefore had a greater claim to fame. What made Ingrid newsworthy had nothing to do with her acting career, rather it was her much more famous spouse. So, having briefly discussed Ingrid's equally brief but revealing appearance in *To Die is not Enough,* the reporter, a perky young brunette with a toothy smile, moved on to her husband's career.

'Is it true that your other half, Rik Haymer, is working on a new album, Ms Sandstrom?' she wanted to know.

Up until this point, the actress had given a smiling, self-assured performance; had clearly been enjoying the attention and renewed interest in her role as femme fatale, Fanny Fairbright. The confident smile began to wrinkle around the edges and those clear blue eyes of hers clouded.

'Um, well I er... I think perhaps you ought to ask him,' she said in a halting voice.

It wasn't the reaction Tudor would have expected from the icy Swede. The Ingrid Sandstrom he had sparred with on several occasions over the past two months would have dismissed enquiries about her husband's career, or anyone else's, for that matter, with a brittle smile and a wave of her hand. He'd never seen her flustered or lost for a frosty rebuke. This interview clip along with the warm, generous Ingrid Sandstrom that Roper, the night manager from The Garden House Hotel, had described, just didn't fit. Something wasn't quite right here. Could it be that the theory he'd been formulating since last night was not only possible, but in fact probable?

He was aware that this presented him with a bit of a problem, for this was yet another theory on top of several that he had already propounded. Before he took it to Dudley, he needed to have some pretty convincing material to back it up with. Mindful of this, Tudor spent the rest of the morning gathering archive images and interview clips which he could safely assume were of Sandstrom and comparing them with those taken at the Bond premiere.

By the time he was done and his findings had been copied onto a flash drive ready to present to Dudley, Tudor was convinced that the woman in the red dress who had posed for the cameras that night was a look-alike – possibly the body-double, who had stood in for Ingrid in her nude scene in *To Die is not Enough*.

Which posed the question – if it wasn't her – what had the real Ingrid Sandstrom been doing that night? The answer to that question seemed obvious. All he had to do now was prove it.

*

'Another day, another theory, eh Glyn?' Tudor was about to lodge a protest, but Dudley waved it down. 'Still, with the chauffeur out of the frame, it does explain who was driving the Jag when it picked up that speeding ticket.' Dudley looked again at the face on his monitor. 'Who is she then, the lady in red?'

'I don't know yet, for certain but she could be this...' Tudor consulted his notes. 'Sally Lawson...'

'The body double...'

'That's right, or Sandstrom may have hired someone from one of those Look-alike agencies. I've got Ferrars looking into that.'

'Bit like looking for a needle in a haystack, isn't it?'

'Oh, I don't know, sir. Ingrid Sandstrom's not exactly a big star, there can't be much call for her look-alike, I shouldn't think. In any case, there's a distinct possibility we already have her fingerprints on the Bond premiere publicity handout that she gave to Mr Roper. That would narrow the search down considerably.'

Dudley snorted. 'He's probably thrown that away, by now.'

'I very much doubt it. He's a Bond film buff and it's got Daniel Craig's autograph on it.'

His boss leaned back in his chair and steepled his fingers. As the seconds ticked by Tudor, sat hunched over his mug of coffee, could feel the tension building in every muscle of his body. He had staked his reputation on this case and everything hinged on him being right this time.

His decision made, Dudley sat up and, leaning forward, tapped the computer screen. 'Right, get onto the night manager – what's his name?'

'Roper, Sir.'

'Roper, and tell him we're sending someone round to collect that publicity handout.'

'He doesn't come on duty until six…'

Dudley shot him a withering look. 'Then phone the hotel manager and get the guy's home number!' he said testily. 'And while you're at it, get his home address. I'll have a word with our friends at the Met and get them to send an officer round with an evidence bag. Let's hope Roper hasn't let too many people handle the damned thing.'

'Right, Sir,' said Tudor, already half out of his chair.

As he walked back to his desk, he was still nursing his embarrassment; how gormless he'd made himself look over the business of contacting the night manager. But he had been distracted, for at that precise moment, the image of the tall, slim man in the black fedora had popped into his head. There was something oddly familiar about the figure; the way he moved, the slope of the shoulders and then it hit him – it wasn't a man at all…

'So that's how she did it!' he exclaimed.

'Talking to yourself, Sarge?' Ferrars was smirking again.

'Never mind what I'm doing, Constable Ferrars. What have you been doing while I've been away from my desk, got that list of look-alike agencies I asked you for, yet?' That wiped the smirk off his chubby face.

'Still working on it, Sarge, but I've tracked down the body double,

Sally Lawson.'

'Let me see.'

Tudor peered at the screen; it was Sally Lawson's profile page on her agent's website. She was described as a dancer, model and actress.

'I don't know about the body, Sarge, but you could hardly mistake them for twins.'

Ferrars was right, Sally Lawson matched Ingrid Sandstrom in height and build but that's where the resemblance ended. When you compared their faces, there was no way that her body double could have stood in for her on the red carpet at the Bond premiere.

'Well, that rules Sally Lawson out. It was a bit of a long shot in any case,' Tudor admitted. He turned to Ferrars. 'So, look alikes, DC Ferrars, where are they? I need that list pronto.'

'Yes, Sarge.'

Tudor took a sip of his coffee, but it had gone cold. He was headed for the coffee machine for a fresh cup when Ferrars called him back.

'Oh, Sarge… I've got some info on those two names you gave me…'

Tudor retraced his steps, the coffee forgotten for the moment. Maybe this would get Paget off his back.

'You were right, Sarge, they are related,' said the young DC. 'Adam Barclay was Jack Barclay's father.'

'What! He can't be,' exclaimed Tudor. '…hang on, what do you mean *was*?'

'He's dead, Sarge; committed suicide two years ago.'

CHAPTER TWENTY-SIX

IT WAS A GREY, overcast morning, the threat of rain hanging in the air, as Harry stepped out of the jewellers, the earrings and a valuation certificate safely tucked away in his inside jacket pocket. After a brief but careful examination, the jeweller and, coincidently, son of the man Harry had purchased them from all those years ago, had declared the stones to be genuine and valued them as such. On being given the news, Harry had breathed a sigh of relief; with this proof in his hands he felt vindicated. The months of pain and anguish were replaced by a joyful exuberance. This feeling was short-lived however; tempered as it was by the knowledge that this same piece of paper would bring only heart-ache to his daughter.

It was still early and the Square was quiet; Harry's footsteps rang out on the flagstones, echoed round the medieval buildings that surrounded it. Pausing by one of the stone pillars of the Old Market Hall, he took out his phone and checked it for messages; he had two. Harry dialled 121 and listened impatiently as the recorded announcement told him what he knew already – he had two new messages – then, Julia's voice...

'Dad, where are you? Phone me as soon as you get this message.'

She sounded anxious, on the verge of panic. The second message was also from Julia but now she was angry, having discovered that it wasn't only her father that had gone missing.

'I can't believe you'd do that!' she shrieked. 'You bring those earrings back RIGHT NOW or I'll never speak to you again. I mean it Dad, RIGHT NOW!'

It was the reaction he would have expected, but the virulence with which she had delivered the message still came as a shock. And worse was yet to come, he realised, when he showed her the valuation certificate. With turbulent times ahead of him, Harry was in reflective mood as he crossed the river Severn at the Frankwell footbridge and got into his car.

All the way home, his mind was preoccupied with what he was going to say and what, if anything, he could do to soften the blow for his daughter. At journey's end he still hadn't come up with anything other than giving her the plain, unvarnished truth. The last thing he wanted to do was to hurt her, but he couldn't see how it could be avoided. He wasn't sure what game her new boyfriend was playing, but he was convinced now that his intentions toward her were not good. Harry was therefore feeling apprehensive, to say the least, as he opened the gate and approached his front door.

He stepped inside and immediately noticed how strangely quiet the house was. He closed the door, shoving it a little harder than he'd intended yet, despite the noise, Julia still didn't make an appearance. He'd expected her to be waiting for him, ready to pounce on him and demand he return the earrings to her. She had been so adamant that he bring them straight back, he found it hard to believe she would go out until he did so.

'Hello, Julia… hello, I'm back,' he called from the foot of the stairs. No reply. Perhaps she was in the garden and hadn't heard him…

As he entered the kitchen, Harry tried the back door knob, but the door was still locked. Illogically, he went to the window and looked for her in the garden anyway. A plump-breasted pigeon stared back at him from his temporary perch on a neighbour's fence and butterflies fluttered amongst the buddleia, but his daughter was obviously elsewhere.

Gripped by a sudden unaccountable sense of unease, he returned to the hallway and started up the stairs. As he did so, his daughter's mobile began to ring, the distinctive ring-tone as familiar to him as his own. Now he was sure something was wrong; she never went anywhere without that phone – a habit she'd got into at her parents' insistence when, on her 15th birthday, they had presented her with her very first phone of her own. The mobile continued to ring as Harry hesitated, unsure what to do next. A floorboard creaked in her bedroom and the phone was abruptly switched off.

'Julia, is that you?' he said, and with a shudder, realised he had whispered it.

And still there was no reply. This galvanised Harry into action. Taking the remaining stairs two at a time, he burst through the door to Julia's room and came to a sudden halt, frozen to the spot once more.

His daughter, dressed only in her underwear, was sat gagged and bound to a chair by the side of her bed. Her eyes were wild with fear and she was desperately trying to tell him something, but the gag – one of those obscene looking, ball gag devices favoured by bondage devotees – made it impossible. Horrified by the sight of his daughter trussed up like some fetish doll, Harry ran forward to release her. Julia's eyes widened and her efforts to communicate became even more frantic as her father

234

struggled to untie the knots that held her.

'I see you got my message,' said a voice at his back.

Harry turned and, as he did so, a light, brighter than the sun seared his optic nerves and his head was filled with pain. He glimpsed a contorted face and then the light went out and darkness engulfed him.

*

Sometime later, he had no idea how long it had been when Harry regained consciousness, he found that, like his daughter, he'd been tied to a chair. Unlike Julia, however, he hadn't suffered the further indignity of being gagged. Apparently, their captor required that he be able to speak. The fair-haired figure was at the window, his back to them, but swivelled round when he heard Harry's chair creak.

'Ah, Daddy's awake at last.'

He came away from the window to stand between them both. A little taller than Harry, with sloping shoulders and muscular arms, he had a narrow face, a small, pursed mouth and unexpectedly dark eyebrows. The pale blue eyes beneath those eyebrows considered father and daughter with a coldness that sent an icy shiver down Harry's spine. The young man hadn't introduced himself, but there was little doubt in Harry's mind that this was Julia's 'Mr Wonderful'.

'Well now, isn't this nice?' he said, placing one hand on Julia's shoulder and the other on Harry's. 'Don't you just love a good old fashioned, family get together?'

CHAPTER TWENTY-SEVEN

TUDOR HAD JUST opened the thin file on Adam Barclay that Ferrars had furnished him with, when Dudley came bursting out of his office and summoned him from the doorway.

'Get your coat, Glyn, and come with me,' he called, and, without waiting for a reply, was off down the corridor.

Tudor glanced at his watch – it was a bit early for lunch, besides, Dudley didn't do lunch, preferring instead to eat a sandwich at his desk. Grabbing his jacket, he hurried off after him. His boss was halfway down the stairs and the unfit Tudor a little out of breath, before he caught up with him.

'You're a man in a hurry today,' he gasped, 'Where are we going?'

'Wolverhampton, we got a match off that Bond premiere handout.'

'Really?'

Dudley thrust a printout into his hand. 'Here, you can read it in the car.'

But one glance at the photo at the top of the page was enough to convince Tudor that they had found the woman in red, who had impersonated Ingrid Sandstrom that night; even allowing for the unflattering lighting of a police photograph, the likeness was uncanny.

Her name, he learnt, as they sped towards Wolverhampton in Dudley's car, was Abigail Harrison. Abigail had two convictions for shoplifting, which was why her fingerprints were on file; unlucky for her, but a real face-saver for Tudor, who had begun to doubt the validity of his doppelgänger theory. Not that he needed any further convincing, but her parentage was the clincher. Her father was British born, as was Abigail herself, but her mother had been born in Denmark and had spent her formative years there. Danish and Swedish weren't too dissimilar and Abigail would have grown up listening to her mother's accented English and presumably that of her mother's relatives. It wouldn't have been too hard for her to imitate Ingrid Sandstrom's Swedish accent, such as it was. How many Brits could tell the difference anyway?

'In one hundred yards, turn left...'

The synthesised voice of Dudley's Sat Nav disrupted Tudor's deliberations. Looking up, he took in his surroundings, became aware that they had left the motorway and were entering the outer suburbs of Wolverhampton.

'Welcome to downtown Wolverhampton,' said Dudley. 'Not the sort of place you'd expect to find a Bond girl, is it?'

They passed a sign for Heath Town.

'She's just the stand-in,' Tudor reminded him.

'Ah yes, always the understudy, never the star... Still, makes you wonder, doesn't it? Another roll of the dice, and this Abigail Harrison could have been the girl who ended up with the rock star husband and the castle.'

'You have reached your destination...'

Dudley brought the car to a halt outside a modest two-up, two-down;

one of a row of terraced houses, each one barely distinguishable from its neighbours. On the opposite side of the road, Tudor noted, the houses were larger semi-detached and the cars parked on the drives were noticeably larger too. The contrast between Ingrid Sandstrom's home and that of her look-alike couldn't have been more marked. Certainly no one could claim that her double was living the dream, and at this stage, he was prepared to believe that she had been no more than an innocent dupe, rather than a conspirator in a murderous plot. He just hoped that the poor girl had been well paid for her red carpet ride and '15 minutes' of fame...

Dudley stationed himself at the gate, leaving Tudor to take the few steps up to the front door and ring the bell. The sound of the doorbell disturbed a neighbour's dog and set it barking, but failed to produce a response from within the house itself. Tudor pressed the bell again with the same result. The upstairs window in the neighbour's house to the left of the property flew open and a red-faced woman with tattooed arms and spiky, blonde hair leaned out. Tudor stepped back from the door and looked up at her.

'There's no one in,' the woman informed him.

Now tell me something I don't know. 'We're looking for Ms Abigail Harrison,' said Tudor. 'Do you know when she'll be back?'

'Couldn't say. She works funny hours,' the woman replied with a shrug, as if to say, *It's none of my business*, though Tudor suspected that she took far more interest in her neighbour's comings and goings than she was letting on.

'Do you know where she works, luv?' This was from Dudley.

The woman turned and stared at him as if seeing him for the first time, and her eyes narrowed.

'Who wants to know? She asked, warily.

Dudley took out his warrant card and brandished it at her.

Tudor doubted if she could read the card from her window, but the West Mercia logo had the desired effect.

'Oh...soz, my mistake' she said. 'I thought you were here to repossess her car.'

So Abigail was in debt or had been until recently...

'We just want to speak to her, that's all.' Dudley assured her.

Tudor couldn't help smiling to himself at the thought of his fastidious boss being mistaken for a repo man.

The woman was prepared to be a little more forthcoming now. 'She's a hostess at that big casino up in the town centre. *The Lady Luck*, it's called.'

No doubt that's where Walker had met and recruited her, thought Tudor. It was the final link in the chain that connected them all.

'Lady Luck? Aren't we all supposed to be gender neutral these days?' Dudley observed, as they got back into the car.

'I doubt if that enlightened concept has caught on here yet,' said Tudor drily.

Before moving off, Dudley put in a call to Ferrars and asked him to dig up what he could on *The Lady Luck's* owners and get back to him ASAP.

*

The Lady Luck casino was housed in a large, nondescript building just off the Ring way. The place looked more like a warehouse than a casino; a bargain basement version of the glittering palaces of Las Vegas, with a pink neon-lit figure of a show girl prancing beside the casino's name. Open 24 hours, a smaller sign below it proudly boasted. Las Vegas had the Nevada Desert for a backdrop; *The Lady Luck* had the urban industrial sprawl of the Black Country.

Barely a dozen cars were spread out over the large car park; a number that, in Tudor's jaundiced view, didn't seem to justify the casino's 24/7 opening hour policy. He didn't approve of gamblers or gambling; Grandfather Tudor had been a lifelong backer of horses that lacked the will to win, and his family – Tudor's father and his two brothers, had gone without because of their father's profligacy. As he'd done in this case, the only thing Tudor was prepared to back was a hunch. To that extent, at least, he was prepared to admit to inheriting some of his grandfather's recklessness.

They were just getting out of the car when Dudley's phone rang. 'Ferrars,' he mouthed to Tudor and, cradling the phone between neck and shoulder, took out his note book. Opening it out on the car's roof, he took notes.

'Casino's owned by a couple of Nigerians,' he informed Tudor when he came off the phone, 'The Kano brothers, Ritchie and Danny. Neither of 'em have previous but rumour has it they're running a string of girls, drugs too. So far the locals have been unable to connect them to either. Still, that's their problem, not ours; at least we know who we're dealing with.'

The doorman, a large, heavy-set man with the obligatory shaved head and neck tattoo, eyed the two detectives with a look of bored indifference as they approached the casino's double-fronted doors and produced their warrant cards.

'We'd like to speak to the owners,' said Dudley.

The man wore one of those head mics which used only to be worn by security men and had since been adopted by everybody from pop stars to supermarket supervisors. He spoke into it, but it didn't seem to be working.

'Wait here,' said the man, and, opening the door just enough to admit his head and shoulders, leant in to have a word with someone stationed on the other side of it. Leaning back out again, he closed the door and the three men faced each other in a silent stand-off.

After several minutes of just standing there, Tudor was becoming impatient when both doors opened and they were invited to step inside by a sharply dressed black man in his mid-thirties. He had the build of an athlete and a face that looked like it had been carved out of ebony.

'Ritchie Kano, head of security,' he said with a wide smile; here then was the youngest of the Kano brothers. 'Sorry to have kept you waiting, gentlemen. 'If you'd step this way.'

He had the disarming manner of a man used to dealing with people. But was it just a front, Tudor wondered. It was hard to believe that the Kanos would welcome a visit from the police.

The doors were closed behind them and they found themselves in a brightly lit lobby facing another burly doorman and a steel security door, which, like the outer doors had a CCTV camera mounted above it.

'I just need you to put one of these on,' said Kano, and handed each of them a visitor's pass. He gave the doorman a nod and, with an electronic buzz, the heavy door opened.

Inside, there had been an attempt to tart the place up with a red carpet at some stage, but it had been a while ago, for now it was stained and sticky under foot where careless punters had spilled their drinks. No wonder Abigail Harrison had looked so at home on the red carpet, thought Tudor – she spent every day of her working life on one. As they passed between the slot machines, roulette wheels and Blackjack tables, he looked for her, but was unable to pick her out from amongst the casino's other female employees, all of whom were dressed in the same gold-fronted waistcoats, white shirts and black pencil skirts.

'Are you a gambler, Sergeant?' Kano asked. 'We'd be happy to stake you two gentlemen, if you'd like to try your luck at the roulette wheel or the blackjack table. Get a couple of nice young ladies to join you, if you like.'

'No thanks,' said Tudor. 'I prefer *Crossy Road* myself.'

Kano laughed, 'Yeah, my kids love that one too.'

Jutting out above the gaming hall was a mezzanine floor with a row of glass fronted offices, and it was towards these that Ritchie Kano led them. A metal staircase took them up to a narrow corridor which ran the length of the offices and at one of the doors, he stopped and knocked before entering.

Danny Kano was a slightly older version of Ritchie. Tudor estimated he was in his early forties. His face was fuller, less sculpted than his younger brother's and his hair grizzled and lightly brushed with grey, but the family resemblance was unmistakeable.

'You're not locals, are you?' he said in a rich baritone, as he came out from behind his desk to shake hands with his visitors.

'No, we're from West Mercia Constabulary,' said Dudley. He produced his warrant card. 'I'm Detective Inspector Dudley and this...' he turned to Tudor, 'is my Sergeant, Glyn Tudor. 'We're here today because we'd like to interview one of your employees, Ms Abigail Harrison. We believe she has important testimony pertinent to an investigation we're conducting in Shrewsbury and in London. But before we go any further, I would like to make it clear that this investigation has no connection whatsoever to you or your business.'

'I'm glad to hear it,' said Danny. 'We're always happy to cooperate with the police, aren't we bro?'

'Always,' Ritchie echoed.

'I'm sure,' said Dudley without conviction. 'We'd like to do this with the minimum of fuss or embarrassment to your selves or Ms Harrison. Is there a door we can use that will avoid taking her out through the gaming hall?'

'There's a fire exit at the far end of the corridor. It has an iron staircase on the outside wall which takes you down to the car park. You can use that. My brother will show you.'

'Shall I fetch Abby then?' Ritchie asked, impatient, it seemed, to move things on.

Danny Kano turned to Dudley, 'Are we done?'

'Yes…' he said to Danny then, lightly catching hold of Ritchie's arm, 'Just tell her your brother wants to see her,' he warned. 'Don't mention us or why we're here.'

With his brother gone and nothing to do but wait, Danny seemed to lose interest in the affair and, wandering over to the large panoramic window, he stared down at the gaming tables below.

'I think the girls are more trouble than they're worth sometimes,' he said, after several minutes of silent reflection.

But which girls was he referring to, Tudor wondered to himself.

*

It had begun to rain as they pulled away from *The Lady Luck,* great viscous drops that exploded on the car's windscreen like grenades. Abby had not seemed that surprised to find two detectives waiting for her in Kano's office, it was almost as if she'd been expecting them. She had admitted impersonating Ingrid Sandstrom before they'd even got her down to the car, but now, back in Shrewsbury, what they needed were the details – the who, the how and the when...

Tudor passed a photo of Walker across the desk.

'Is this the man you knew only as Alex?' he asked. Interesting that Walker had used Rainesford's diminutive as an alias.

'Yes, that's him,' she said, without hesitation.

'His real name's Roderick Walker,' Tudor informed her. 'He's Ingrid Sandstrom's chauffeur. Was he a regular at *The Lady Luck*?'

Abby took a sip of water before replying, 'I wouldn't say he was a regular, exactly. He'd been in a few times and always gave me a big tip no matter if he'd won or lost. We became quite friendly and one night he asked me if I would go for a drink with him. I was on days the following week, so I said yes.'

'And that's when he asked you to impersonate Ingrid Sandstrom?'

'Said I was a dead-ringer for her.'

'And you agreed to do it though you barely knew the man?'

'I needed the money,' she said, and lowered her eyes. 'I was behind with the rent. My landlord was going to evict me.'

She looked as if she was about to burst into tears.

'Do you need a few minutes, Ms Harrison?' Dudley, in his role as nice cop intervened.

'No, I'm all right, thank you,' she said.

'Did you know who *she* was?' Tudor asked.

She shook her head. 'I'd never heard of Ingrid Sandstrom, but Alex – I mean, Mr Walker, showed me clips of interviews she'd done and the Bond film she was in, of course.'

'And where did all this coaching take place?'

'At my house... he always came to me; said he was having a lot of work done at his flat.'

She'd watched the clips endlessly, she told them; learning how to speak, how to hold herself, how to move like Ingrid; become Ingrid…

'And what explanation did he give you for this little charade he wanted you to play?' said Tudor.

Abigail looked uneasy.

'He told me that Ingrid Sandstrom had to be at that Bond premiere or her career was over, but she was depressed and on the booze and would make a fool of herself. It was just to keep her out of trouble,' he said 'until she'd sorted herself out.'

'And you believed that, did you?'

'It sounded reasonable enough at the time; a lot of actors get stage fright, don't they? Even really famous ones.'

Tudor wondered how the Swedish ice maiden would react to being regarded as a B list actress by her stand-in. He doubted if the lady would be amused…

In the interim, Dudley took over. 'I'm more interested in the mechanics involved. The night porter at the Garden House has told us that you came downstairs with Mr Walker – does that mean you were staying there with him?'

Ms Harrison seemed offended by the suggestion. 'No way,' she said. 'I went down on the train and from the station went straight to the hotel. I walked in wearing a dark wig and with just the clothes I stood up in. I used Mr Walker's room to get changed in and nothing more.'

'What about Ingrid Sandstorm – did you see her at all while you were there?'

'I've never *met* her,' she said, with some vehemence. 'Walker reckoned it was best that we didn't. She wasn't her usual self, he said, and I'd learn nothing from meeting her. The first I knew she'd been at the hotel that night was when I saw her on the news the following day.'

'When it was announced that her rock star husband had been found drowned in his own swimming pool, that didn't give you cause for concern, Ms Harrison?'

'At first, yes, but then they said he'd committed suicide and I thought no more about it.'

Tudor wasn't entirely sure he believed her, but then others far more involved in the case than Abby had been convinced that Haymer's death was a suicide.

'Thank you, Ms Harrison,' said Dudley. 'You have been most helpful.'

'Does that mean my client is free to go?' the duty solicitor, a fresh-faced junior from a local firm of solicitors asked.

'She's not under arrest, Mr Clarkson, but I believe it would be in your client's best interests to stay where she is a while longer.'

'Ms Harrison?' enquired Clarkson, his head cocked to one side like an inquisitive bird.

She didn't look too happy about it, but after a Pinter length pause, she agreed to stay put.

Dudley got to his feet. 'Rest assured, Ms Harrison, your cooperation will not go unappreciated,' he said. 'You must be hungry, I'll arrange for some tea and sandwiches to be brought in to you.'

As he and Dudley walked back upstairs, Tudor voiced his thoughts, 'I think we've got enough now to arrest them, don't you, Boss?'

'Enough to hold them for 36 hours, at any rate, I'll sort the warrants for Walker and Sandstrom,' said Dudley. 'You get the team together for a briefing at...' he consulted his watch, '5 o'clock.'

'OK Boss, but I think we should bring Alex Rainesford in as well.'

'She's already on bail for manslaughter, in case you'd forgotten,' Dudley reminded him.

'I know… which is why she won't want conspiracy to murder added to her charge sheet and that gives her a strong incentive to help us.'

Dudley looked doubtful. 'I don't know, Glyn. It's going to look very much like police harassment to that hot-shot lawyer of hers…'

'Maybe, but come on, she lives in the same house as our chief suspects – even if she's not directly involved, she can't have been totally oblivious to what's been going on… she must know something and we can use that to crack those other two hard nuts wide open.'

They had reached the top of the stairs. 'All right, I've backed you so far… all three it is then.'

After informing the team of the 5 o'clock briefing, Tudor got himself a cup of coffee and took it back to his desk. He took a sip and, finding it too hot to drink, he left it to cool. While he waited, he idly flipped open the Barclay file and what he read there had him reaching for the phone and dialling Harry Paget's number.

CHAPTER TWENTY-EIGHT

HARRY CAME TO with a start. He must have nodded off, he realised, and the rain that hammered against the windows had woken him. Light passing through the streaming panes dappled those areas of the varnished floorboards not covered by the large patchwork rug at the side of Julia's bed. Harry found an unexpected stillness in these watery shapes that soothed his jangled nerves, but this shimmering provided no more than a temporary distraction from harsh reality. They were still tied to their chairs; his daughter with that obscene looking ball gag in her mouth and he with a strip of gaffer tape over his. The only difference being that Adam, or Jack, as he would now have to call him, was no longer in the room. Having delivered his bombshell had he deserted them; left them to die of starvation? It seemed unlikely; it would take weeks, and long before the end came, his friends, concerned by his absence, would alert the emergency services. But where was he and what was he planning to do with them?

The hammering of the rain ceased as abruptly as it had begun and in its absence, the house seemed eerily silent. This silence served to confirm Harry's growing belief that Jack had, temporarily at least, left them to their own devices. If she had stayed awake, Julia would already know this, of course. As if in answer to his unspoken question, his daughter nodded towards the window. From this gesture Harry gathered that his assumption had been correct.

Barclay's absence presented them with an opportunity to escape, but how? They were both trussed like turkeys ready for the oven.

But Julia was ahead of her father and she began to hop up and down in her chair. For a moment, Harry was afraid that his daughter was having some sort of seizure, until he realised that she was trying to turn her chair around. If he did the same and, if they could bring their chairs close enough together, it might be possible to untie each other's bindings; a simple enough idea which proved far more difficult to put into practice. Young Jack appeared to have a sailor's skill with knots and had bound them so tightly to their chairs, that movement was severely restricted. No doubt his intention had been to cause them as much discomfort as possible, as well as ensuring that they didn't escape. It was exhausting. His cramped muscles protested at every jolt and he had to break off frequently to get his breath back before continuing. By the time Harry had succeeded in turning his chair through 180 degrees, his shirt was damp with sweat and his arms were chaffed and sore with rope burns. It took a further 10 minutes of shuffling before he and Julia were finally able to touch hands.

Harry could no longer see Julia's bedside clock, but he estimated that all this manoeuvring had taken the best part of 20 minutes. How much time they had left before Barclay returned was impossible to estimate without knowing where he'd gone and how much time had elapsed since his departure. Harry knew only that whatever time they had left, they couldn't afford to waste it. His hopes of early success were quickly dashed, however; Jack Barclay's knots were fiendishly Gordian in their complexity. And though he continued to probe and pull at them for some time, they remained impenetrable. Sensing her father was tiring, Julia took over for a while, but like him, was forced to admit defeat when she tore off one of her fingernails. Moments later the front door slammed, footsteps sounded in the hall and the final bell was rung on their escape attempt.

Harry's heart rate rose with every step that Jack took on the stairs, as he made his way up to them. As Barclay entered the bedroom, Harry and his daughter turned as one to meet his sardonic gaze.

'What have you little mice been playing at while I've been away, umm?' he said and, raising a hand to his chin, stroked an imaginary beard. 'Musical chairs, was it? But you need music for that, don't you? Yes, of course you do. Fancy you not knowing that. Good job DJ Jack is here...'

And with that, he took out his iPhone and began playing a popular dance track, with a thumping base line.

'On your feet, then,' he said. 'Let's see you dance. Come on, you can do it. I know you can. You were dancing on the ceiling just a few minutes ago...'

Harry felt sick. The little shit had been downstairs all the time; just wanted to see what they would do, when they thought he wasn't there. He'd been toying with them; playing a nasty little game for his own sadistic amusement. How could this twisted young man be his grandson?

Two hours earlier, when he had made that crack about a 'family get together', Harry had been as puzzled by it as Julia must have been. It hadn't immediately occurred to him that this madman could have any connection to the baby boy that he and Annie had been forced to hand over for adoption all those years ago. And even when Jack had referred to the two of them as Grandad and Auntie Julia, Harry had assumed that he was just being sarcastic. And to some extent he was, of course, but it took a while longer for Harry to see that too. In the course of the hour long tirade that followed, Jack Barclay did not spare his captive's feelings as he narrated the sad history of his father's life and his death by his own hand at the age of 43.

*

Annie wasn't quite sixteen when David, as they had named him, was born. A beautiful, blond-haired boy with his mother's eyes, but there had been no prospect of them being allowed to keep him. Both sets of parents had been adamant on that point. Although Harry had always been welcomed in their home, Annie's parents didn't view him as a suitable husband for their clever daughter. There were other reasons too, lots of them, from both sides;

"You're far too young to be bringing up a child"

"You won't be able to support it"

"What will the neighbours think?"

And on it went… a daily barrage of hectoring until they had bowed to the inevitable.

In truth, it would have been a struggle for them; in those days councils didn't dish out flats to gymslip mums and parents didn't collude with their offspring to get one. But despite all the obstacles put in their way, if they had been allowed to, they would have kept the boy.

Throughout their long marriage, Annie had maintained that giving David away was the hardest thing she had ever had to do in her life and, until death parted them, Harry would have said the same was true for him, too. Rarely a day went by when they didn't think about David and yet despite this, they had decided, long before Julia came along, that they would keep his existence a secret from any other children they might have. A terrible misjudgement, it was easy now to see, and one that, like Banquo's ghost, had come back to haunt him. But to their youthful selves it had seemed the right and proper course to take. Why burden their future offspring with the knowledge of a lost sibling who would be as good as dead to them anyway?

And now David, as Harry would always think of him, *was* dead and it had all been for nothing. For once Harry was grateful for the fact that Annie wasn't here to share this moment with him.

But his main concern was reserved for his daughter who, in many ways, had been dealt the cruellest blows by Jack's revelations. To learn that her parents had kept the existence of an older brother from her was bad enough. To discover that her Mr Wonderful was in fact her nephew, and that he'd just been using her to get to the grandfather he blamed for his father's unhappy life, must have broken her heart. God alone knew what it had done to her mind.

It was these darker aspects of Jack Barclay's relationship with his daughter that troubled Harry the most. How far had he been prepared to go in his role as her boyfriend in order to win her over? It didn't bear thinking about and so, for the moment at least, he tried very hard not to.

But he could not escape his own overwhelming sense of guilt for the part he had played in bringing about all this misery.

According to Jack, for the first 5 years of his life, his father enjoyed a warm and loving relationship with his adoptive parents, who treated him just as if he was their own. But all that changed when, shortly after he started school, his adoptive mother became pregnant and by the time the baby, a boy, was born, they had come to look upon Adam very much as the cuckoo in their nest. Years of casual neglect and physical abuse followed and as soon as he reached 18, he left his adoptive home and never went back.

Adam Barclay drifted from job to job and town to town until finally settling in Manchester. There, in that city's lively club scene, he discovered the numbing effect that alcohol can have on a man's pain. It was in one of these clubs that he met Sarah, the woman who would later become Jack's mother. But from the start their union was dogged by Adam's excessive drinking and though he tried many times to curb it, the solace he found at the bottom of a glass always drew him back.

When Jack was 9 years old, his parents separated and though the boy spent every other weekend with his father, it would be another 10 years before he spent enough time with him to finally understand why his father drank so much.

*

Jack glared down at Harry and for a moment he thought the boy was going to hit him. Instinctively, he braced himself, but the blow never came. Instead, Jack leant down between the chairs and checked that their bindings were still intact. As he did so, he whispered something in Julia's ear. She pulled away from him and he laughed. Still grinning he walked over to the window and, leaning against the frame, stared out at the lowering clouds.

'Your parents fuck you up, that's what Larkin said,' he mused, as if to himself, then, turning back into the room, jabbed a finger in Julia's direction. 'What do you think, Grandad, is she a fuck up?'

The only fuck up here is you, son, Harry wanted to say, but as the gaffer tape over his mouth prevented him from speaking, he had to be content with merely thinking it.

But Jack, it seemed, wasn't interested in having a conversation, he was just thinking out loud.

'No, not her, she's a keeper, isn't she. Didn't give her away, did you?'

'That's not how it was,' Harry tried to say, 'we wanted to keep your father too,' but with the gaffer tape in place, all he could manage was a series of animal grunts, as he tried desperately to make himself understood.

'What's that, Grandad?' Jack asked, a hand cupped to his ear, 'You're what... sorry?'

It was maddeningly frustrating. If only the boy would remove his gag, he could explain. And yes, of course he was sorry, but he couldn't have known how badly things would turn out. He and Annie had acted in good faith and with the best of intentions, to do what they thought best for their child at that particular moment in their lives.

But Jack wasn't finished with him. 'Well, you know what, Grandad?' he said. 'Being sorry just isn't good enough.' He came and stood over Harry again. The tone of his voice was a menacing growl. 'You have to pay for what you did to my dad,' he said, and Harry felt the boy's spittle on his face. 'Not money. Did you think I meant money?' In one step he had moved to stand beside Julia's chair. His fingers brushed her cheek. 'You see, it has to be an eye for an eye...' he explained. 'Nothing less will do.'

Harry couldn't see what the boy was doing to Julia, but that vengeful quote from the bible made Jack's intentions clear enough; he would avenge the loss of his father by robbing Harry of the one thing he held most precious – his one remaining child. The mere thought of losing her filled him with horror. Bound and gagged though he was, as a father he had to do something; had to try and save her. He had no rational plan, it was instinctive – a parent's default response when their child is in jeopardy. Fuelled by the adrenalin of fear lest Jack intended to kill her immediately, Harry thrashed about in his chair and strained against his bonds, as he tried to turn the chair round so he could see what Barclay was up to.

Jack's response was to seize the chair-back in both hands and, using the same upper body strength that had overpowered Harry the night of the break-in, rendered him impotent. All Harry could do now was twist his head from side to side.

'Whoa, Grandad, calm down. You're going to have a heart attack if you carry on like that. What are you trying to do – turn your chair round?' he said, in the cooing tones of a carer addressing an elderly long-term resident of a nursing home. 'Relax, save your strength, let me do it.'

And with apparent ease, Jack dragged Harry's chair back round to its original position, facing the window. 'And while I'm at it,' cooed Jack, 'Why don't I turn Aunt Julia round too?'

So that was that. They were right back where they had started. All that effort had been for nought and escape was still as far away as ever.

'Now, where…' but Jack was interrupted mid-sentence by the ringing of the front doorbell, and like a participant in a game of musical chairs, he froze on the spot the moment the ringing stopped.

Seconds later the bell was rung again and as its echo died away, the letter plate was raised and a woman's voice called out.

'Mr Paget, are you there?'

Harry recognised the voice at once and he felt a surge of hope rise in his breast. It was the voice of the young policewoman who had been so kind to him after the burglary – PC Maggie Mellor.

Fate had offered him one last chance and Harry didn't hesitate to take it. Summoning all his strength, he hurled himself sideways and went crashing onto the floor.

'Mr Paget, are you all right?' An alarmed Mellor called through the letterbox.

Cursing under his breath, Barclay knelt down beside Harry and, in a re-run of that awful night two months ago, punched him hard in the stomach. The blow knocked the wind out of him with such force that the expelled air loosened one corner of the gaffer tape that covered his mouth.

As her father lay gasping for air like a landed fish, Julia threw herself onto Jack Barclay's kneeling form. Taken by surprise, he howled with pain as the edge of the chair-back caught him a nasty blow on the side of his head and he went down like a man who had been shot.

All three now lay on the floor in an untidy heap; Harry and Julia on their side and unable to get up, Jack Barclay face down, a thin ribbon of blood trickling down the side of his face. But how long would he stay that way? Harry didn't have long to wait for an answer. As he watched helpless to do anything about it, Barclay slowly hauled himself up onto his hands and knees. He might be groggy, but he was still dangerous. Harry didn't know how he managed it, but somehow he summoned enough breath to utter a feeble cry for help.

Things moved quickly after that. There came the sound of breaking glass, of heavy boots running up the stairs and, to Harry's great relief, PCs Mellor and Crawford burst into the room.

CHAPTER TWENTY-NINE

DAWN TINTED the sky a rosy pink as the small convoy of police vehicles converged on Morecroft Hall. These dawn raids always set the adrenalin pumping. So much so, that Tudor had been awake half the night and had arrived at the station bleary-eyed and hopped up. It was the kind of high junkies paid good money for. But like any high, it inevitably ended with a low once the raid was over and the suspects were banged-up in the cells. This was usually Tudor's cue to crash-out and catch up on the sleep he had missed.

Last evening's briefing had been long and far more detailed than most raids called for. As a building, Morecroft Hall presented several problems. For a start, it contained a large number of rooms and the internal layout was complex. They had obtained a copy of the original plans for the building, but there had been some changes and additions made in the intervening years. It also had several entrances. Going in by the front door was out of the question; it was made of solid oak and reinforced with iron bands. Walker, on the other hand, was quartered in a self-contained flat above the garage block. So it had been decided that they would secure him first and use his keys to gain admission to the main house. If cooperative, he would also prove a useful guide through the labyrinthine interior.

By the time the briefing was over, Tudor had been in need of a smoke and he headed for the car park. Downstairs he'd found PCs Mellor and Crawford booking Jack Barclay in with the custody sergeant. The lad's face was ashen and bloodstained, he noticed.

Tudor drew Maggie to one side. 'What's the story with Barclay and where is Mr Paget?'

'Harry's OK, he and his daughter have been taken to A & E,' she told him. 'His daughter has a suspected broken arm and Mr Paget is bruised and shaken, that's all. It could have been a lot worse.'

'I'm relieved to hear it,' he stole a glance at the handcuffed prisoner. 'And boyo over there – how did he come by that cut on the side of his head?'

Any further thoughts of having a cigarette were forgotten as Tudor listened intently to Mellor's precis of events at the Paget residence.

'And *he's* Paget's grandson? Bloody hell!' he exclaimed, when she had finished. 'Burglary, incest and kidnapping, he doesn't believe in doing things by halves, does he?'

'According to Paget, he was intending to add murder to that list.'

'Je-sus,' said Tudor shaking his head. He took another look at Barclay. 'I don't think they'll feature that one on *Long Lost Family*...'

'Perhaps not,' said Mellor, 'though I reckon Jeremy Kyle would lap it up.' She'd taken hold of Tudor's arm then and pulled him further down the corridor.

Mistaking her motives and thinking she was about to kiss him, Glyn had cautioned her, 'Not here, Maggie,' he rasped.

'What? No, don't be silly; I was just wondering what made you think

Paget might be in danger?'

Tudor lowered his voice. 'When he told me his daughter was going out with a guy called Adam, I wondered if he could be Jack's brother. But I got a bad feeling when I found out that Jack Barclay had a father called Adam and he committed suicide two years ago at the age of 43. It could simply be a coincidence, of course, but what were the odds on that? And that was it really; nothing concrete – just a feeling that something wasn't right.'

When calls to Paget's landline and mobile had gone unanswered, he had asked the dispatcher to get a patrol to swing by Paget's house and investigate.

'Well, whatever it was, Sherlock, you made the right call.'

'Elementary, my dear Mellor. Elementary...' he said.

*

Tudor smiled at the memory.

'You're looking very pleased with yourself,' Dudley observed from the passenger seat.

His boss had been so quiet for most of the journey, Glyn had all but forgotten he was there.

'Oh, it's nothing, just something someone said, that's all.'

'A joke was it? Do share...'

'It really wasn't that funny, Boss. I'd be embarrassed to repeat it,' said Tudor, and hoped Dudley wouldn't press him; he'd suffered enough embarrassment at his hands already, as far as his love-life was concerned. Mercifully, Dudley wasn't in the mood to pursue it and he relapsed into silent contemplation once more.

They planned to mount their assault from the service road entrance at the rear of The Hall. This was the gate Tudor had used the day he'd taken

Ingrid Sandstrom to the mortuary to identify her husband's body and for which he had the access code. They were banking on Ingrid not having thought to change it in the interim. If the code had been changed, they had come equipped with chains and were prepared to pull the gates off their hinges if necessary.

Tudor was wound as tight as a spring as he walked up to the gate and punched in the access code. A breathless second in which a wood pigeon could be heard cooing in the trees nearby and then with a soft whir, the gates began to open. He jumped back in the car and, as soon as the gap between the gates was wide enough, drove in. Tudor brought his car to a halt behind the garage block and switched off the engine. A second car made its way round to the front of the house whilst a police transit van disgorged its cargo of 5 constables, among them DC Ferrars, Maggie Mellor, PC Crawford and Sergeant Tom Corfield. Dudley had press-ganged just about every man-jack available. If there was a major incident in Shrewsbury, there wouldn't be enough officers left to deal with it.

With everyone in position, Tom Corfield, carrying an enforcer, closely followed by Tudor and Crawford, tip-toed up the iron staircase at the side of the garage block. All three wore stab vests.

When the trio were lined up on the balcony outside Walker's front door, Glyn gave the signal; the constable swung the battering ram at a point just above the Yale lock and the door burst open. As they ran in, Tudor had a fleeting impression of oak beams, framed modern prints, honey-coloured floorboards and then they were through a connecting door and running down a narrow corridor. Through a half-opened doorway he glimpsed a bathroom before bursting into the bedroom, which lay at the far end of the hallway. Walker was sat up in bed, a mobile in his hand. Tudor's first thought was that the chauffeur was phoning the main house and, rushing at him, he kicked the phone out of his hand. The man let out a yowl of pain, or it may have been anguish, as the iPhone hit the wall behind him, bounced off and went skittering across the wooden floor. Crawford snatched it up and handed it to Tudor.

'All right, Walker. It's over. Get some clothes on, you're coming with us.'

Tudor stood back as Tom Corfield offered the scowling chauffeur a pair of trousers and a white, long sleeved shirt he'd taken from the back of a rattan and oak chair. Walker swung his legs out of bed and got to his feet. Hitching up the Calvin Klein boxers he was wearing, he displayed an impressive six-pack that Tudor could only hope to attain with prosthetics or CGI enhancement. His hard-eyed stare took in the three police officers. He was powerfully built and Tudor could tell he was weighing up his chances.

'There's another half dozen officers downstairs, Tudor warned him.

Walker gave a grim smile and, taking the garments the sergeant was holding out for him, pulled them on.

'Roderick Walker. I'm arresting you on suspicion of conspiracy to murder. You do not have to say anything. But it may harm your defence if you do not mention when questioned, something which you later rely on in court. Anything you do say may be given in evidence,' Tudor recited when the chauffeur had finished dressing.

'Cuff him, Sergeant,' he ordered.

Crawford stepped forward with the handcuffs and Corfield told Walker to turn round and place his hands behind his back.

Walker did so but, as Crawford leant down to place the handcuffs on his wrists, the chauffeur whirled round and rammed his left fist into the constable's solar plexus. As Crawford sank to his knees, Walker headbutted Tom Corfield and he staggered back against Tudor sending the two men sprawling onto the floor. The chauffeur ran past them heading for the door, but quickly recovering his wits, Glyn scrambled to his feet and performed a flying rugby-tackle that brought Walker down flat on his face. Though winded, Walker still tried to scramble across the floor until Tudor planted a knee in the small of his back and, grabbing a handful of Walker's slicked-back hair, jerked his head back sharply.

'You're not going anywhere, Mr Walker, and if you want to get out of prison while you're still young enough to enjoy your freedom, he said, 'I strongly advise you to cooperate with us.'

Blood dripping from his nose, Tom Corfield joined Tudor and kneeling down beside the prostrate Walker, pulled first one wrist behind his back then the other and without further struggle handcuffed him.

At that moment, Dudley appeared in the doorway, 'What's taking so long?' he demanded then, taking in Tom Corfield's bloody nose and behind him, PC Crawford still on his knees, he moderated his tone, 'Will you two be all right?' he asked.

'Yes, sir,' both officers assured him.

'All right, gentlemen, the clock's ticking, let's get him up. We need those keys.'

Together Tudor and Corfield hauled the prisoner to his feet. Standing face to face, he and Dudley eyeballed each other like a couple of heavyweights at a pre-fight weigh-in, neither man prepared to be the first to blink.

'The game's up, Mr Walker so, do yourself a favour and cooperate. We'd like your keys. Are you going to tell me where they are or do we have to turn this place over?'

'You'll do that anyway,' said Walker sullenly.

'That's a no then, is it?' said Dudley. He gave it a moment longer before giving the nod to Tudor to proceed with the search.

It didn't take long to find them. Walker, it seemed, was a creature of habit and each time he came in, he left his keys in a shallow dish which sat on a small table just inside the front door. Brief though the search had been, it and the extra time taken to secure Walker meant precious minutes had been lost. They couldn't afford any more delays or they risked the possibility of Mrs Harris or her husband being up and about. Servants might well be considered an anachronism in this day and age, but Dudley had little doubt that they were still expected to be about their duties well before their masters were ready to get out of bed.

Dudley dangled the keys in front of the chauffeur's face. 'Now, I'm going to give you one last chance to reduce your sentence,' he said. 'You may think you're off the hook for Haymer's murder but, in the light of recent events, we're going to be taking another look at the sudden and, some might think, convenient demise of the late, Mr Moretti.'

Walker's smoke grey eyes smouldered. 'That's down to Alex and it was self-defence,' he said.

'Allegedly,' Tudor broke in. 'You see, the pathologist thinks it's possible that the paperknife may have been pushed not plunged into Moretti's eyeball; which means somebody had to have held him down while she did it.' This wasn't strictly true, but Tudor was beginning to think that may well have been the case. He just hoped that if the pathologist was prepared to take another look at it, the results would bear him out.

The chauffeur laughed; a low bark that was quickly cut short. 'You still don't get it, do you?' he said.

'Get what?' Dudley asked.

Walker just grinned and Tudor found himself wanting to wipe that smug smile off his face, but resisted the urge to hit him. He and Dudley were still trying to work out what he'd meant by his enigmatic statement when, below them, they heard one of the garage doors fly open and a powerful motorcycle engine burst into life. Tudor ran out onto the verandah in time to see a black and silver motorcycle with two leather clad riders, their helmets glinting in the early morning sun, racing towards the front gate which opened at their approach.

'They're making a run for it,' he shouted, and without waiting for Dudley, charged down the iron staircase, the acrid whiff of the bike's exhaust fumes filling his nostrils.

As he reached the foot of the staircase, he heard the noisy clatter of rotor blades. He glanced up in time to see the police helicopter swoop down over the house like a giant bird of prey and shadow the runaways. Tudor ran round to his car, jumped in and went roaring after them. At any moment the automatic gates would close again. If he didn't get through before they shut, he would be forced to go back to the service road gate and drive all the way round. They couldn't outrun the chopper, but this case had become personal and he was determined to be the one to make the arrest. As Tudor neared the gates, they began to close and he gunned the engine. Hunched over the wheel and gritting his teeth, he willed the Mondeo forward. He was beginning to think he was home free, when there was a clang at the rear end followed by the screech of metal against metal that set his teeth on edge, and then he was through. In his rear view mirror, he could see the damaged gates open and close repeatedly like a demented robot whose circuits have blown. Collateral damage... there would be time enough to worry about that later.

He took the turn into the lane far too fast, was forced to brake hard or overshoot and drive straight through a hedge into a field. The wheels locked and the back end of the car slewed round throwing up a cloud of dust and debris. It was touch and go for a moment, but he managed to bring the car under control. Easing his foot off the accelerator, he spoke over the radio to the police observer on board the helicopter and was told the suspects were heading north on the A49 towards Shrewsbury.

Siren blaring, he tore down the A4117 to The Nelson Inn and at the island turned right onto the A49. Without much traffic to get in his way, he slammed the accelerator to the floor and held it there. He didn't yet have a visual on the bike, but a mental image of the black and silver motorcycle as it had sped away flashed into his mind and he wondered if it was the same bike that had knocked him down outside The Garden House Hotel. Clearly the fugitives had to be Rainesford and Sandstrom (it was unlikely to be Mr and Mrs Harris, the only other occupants of the house) but which one of them had tried to run him down? Either way, if confirmed, it meant further charges would have to be added to what was already a lengthy list.

He was approaching Ludlow Town's football ground when the police observer on the helicopter radioed that the suspects had turned right onto the B4365 which bisected Ludlow racecourse and the golf greens. Minutes later, Tudor pulled onto the same road and brought the car to a halt, the engine still running. Across the greens to his left, the black and yellow police helicopter hovered high above the club house. It was a beautiful day; the sun burning brightly in a cerulean blue sky and the golf course's greens were lush and still wet with dew. Tudor couldn't see the suspects, but was advised by his 'eye in the sky' that they were stood beneath a tree on the club house road. Tudor drove on slowly until he drew level with the turn-off and stopped. They were a good distance away but, even in the shadow of the tree, the silver helmets of the riders and the bike's silver paintwork were clearly visible. What were they doing there – attempting to hide? They must know that the helicopter crew had a fix on them. What then? It was puzzling.

As he considered whether to go in or wait for back-up in the form of Crawford and Mellor, who were, he had been informed, just minutes away, Tudor became aware of the low drone of an aircraft engine. Stepping out of the car, he turned to his right and looked up. Coming in low over the golf links was a single-engine aircraft with short stubby wings and it was heading straight towards him.

So that's why we were all here, but surely, he thought, the pilot wouldn't risk a landing with the police helicopter there. Tudor glanced back to the club house, but from this angle the sun was in his eyes and he could no longer see the chopper, so perhaps the pilot couldn't see it either. The plane was level with the bonnet of his car now, its wheels almost touching the ground and he could clearly see the pilot at the controls. The two women stepped out onto the tarmac road bordering the flat stretch of green the pilot had chosen for his landing strip. The moment the plane touched down, the two women began to run towards it. Tudor saw the cabin door swing open and leaning out, the pilot urged them on with increasingly frantic waves of his arm.

Where the hell was his back-up, Glyn wondered. He couldn't allow Rainesford and Landstrom to get on that plane. If he hesitated any longer, they would get away. Jumping into the Mondeo, he revved the engine until it screamed and, releasing the handbrake, aimed the car's bonnet at the aircraft's tailplane. At the sound, the two women turned, as did the pilot, whose face registered his horror as Tudor's intention became apparent. Quickly shutting the cabin door, he opened up the throttle and the plane began to gather speed. His would be passengers continued to run after him but, as the plane neared take-off speed, were unable to keep up with it and they turned away.

The plane's wheels lifted, came down with a bump, rose again. Still just 30 feet off the ground and in danger of ploughing into the club house, the pilot pulled back hard on the stick and banked to the right. It was a fatal error; the plane shuddered, stalled then fell earthwards. The starboard wing hit the ground first, flipping the little plane over onto its back and the propeller gouged a deep rut in the pristine turf.

In a freeze-frame moment nobody moved, and in the sudden stillness that descended over the scene, Tudor could hear the distant sound of a police patrol car siren. Then, as if some unseen hand had pressed play, normal life, if this could be described as being in any way normal, was resumed.

Whipping out his phone, Tudor called the emergency services and briefly explained what had happened. With the fire service and an ambulance on their way, he got out of the car and cautiously approached the wrecked plane. The sickly sweet smell of high octane aviation fuel pervaded the air, and he found himself praying to a god he didn't believe in that the damned thing wouldn't blow up. The two runaways had not moved, but seemed rooted to the spot; stunned by the sudden turn of events and the cataclysmic end to their getaway. Both women had removed their helmets and Tudor could at last confirm that the leather clad riders were indeed Ingrid Sandstrom and Alex Rainesford. Ingrid had a comforting arm around the red-head's shoulder. Both appeared to have been crying. Neither woman acknowledged Tudor as he walked past them and went over to the upturned plane.

Tudor didn't know it, but he was looking at a Cessna Skyhawk; only one previous owner (and he wouldn't be flying for a while), though some work required to make it airworthy. In fact, the Cessna had broken in two on impact and a large section of the fuselage, including the tailplane, though still tenuously connected by the steely ligaments of the control wires, lay at an awkward angle to the main body of the plane.

Walking around the wing to the plane's nose, he found himself staring at a piece of modern art – the propeller blade, bent and twisted into a new and fantastical shape as it had burrowed into the ground. Behind that, the engine cowling, spattered with clods of earth and oil. Beyond that, the shattered windscreen, through which Tudor could see the unconscious pilot, still strapped in his seat and hanging upside down like a bat. The man appeared to be unconscious and a steady trickle of blood issued from a nasty gash on his forehead. The reek of aviation fuel was almost overpowering here, but much to Tudor's relief, there was no sign of fire. Still, as the ticking of the cooling engine reminded him, the plane's ruptured fuel line was a veritable time bomb just waiting to go off. Regardless of the danger, he would have to get him out of there and quickly.

Tudor returned to the cabin door, normally to be found below the wing, but in its present configuration, above it. The underside of the metal wing was slicked with oil and slippery. It was like stepping onto an ice rink or frozen pond. Alarmingly, it also made the same crackling sound that thin ice makes when any weight is placed on it. Glyn felt his left foot slide from under him and reached for the nearest support – the landing wheel strut. Steadying himself, he reached down with his left hand and released the cabin door latch. He gave the door a tug and it swung open. Glyn crouched down and peered into the cabin's interior. It was much smaller than he had expected, despite the two seats and twin control columns. The pilot's head was down by Tudor's feet. It was only then that he realised he would have to get down on his knees in all that oil if he was to get him out.

'Shit!' he said, straightening up. He was wearing a brand new pair of trousers that had cost him thirty quid.

He took another look, hoping to see some other way to get the unconscious man out; one that didn't involve ruining his M & S trousers. But unless he could turn the Cessna the right way up, there was no other way to do it. Where was Superman when you needed him, he wondered ruefully.

Carefully lowering himself onto one knee, Tudor reached in with his right hand and took a firm grip on the collar of the pilot's leather jacket. With his left hand poised above the harness release button, Tudor readied himself to grab the other collar the second he punched it. 1-2-3, he counted in his head, and punched the release.

The weight of the man surprised Tudor and he almost dropped him. But those miner's shoulders of his took the strain and he managed to drag the pilot's head and torso out onto the wing. Once he'd got him that far, the oily surface made it a lot easier to slide the rest of him out. Slipping his hands under the man's armpits, he pulled him onto the grass and away from the wreckage. He was perhaps 30 yards away when there was a bang loud enough to set his ears ringing, followed by a whoosh, and he felt a hot wind fan his face. He looked up and saw that the plane was on fire and hot debris was raining down on his car.

Finally, sirens blaring, blue lights flashing, the cavalry arrived; two squad cars and an ambulance. They screeched to a halt and the sirens were switched off, but more could be heard on the approach roads.

Leaving the injured pilot to the paramedics, Tudor looked to his suspects. The two women hadn't moved from where he'd last seen them. But now, standing in the glare of the squad car's lights, it was if they were stood on stage. All they needed was an audience and very obligingly, the West Mercia Force had provided them with one. As Tudor approached them, Ingrid Sandstrom, in a final reveal, took Alex's pale face in both hands and, eyes closed, pressed her lips to hers; their passion for each other apparent in this last, lingering farewell kiss.

Trust the ex-Bond girl to provide a surprise plot twist, he thought. She had wrong-footed him at various stages of this investigation, but very cleverly, she'd held her best card close to her chest until her final scene.

With firemen spraying a layer of foam down onto the fire and the two prisoners handcuffed and ready to be driven off in separate cars, Maggie Mellor came looking for Tudor and found him standing alone.

'Are you all right?' she asked, her voice full of concern. 'Your face is looking very red.'

'Yeah, just a bit shaken, that's all.' He gave her a reassuring smile, 'Nothing that this weekend in Wiltshire and a little TLC won't put right, anyway.'

Maggie stared past him at the conflagration at his back. 'You think you'll have the paperwork for this lot written up by then?'

Tudor followed her gaze; took in the burning plane, his damaged car.

'What that? Just collateral damage,' he said.

ABOUT THE AUTHOR

Chris Niblock was born in London, but now lives in Shropshire. *A Stirring in the Blood* is his third novel. He is also an artist and amateur musician and regularly sings and plays guitar in his local café bar. You can read his blog and view a selection of Chris's artwork on his website at www.chrisniblock.com

www.ingramcontent.com/pod-product-compliance
Lightning Source LLC
Chambersburg PA
CBHW061557170626
46811CB00001B/238